El Indio Jesús

AMERICAN INDIAN LITERATURE AND
CRITICAL STUDIES SERIES

GERALD VIZENOR AND LOUIS OWENS
GENERAL EDITORS

El Indio Jesús
A Novel

Gilberto Chávez Ballejos
and
Shirley Hill Witt

UNIVERSITY OF OKLAHOMA PRESS : NORMAN

This is a work of fiction. Names, characters, places and incidents are either the product of the authors' imaginations or are used fictitiously, and any resemblance to actual events, locales, or persons, living or dead, is entirely coincidental.

Library of Congress Cataloging-in-Publication Data

Chávez Ballejos, Gilberto, 1935–
    El Indio Jesús: a novel / Gilberto Chávez Ballejos and Shirley Hill Witt.
        p. cm. — (American Indian literature and critical studies series; v. 35)
    ISBN 0-8061-3230-2 (cloth: alk. paper)
        1. Indians of North America—Southwestern States—Fiction.
    2. Mexican Americans—Southwestern States—Fiction.
    3. Southwestern States—Fiction. I. Witt, Shirley Hill, 1934–
    II. Title. III. Series.

    PS3553.H3465 E4 2000
    813'.54–dc21
                                                                99-088182

El Indio Jesús: A Novel is Volume 35 in the American Indian Literature and Critical Studies Series.

Text design by Gail Carter.

1 2 3 4 5 6 7 8 9 10

This book is dedicated to
Butch and Sundance
"Hasta el último cartucho . . ."

Para mejorar de vida
Me enamoré de la muerte,
Y tuve tan buena suerte
Que la hice mi querida:
Ahora me siento más fuerte
Porque la tengo paridad . . .

To make life better
I would court death
And I was fortunate
That it became my lover:
I feel stronger now,
Now that we are equal . . .
                    —ANONYMOUS

Haven't you ever thought, you gringos,
that all this land was once ours?
Ah, our resentment and our memory
go hand in hand.
                    —CARLOS FUENTES

There is no greater sorrow on earth
than the loss of one's native land.
                    —EURIPIDES, 431 B.C.

Contents

Acknowledgments   xi

Prologue   3

1. *Monday*
    Attitude   9
    Clients   15
Consultants   20

2. *Tuesday*
    The Right On Time Construction Company   29
    Miguel Olson   33
    Waldo   41
    Goodwill   55
    The Art of Lowrider Maintenance   61
    The Columbus Air Force   75

3. *Wednesday*
    Grafitismo   93

4. *Thursday*
    ¿Quién Ganó?   111

5. *Friday*
   El Rancho En El Bosque   121
   Conversation   127
   Sister Kateri   143

6. *Saturday*
   La Familia Que Vendieron Dos Veces   157
   Fly By Night Company   165
   Foreign Service   183

7. *Sunday*
   Checkpoint Carlito   215
   La Majada   226
   La Jornada del Muerto   234
   And Again   247

Glossary: Terms and Phrases   251

Acknowledgments

El Indio Jesús is the product of a long period of gestation. His conception should be dated from the time when a former governor cum *grafitero* fired one of the authors.

Encouragement came from William H. Meyer and Joanna Meyer, María Ines Huizi de Campbell, Edward Franco, and Dr. Mimi Gladstein.

During the novel's preparation for parturition, the authors appreciated the guidance of Louis Owens, Gerald Vizenor, Luis Tovar III, Kimberly Wiar, Karen Wieder, and Larry Hamberlin. We thank them for their patience and attentiveness to our needs.

The authors also herein acknowledge those who gave of themselves, sometimes with their lives, for the ideals of justice and equality. Among them are Pípila and his heirs, the rock throwers of history, whose too-few statues we have seen in Guanajuato, Mogadishu, Victoria, Nairobi, and Caracas.

Saludamos a esos gran pendejos que forman la vanguardia para mejorar las vidas de los que vienen atras.

El Indio Jesús

Prologue

El Indio Jesús drove his *caro troquita* south on Rio Grande Boulevard past Indian School Road and Wells Market in Duranes. A shrill siren interrupted his thoughts. In the cracked rearview mirror he could see a squad car gaining on him. He saw whirling lights. Pulled over. Stopped. Gripped the top of the steering wheel with both hands. He sat motionless. Didn't move. Waited. He watched as the officer used the radio. Minutes went by.

The officer opened his car door, got out ponderously, slammed the door shut, and slowly paced toward the *caro troquita*, snapping his gun holster. He surveyed the rear, the sides, and the front of the vehicle with quick swipes of his head behind the mirrored sunglasses. He approached the open window.

"Keep your hands on the steering wheel."

"Good morning, officer," said El Indio Jesús.

"May I see your license and vehicle registration, please?"

"Of course, officer."

The policeman examined the papers El Indio Jesús fished out of the glove compartment, his lips moving as he read slowly, silently. In the early Sunday morning there was no other traffic, and the stillness of the bright day lengthened while El Indio Jesús marked time. At last, the office pushed back his hat from his forehead and said, "This is no registration. What is this?"

"It is a notarized bill of sale, Officer Ward," reading the name tag on the policeman's pocket.

"This thing?" He waved the dingy, creased piece of paper.

"Yes, sir. It's a legal bill of sale.

"Well, it don't look like no bill of sale I ever seen. And it sure as hell ain't no registration. Where's your registration form?"

"This is all I have, Officer Ward. I just bought this car and I am waiting for the title and registration form from the Motor Vehicle Department. I have eight more days . . ."

"And where's your proof of insurance? This state requires you to show that you have proof of insurance, or else you have to have a surety bond or show me a cash deposit in the amount of twenty thousand dollars. Failure to have evidence of . . ." He launched into a recitation of the list of penalties facing El Indio Jesús, finishing up with, "You have the right to . . ." tediously reeling off Miranda rights granting legal counsel and the right to remain silent.

When he paused to take a breath, El Indio Jesús remarked, "Ah, yes, *mi primo* Miranda from Arizona, 'Flaco' Miranda."

Office Ward pulled his hat back down to his eyebrows, scowling. "Get out of the car, slowly. Face the car and put your hands on the roof. And spread them!"

He roughly ran his hands over El Indio's body. Finished with the patdown, he clasped handcuffs on El Indio Jesús' wrists, arms behind his back, and marched him to the squad car, where he was guided, hand on head, into the caged back seat. The officer climbed into the driver's seat and worked the car radio.

"Got to call the tow truck, too," he murmured, attempting to reach the station. But the radio bathed the squad car with electronic screams. "Damned thing ain't working worth a diddley squat." He thumped the steering wheel with his fist in exaspera-tion, then tested the lock on the shotgun installed next to him, shaking it by the barrel to feel if it was securely in place. He tried the radio again. It would not cooperate.

Just then another squad car coming down off the Interstate ramp pulled up alongside them.

"What's up, Ward?" the new officer yelled across his front seat.

"Hey, Trujillo, call this in for me. The lousy radio's not working again. No, let me do it."

Officer Ward got out and leaned in the window of the second squad car. Grabbing the mike, he fingered the on-button and reported in. "This is eight-nine-seven reporting in with suspect for questioning. Double check computer for car license number Alpha Cat 311 and driver's license 32725872 under the name of Jesus Martinez. Yes, that's right: Jee-sus. And send the tow truck to Indian School and Rio Grande."

Finishing his call, he withdrew his head and stood between the two squad cars addressing the second officer, all the while keeping an eye on El Indio Jesús.

Chuckling, he said, "I just don't know how you people come up with names like that, Trujillo, naming a kid Jesus. Wow. " He shook his head in disbelief.

Trujillo again leaned over to the passenger side window, took a look at the prisoner, and then spoke to Officer Ward.

"Well, Roy, Roy, Roy, I don't think you're no damn French king, which is what your name means. As for me, you should say 'Troo-*hee*-yo,' not 'Troo-*jil*-lo,' like you always do."

He revved the car's engine, shouting above the roar, "And it's 'Hey-*soos*,' not '*Jee*-sus.'" He idled the motor for a moment and said thoughtfully, "Officer Ward, you have just busted El Indio Jesús—Hey-*soos*—again. *Buena suerte.*"

He drove away.

MONDAY

Attitude

As sure as farts follow *frijoles*, El Indio Jesús found himself in the custody of the police at fairly predictable intervals. There was always that phase of his life cycle.

La chota apprehended him with or without due cause. Sometimes they charged him with being drunk and disorderly. Often enough, they said he was driving an unsafe vehicle. Most likely, they were stimulated to make the arrest because he looked Indian or Chicano or Genizaro or poor or vulnerable.

They booked him for driving while intoxicated or for operating an unsafe vehicle or reckless endangerment of the citizenry or whatever. But no matter what the charge, to it was invariably added the unwritten "attitude," as in "I don't like your attitude."

But it was more. This uncommonly common man, so ordinary, so invisible, carried himself in an unassuming way that spoke of strength. He was *duende*. He had seen and felt death. Death meant nothing to him. Except that it made him respect—love—life all the more.

Many survivors of death recognized their kinship with him. They were attracted to him. They *liked* the edge of life that they had experienced, that bonded them. *Duende* gave them that gift. What is more, it was sometimes said as warning in the barrios that those without that touch of mortality fear those with it, fearing them for their courtship of the edge of life.

A policeman like Officer Ward, who might daily face sudden death, may forever live without reaching a state of *duende*. He never savored death, reconciling himself to it, never embracing its possibility. He keeps his fear, equipping himself with more and more physical and mental weapons to combat it. He will never have *duende* and resents—hates—those who carry themselves in ways that separate them from those who fear. These the police cannot intimidate. These simply madden them.

And so, derived from *duende*, the matter of "attitude" did not rest upon anything that El Indio Jesús actually said, for he was ever studiously polite and deferential. When slapped with sarcasm or paternalism or naked hostility, he still maintained a composed demeanor.

It was not language distance, either. He spoke perfect *gabacho*— accentless English—with a vocabulary generally larger and more imaginative than that which any arresting officer, especially Officer Ward, could command.

The word *atufado* described his way of passive resistence when faced with a threat. For centuries the term was applied to the maddening stoicism of the natives of the land.

So, there it was: a combination of *duende* and *atufado* that was so enraging.

And then there was the matter of transportation, what he called his *caro troquita*. This obsolete vehicle that, despite all odds was still operating, modified into a trucklike thing capable of carrying a half-ton for short distances, well, it was a public eyesore and should definitely be off the streets, paperwork be damned. Whereas that *chota* Officer Ward struggled to pay off his twelve-thousand-dollar Chevy pickup with the camper body at 17 percent interest, this lowlife Chicano or whatever rode around in a vehicle insulting not only to visions of the Chamber of Commerce but even dared to slogan the monstrosity with AQUÍ VIENE TU DADDY.

In the past, and not infrequently, El Indio was booked on the kinds of charges laid upon those with a problem of attitude. Also, and typically, his *caro troquita* was now impounded, towed to a holding lot some fifteen miles from the jail, almost into the mountains.

He was set free again when a priest, after a few days, delivered his mail, which included the *caro troquita's* proper registration and title. He left with a set of new friends and new ideas. And messages to deliver.

To retrieve his *caro troquita*, he had to come up with the three-dollar-a-day storage fee tacked onto the forty-dollar towing fee, swelling the ransom beyond what he had originally put into the erstwhile Volkswagen bug. It must languish in the impound lot until or unless he decided to liberate it.

More often than not, when faced with this same sort of situation and recognizing the value of cost effectiveness, the Robert O. Anderson School of Business not having exclusive rights to the concept, he would abandon his creation. He knew that within days the pan with its serial number and all its vital organs would be stripped from the body by his *carnales* from Juárez who worked and controlled the lot. When he was released, he could make arrangements for the pan to be transferred to an intermediary, a former 187th Airborne Regiment paratrooper with Chosen Reservoir experience. The rest of the parts, or better parts, would be collected through barter until it all coalesced and was born again, like a Frankenstein monster VW beetle, atop the original pan, but bigger, stronger, and uglier. The new *caro troquita*, complete with title, license, and registration form down to matching serial numbers, would then be christened, perhaps as "Juanabago," "La Unica," or "Chipita."

El Indio Jesús sought to recover his tools stored in the *caro troquita*, however. This was a problem for him, for he truly loved his tools, cherished them, and mourned their loss. He wished that he did not care so much for his tools, because that complicated the simplicity of his life. But all too often, they were lost. He believed that there was a descending system of tool theft whenever his vehicle was taken from him whereby the officers took the very best, the tow truckers the next in quality, and the operators of the impound center whatever remained. This assumption lay in his observation that none of his tools ever showed up in pawn shops. As a rule, tools stolen by a thief eventually appear for resale at pawn shops or at flea markets. But he would remember his tools always.

El Indio Jesús never lounged in jail for long. First of all, jail was not punishment for him, and his jailers perceived this quickly and considered him more dangerous inside than out. He really enjoyed this opportunity to meet the inmates and guards because there was a great deal to be learned from them. And there was much that he could teach during the long hours of waiting. Then, too, it was clear that El Indio was no criminal and that his arrest was at least a misunderstanding or, at most, a miscarriage of justice.

Another thing bothersome to the jail authorities was the profile of the guests who visited him, who demanded information about the charges and conditions under which he was arrested. These guests included hotshot attorneys from the American Civil Liberties Union and representatives of the Archbishop's Office of the Catholic Church. These visitors made the jail administrators uncomfortable. Before long, the Irish priests from the Old Town Catholic Church saw to it that he was released to perform community service under their guidance. These priests recognized and respected his multiple skills for building and repairing, for tasks that required manual labor, a strong back, and a mind willing to absorb monotony. In Old Town, La Plaza Vieja, they would see to it that he discharged his debt to society by working in that barrio under their benign supervision.

But El Indio Jesús made arrangements, too. He established an understanding with the priests about the specifics of his labor. Years ago, when he first fell into their hands, he offered them a deal. Either he would give them forty hours a week of *gabacho* work or twenty hours of *nongabacho* work, or some mutually agreed upon combination.

El Indio Jesús saw *gabacho* work as laying things in a straight line, such as stacking cement cinder blocks to make a wall, installing electrical wiring, setting up a hot water tank, or painting and posting signs saying, NO PETS, NO ADMITTANCE, PRIVATE, KEEP OFF THE GRASS, VISITING HOURS 8 TO 4, or NO PARKING, VIOLATORS WILL BE TOWED AWAY AT OWN EXPENSE. The cognitive category also included assembling prefabricated items with assistence of instructions in English, French, or German, but rarely in Spanish.

Nongabacho work, as he defined it, allowed him to be creative, imaginative, and insightful. Walls that seemed to undulate like waves yet were firmly based or capturing sunlight as a friend and not an enemy were some of the challenges that *nongabacho* work inferred. Although it contained a certain degree of freedom, it was highly taxing of his mental energy and, often enough, his physical energy as well.

It was up to the priests to decide the condition of El Indio Jesús' servitude. At base lay the ever present need to repair, shore up, buttress, weatherproof, winterize, summerize, and beautify the church and support buildings and grounds. The priests, and those responsible for the operation of the church as a structure, were completely ignorant of eighteenth-century construction techniques and architecture. They were at the mercy of a native, such as El Indio Jesús, who gave the impression of commanding a genetic knowledge on how to do what must be done. And they knew it.

This day, El Indio Jesús left the city jail in the company of a Legal Services lawyer and a priest. As they turned the corner of the building, they came upon a knot of men engaged in conversation in the parking lot. There was a physical similarity among them that almost suggested consanguinity—tall, thin, pale, sharp-eyed. In one simultaneous movement, they turned to look at El Indio Jesús and his companions as though programmed to extraordinary high levels of alertness.

When the three came abreast of the group, El Indio and one of the tall men separated out from their companions, moving away to talk in intense, soft, but rapid Spanish. To the two sets of watchers, nothing could be interpreted from either the words or the body language of the two.

Then they split apart and moved to rejoin their companions.

"*Hasta luego*, Martínez," the tall man called back.

"*Hasta pronto*, Beserra, *hasta muy pronto*, " responded El Indio Jesús.

"Friend of yours?" the lawyer asked, with an astonished expression on his face.

"Friend? No. But we go back a ways," he replied.

The lawyer and the priest exchanged surprised looks as they continued walking toward the lawyer's car.

Across the parking lot the other group of men walked toward the city jail and courthouse.

"Friend of yours, Captain Spencer?" one asked the man who had talked with El Indio.

"Friend? No. We just go back a ways," he answered.

"You can sure dish out that spick lingo, Jack," another remarked.

State Police Captain Jack Spencer regarded him thoughtfully, then replied, "Throw enough of these guys in jail and you get to know the language pretty good, Charlie." Then he laughed, but without humor.

Clients

El Indio Jesús accumulated a body of understanding about the church, the activities around La Plaza Vieja, the priests, and the parishioners. He let his eyes, ears, and mind work out the answers to questions before resorting to words for explanations.

He had a unique perspective. It drew its own conclusions about cause and effect. He was pleased to learn, for instance, that God is not only living but is actually living in France. This he deduced from the Blood of Christ bottles he had taken to the dump each Sunday morning after the communion service. The eucharistic wine was imported from France.

El Indio Jesús noted a preponderance of women in the church despite the male control from the pope on down. Women far outnumbered in frequency the attendance of men. Women often came twice a day, early in the morning and again in the late afternoon or early evening.

The priests explained to him that women generally feel that they are visiting a dearly beloved friend in the friend's own home—the church—when they come to pray to the Virgin Mary,

Nuestra Señora, and especially La Virgen de Guadelupe. From them they could count on receiving love and sympathy if not necessarily solutions to their problems, the priests assured him.

Ever a devotee of the experimental method, El Indio Jesús tried out the devotional pattern of the women to see what it might do for him. After several sessions, he concluded, among other things, that the practice offered the Catholic women of America an unparalleled opportunity for planning. In the morning one could plan out the day's activities and goals, and in the evening one could assess the level of success or failure and make preliminary plans for refinement at tomorrow morning's devotional. One of his clients even went so far as to vocalize and affirm his observations. She said that when she entreated Las Virgenes to grant her the necessities of life such as a new car, a microwave oven, or space, on good days they put into her mind ideas about how to gain even her most desired far-reaching goals.

Why men attended church less often than women was a question El Indio wanted answered. The priests were quick to tell him that since it was Adam who fell to woman's temptation—Eve—their major charge from God and the church hierarchy was to bring men back into His Grace, a very hard thing to do.

The priests blamed their limited success in the barrios on what they called *machismo*, using the term in the familiar but uncomfortable way nonspeakers of a language often adopt to gain linguistic congress with native speakers. In this case, however, El Indio Jesús had not the faintest idea what the priest meant when they dropped the term *machismo* on him in conversation. To him, *macho* simply meant the male part on a human or animal, which makes masculine different from feminine. It turned out, after a fair amount of probing, that what the priests meant by *machismo* was what they had picked up from their female parishioners of the younger generations who read *Cosmo* and *Redbook*; in effect, it was supposed to convey the idea of male supremacy, which, in turn to the priests, translated into a male obtuseness and unwillingness to spend time on their knees before Nuestra Señora humbly asking for things.

El Indio Jesús approached some of his *amigos* with a question about their fidelity to the church. They gave him a number of answers, none of which seemed to match the prevailing *machismo* concept. Some of them had never recovered from their resentment of demands in childhood for attendance and stiff clothes and boring Latin liturgies. Some linked together the transitional ceremonies of life that had taken place in the church, and felt that cumulatively their lives had not been particularly enhanced by the weddings, funerals, and baptisms. But for most of those who discussed the matter at any length with him, they said that there was just not enough time to catch up on weekend chores and also respond to the demands of the Lord as set forth by the priests. Transportational needs alone most often precluded such allocation of time if one were to make it to work on Monday morning. For most, Sunday morning first and foremost meant automobile repair. One reminded him of the cliché that the best time to teach someone how to drive in the city was on Sunday mornings, when the gringos were still abed or in church and the Chicanos were busy repairing their cars.

■ ■ ■

During his indenture to the priests who had bailed him out of jail, women of La Asociación de Señoras de la Sangre de Cristo and the Knights of Columbus Auxiliary would from time to time request his help with chores at their homes. They needed the bathroom tiled or a room plastered or a flowerbed laid. They asked him to perform those tasks that the man of the house could not or would not do. No matter what the request, El Indio would always say yes, *pues sí*, and if it was something he did not know how to do, he would scout out his think tank for a quick briefing to enable him to proceed, relying on his natural talent for improvisation to carry him through to completion of the task.

Some of the requests he handled while still under community service. The rest he took on once his debt to society had been paid back. To his clients in either case, his first question always was, "How much money do you wish to invest in this job?" And then he would inform them, "I will need half that amount now in order to buy the materials that are needed, and I will finance the remainder and provide the labor. When I have completed the job, if it is satisfactory to you, then you may reimburse me for the remaining cost of the materials as well as pay me for my labor."

He would further say, "If you like, since I have no car at present, you may take me to buy the necessary materials and then you can pay for them directly. Or, as I have suggested, you may give me half of the money and I will make my own arrangements for their purchase and delivery."

Since the *señoras* of La Plaza Vieja dared not be seen with men not their *esposos*, they always gave him the cash and required that he bring back receipts "because my husband wants receipts for what I spend." Coming up with receipts was the easiest part of the job, since, as a firm rule, every parking lot outside hardware stores and lumberyards is alive with fluttering sales receipts. He made it a habit to collect handfuls of them whenever he stopped by, enabling him to produce slips with appropriate and approximate amounts whenever necessary *para el esposo*.

He made it clear to his clients that he was tied to the church for church and barrio labor for that first week. He then collected the up-front money from each of them, usually between five and ten clients in all, becoming fully subsidized by Friday for the purchases needed to launch his handyman business all over again.

El Indio Jesús used what others considered weekend leisure time to become mobile. On Saturday he bought a disabled Volkswagen beetle, abandoned or nearly so, which he had spotted during prior weeks. He kept a mental list of such vehicles for just such arising needs. He then prevailed upon a friend to recondition the motor enough to work reasonably well, promising labor in exchange, labor that could be counted on. The exchange of goods and services were ever the currency of the poor, since outright cash purchases were so unlikely. The exchange system in which El Indio participated was complex but efficient.

On Sunday, El Indio Jesús scavenged the Chicano Flea Market on South Coors Boulevard for tools. He would say, "*Voy a comprar los fierros de los que tiraron la toalla.*" He knew that as the economy shrank and times became harder for the people, the quality of the tools they were forced to sell became increasingly better. Their loss became his gain, he thought joylessly. Besides, next time around, they might well be the buyers and he the seller. And maybe he would spot some of his old tool "friends" among the greasy piles on the sales tables if he were lucky.

In the afternoon he turned the VW bug into a pickup truck, his *caro troquita.* Since the time of the Arab oil embargo, he had forsaken Chevy pickups for VWs, which he could then cut up and install with small flatbeds. He ceremonially lettered names or slogans across the brow of each vehicle now risen Phoenix-like from curbside ashes.

By Monday morning he was capitalized, mobilized, and equipped with tools and materials.

Thus began El Indio's second week after incarceration. He started each day with customer work. This took him till noon. He handsomely repaid the ladies who financed him by giving them top-quality work, proving that he was a man of his word. It was his code to give them more than what was asked for. He always asked them what else they needed to have done—a leaky faucet tightened, a stubborn cupboard door—an extra something he could do for them.

His clients were more than pleased to give him referrals to friends and neighbors. Before long, he found employment both in the Valley and the Heights, even as far as the Kirtland Nuclear Weapons Research Center fence. It amused him to notice that in that neighborhood, customers associated with the military also drank the Blood of Christ—imported from France, no less—but did so without ever having to set foot in church. Or into a dumpster.

Consultants

To accomplish his various projects, from time to time it was necessary for El Indio Jesús to contract for consultant work. On these occasions, he took his problems to the Unauthorized Safeway Shopping Center Board of Directors, or the USSCBD. This resource bank had among its personnel a variety of engineers, historians, attorneys, artists, inventors, and physicists. It was rumored that it contained a wider collection of talent than the original Los Alamos Trinity Project in that it had also an array of humanitarians and social scientists. In fact, some members of the USSCBD were said to have been part of the atomic bomb team, but since board members were especially sensitive to probing questions about their past, they were treated with the consideration they deserved.

The USSCBD met regularly at dawn near the dumpster beneath the old cottonwood tree across the street from the Safeway shopping center. The site was crucial to monitoring the mall activities, particularly the movements around the liquor store. Since the church was only a block and a half away, it was convenient for El Indio Jesús to seek the board's advice.

El Indio Jesús and the USSCBD enjoyed a climate of mutual respect, and the terms and conditions of the contractural responsibilites were never abused. Virtually any subject matter came within the board's command: if expertise was currently lacking owing to personnel shifts, a talent search was launched, soon producing the required master hand.

With regard to reimbursement, the USSCBD was quite specific—hard cash, La Copita wine, or an acceptable substitute. On Mondays, the agreement involved the Blood of Christ found in bottles at the church. This was when El Indio Jesús' credit soared, when he could count on unlimited information as long as the blood flowed.

The contracts took a number of forms depending on the mission. Once El Indio Jesús was confronted with the problem of connecting a 220-volt clothes drier to a 1930s 110-volt fuse box in the three-hundred-year-old *granaria.* It was a challenge more properly solved by an electrical engineer than an ordinary electrician, and the never-failing USSCBD produced the correct resource person within a day.

Another time, he needed to determine the stress or pressure level an adobe wall could withstand. The task called for placing an additional half-ton of mud against the corner of the two-century wall in order to construct a half-shell to enclose a statue of La Virgen. An aeronautical engineer, working with stress and weight concepts, guided El Indio Jesús until the work was completed. More was accomplished, however, than was intended: the niche with La Virgen reached such aesthetic heights that pilgrims began arriving from around the world, even from Lourdes, to view La Virgen here. She gave every indication that She was about to take flight into the turquoise skies. Indeed, it was said that La Virgen incited more than a few church matrons to try their own wings. They were never seen again. Feminists from the university referred to La Virgen, too, as a pure embodiment of a woman's quest for serenity, self-actualization, the achievement of space—albeit inner space—and fulfillment.

One of El Indio Jesús' most intriguing problems to solve was the matter of the red clay roof tiles. The church had been covered for three centuries with such tiles. Several were broken, missing, and in need of repair. Beyond being functional and attractive, the tiles over time proved to be functional, attractive, and flaming-arrow proof, an aspect not unappreciated by the early priests.

Red clay tiles were no longer produced in the area as far as El Indio Jesús and the USSCBD could ascertain. An artificial variety of compressed concrete was on the market, but its inauthenticity was a dead giveaway. There was even a vinyl tile available in a world surely converting itself into plastics.

He needed a few tiles for replacement nonetheless. He decided to learn how the red clay roof tiles could be made from the valley mud as they once had been. He was informed by his consultants that the last such tiles to enter the area had come up along the Jornada del Muerto from Mexico for the construction of the Alvarado Hotel. This historic landmark, now demolished, was replaced by a parking lot, thanks to the urban renewal program supervised by then-City Commissioner Pete Dominici. The Alvarado now shared a sandy grave with Pete's brainchild, the multimillion-dollar city jail farm, which disappeared beneath the ground within years of its construction.

One member of the USSCBD reported that tiles could be found in the lot at El Conquistador Salvage Company for four or five dollars apiece. Sometimes nonstarving Corrales artists bought them to ethnicize their *casitas* up valley, inflating prices over time.

El Indio Jesús' determination to learn how to manufacture tiles himself increased when he asked himself, Why is it that nuclear bombs can be constructed in the reaches of La Jolla del Rio Grande—the Jewel of the Rio Grande—but not clay tiles?

At the university, the industrial arts faculty members told him he would have to buy a five-thousand-dollar kiln (gas or electric) to reach the required temperatures for such a tile. The department had kilns like this, but since El Indio was not enrolled as a student, he could not have access to them. Besides, the small number needed was not worth their bother.

He then asked himself: How did they reach correct temperatures for baking the tiles in the eighteenth century? The Pueblo Indians were no longer making such tiles. It was a matter for the USSCBD's serious attention, and it would cost more than one bottle of La Copita.

A task force of architects, historians, archeologists, and physicists convened. It was soon decided that the issue demanded a meeting of the entire board. He was notified that they would get back to him after consulting with colleagues at Kirtland, Sandia, and Los Alamos, as well as other research facilities and think tanks.

Get back to him they did, and to his surprise, it was one of their own members who turned out to be the consultant who could answer the mystery of the red clay roof tiles and their manufacture. It was none other than Tony the World Traveler from Laguna Pueblo.

Tony the World Traveler was a war veteran who had served two hitches during the Vietnam War. The first was in the navy, working in the engine room of a supply ship that loitered off Cam Ranh Bay for most of his duty. On leave in Saigon, he succumbed to the beauty of the Vietnamese people, who looked to him like Hopis. Second hitch was as a Marine. He served as a gunner in a Huey troopship, working out a method by which he expended all a mission's ammunition in what looked like precision fire without ever actually hitting any human targets. And he certainly did get to see Vietnam.

After Tony the World Traveler's second tour in the military, he left Laguna for New York, where because of his many experiences and the need for his skill as an engine room wiper, he was able to get a National Shipping Card, which gained him membership in the International Organization of Masters, Mates, and Pilots. This meant he could go to the union hiring hall in Charlestown, Boston, or New York for merchant marine duty, either for a berth in his specialty or as a P.A.C.—Person in Addition to Crew—the latter allowing him to sail on voyages over the seven seas without pay or fare, but with plenty of decent food.

In Italy he jumped ship and got a job making Mediterranean-style red clay roof tiles. Being the newest hire, he was put in charge of feeding the kiln. He soon learned, using the local wood, how much time clay took to produce the correctly fired tile. It was also a matter of gauging by color of flame and color of tile, taking altogether a period of forty-eight to fifty-five hours.

When he returned to Laguna, he experimented with different varieties of the local wood—cedar, piñon, juniper, cottonwood—consuming some six cords until he approximated the required conditions. As far as the USSCBD knew, he successfully produced red clay roof tiles from Rio Puerco clay, which was not much different from Rio Grande Valley clay.

At that point, however, Tony the World Traveler was not able to share his hard-won knowledge. He had been arrested in the Safeway supermarket parking lot for performing a rain dance with his colleagues. The arresting officers accused him of creating a public nuisance—worse, of being a public nuisance—even though anyone in the entire state that July could verify a pressing need for rain. Tony the World Traveler unsuccessfully protested that only Mrs. Safeway had legal right to bring charges against him, since it was her parking lot. He was booked as a common vagrant.

The USSCBD shook its collective head in dismay. Why would Mrs. Safeway treat the natives like this now that fifteen of her supermarkets were in Mexico? She was said to be studying Hispanic preferences and habits, looking toward the day when Chicanos—that is, detribalized Indians—would be the majority population in the western states where her chain was based. Her treatment of Tony the World Traveler, well, that was no way to treat a *compadre* and a member of the august Unauthorized Safeway Shopping Center Board of Directors.

Then it rained for six days. As the surf came up on the Rio Grande, the police asked Tony if he could please do his civic duty and perform a stop-the-rain dance. Although he was released on his own recognizance, he steadfastly refused to cooperate until Mrs. Safeway personally apologized. He felt that his constitutional right to be confronted by his accuser had been violated.

Once back with the USSCBD, however, his and the board's resolution dissolved along with the board room, which was now well underwater. His fellow members looked distinctly pruny at this point. Tony the World Traveler convened an impromptu group that, by morning's first light, performed a reverse rain dance.

The Middle Rio Grande Conservancy District discussed awarding him some special recognition for his efforts, but the meeting's minutes fail to indicate if anything was actually done about it. Jealousy may have squelched that generous impulse.

Tony the World Traveler offered El Indio Jesús the product of his tile experiments in exchange for the Blood of Christ and a ride to Laguna, where the red clay roof tiles were made. They anticipated some breakage during transport, but there would be enough for what was needed. Once the tiles were in place, they could be expected to last for some eighty to ninety years.

It was important to El Indio Jesús to learn how to make the tiles, but Tony the World Traveler left for the annual John Steinbeck celebration in Salinas, California, and then up to San Francisco to reunite with surviving Beat Generation poets with whom he had traveled in times past. In time, rumor filtered to the USSCBD that Tony the World Traveler was seen in Latin America, someone said Chiapas. And then El Salvador or maybe Guatemala.

1 2 3 4 5 6 7

TUESDAY

The Right On Time Construction Company

Early Tuesday, El Indio Jesús entered the small building housing the newly formed Right On Time Construction Company. The ROTC, as it was ever called during its lifetime, derived its name from the prevailing attitude of its job corps, that whenever they arrived at their destination, it was indeed right on time, no matter what. Composed of unemployed *carnales*, all wore identical white hardhats with ROTC lettered across the front, with no indication that one person was more important than another. This replicated reality. There was no established hierarchy. All were equal.

Other things lacked formalization as well. The ROTC had no contractor's license nor bonding capability, no construction materials nor money, nor credit with which to buy equipment. No tax number had been bestowed upon it either.

The contractor's license was not considered obtainable by the personnel and management of the Right On Time Construction Company, the personnel and management being, of course, one and the same. To obtain the license it was necessary to pass a written test at the state office in the capitol, a test that was known to have been failed by a Chicano with a doctorate degree in landscape architecture from the University of Pennsylvania. How, then, could an ordinary *vato* expect to pass such a test? There might be other ways, of course. Not long ago a Hispanic *politico* was indicted, tried, and convicted of receiving bribes in exchange for contractor's licenses passed along to Chicanos. Only *gabachos* from Oklahoma and Texas seemed to have what it takes to pass the test and start up their own construction companies with the blessing of the state.

What ROTC did possess was a flexible but ample labor pool of highly skilled workers. Since most of them were chronically unemployed, the team could be expanded at a moment's notice as need be. The several Mexican nationals on the ROTC roster provided enormous skill. El Indio Jesús could recruit laborers able to work with adobes or stonework without requiring training. He knew where to find an undocumented worker whenever staff was short. With them, it was the ROTC that gained the most advantage because the Mexican inspiration lifted the quality of all their work.

El Indio Jesús was especially friendly with the one Mexican national on permanent staff with whom he exchanged *abrazos* of welcome each time they met. Then they would retreat to quiet corners to discuss adobe concepts on the level of subatomic particle physics.

The Mexican *adobero* was called El Chuy Jiménez, although on the books it was spelled "Chewy." He began his career as a *grafitero*—a wall artist—frequently representing the northern tier of Mexico when he was in El Norte, north of the border, but whose true genius was in adobe.

El Chewy Jiménez was an unassuming, quiet man who was always pleasant toward the other workers but who tended to keep to himself. At noon, when all the rest went off together to KFC or Taco Bell or McDonald's, he stayed behind and ate tortillas and tamales from a brown paper bag he packed himself.

His function on the job was to bring fresh Mexican creative juices to the task of determining how the windows and the *portales* should be placed and where the arches and doorways should be set, and to make sure the lines of the walls were graceful with the spirit of endlessness. His judgment and authority were never questioned.

The work progressed well, contracts were regularly won, and the ROTC built itself up to a full functioning entity. Workers bought pickup trucks with camper bodies for themselves, avocado-colored compactors for their wives, and pit bulldogs and BMX bikes for their children. It looked as though the ROTC had made the big time, the American Dream within its grasp.

Then one day El Chewy Jiménez was seen with a stacked Swiss stainless steel food warmer instead of his usual crumpled brown sack. While the workers regarded this curiosity with sidelong glances, a yellow MG midget sports car approached the site with a slender, fair-haired woman at the wheel. Unwinding her long legs from the low car, she collected the food warmer, waved bye-bye to El Chewy, and dusted away, gravel spewing.

In days to come, La Blondi—as the workers called her among themselves but never in El Chewy's presence—punctually delivered food in the warmer at noon and picked up the container again at one-thirty every day. In the length of time it took them to build two handsome walls, El Chewy's schedule became an accepted fact.

One day he called his coworkers together.

"*Lo siento mucho, compadres, pero tengo que irme . . .*" He would be quitting when their present job was completed. "*Ha sido una estancia muy bueno, muy feliz, pero tengo que irme . . .*" For a man who was ever poised, he awkwardly, hesitantly explained that it was time for him to branch out on his own.

An audible gasp went up. The ROTC depended on him for almost all of the creative aspects of the work. The artistic part being the most important, the company had reached its success because of El Chewy Jiménez. What would the ROTC do without him?

The men speculated about why this sudden unfortunate change.

"Perhaps it is a problem with *la familia* in Chihuahua?" suggested one.

"Is there something we can do to help you out?" asked another. "Transportation?"

"Money? We could take up a collection?"

"La Migra—immigration?"

Lowering his head and giving no explanation, he said once again, "*Tengo que irme . . .*" He was leaving.

At just that moment, La Blondi squealed up in her *carito*. Collecting a few tools and the food warmer, El Chewy Jiménez slid into the MG, waved *¡adiós!*, and was gone in a puff of *caliche*.

With two contracts yet to be filled, the ROTC continued on with the work, but the walls lacked the magic of the others. These were very straight, very *gabacho*, not sensual, looking almost like cinder block walls. In truth, they were ugly, without soul.

The ROTC broke up shortly after those disasters, mainly because of shame. Just before its dissolution, the workers spotted El Chewy Jiménez building a greenhouse at La Blondi's house in the Heights. They noted that he was gaining weight.

■ ■ ■

Some six months after the ROTC disbanded, El Chewy Jiménez looked up El Indio Jesús in La Plaza Vieja. He asked what had happened with the company.

El Indio delivered the workers' message to him. "*La Blondi desbarató la compañía.* It no longer exists."

"*Pués,*" sighed El Chewy, "*a mí también.*"

Thus it was that El Chewy Jiménez and the ROTC met and were defeated on the battleground of life by one of the most powerful weapons in the arsenal of the gringo world—the blonde.

Miguel Olson

After lunch on Tuesday, El Indio Jesús drove to Joanie's apartment in the city core, where a few single-family dwellings, now split up into haphazard apartment units, awaited execution at the hands of the urban renewal program. These rentals had life expectancies of only a few months: they had already been sold to the city, and although not legally eligible for leasing by the previous owner, the urbans never bothered to check, so the original owners continued to rake in rent money—and would continue to do so until the loophole was permanently closed by demolition.

Joanie was the widow of El Indio's colleague Miguel Olson, formerly of the 187th Airborne Regiment and occasional transfer man for the impounded *caro troquita* parts. Not long ago the newspapers reported that Miguel Olson had been found burned to death behind La Paloma Blanca Bar on South Second Street.

El Indio Jesús could not help musing over the life of his friend, the Chicano Swede, as he made his way to Joanie's home.

■ ■ ■

Miguel Olson owed his life to the sharp ears and kind hearts of barrio children.

The Atchison, Topeka, and Santa Fe Railroad maintained a siding in the Barelas barrio where the Pullman cars were shunted for cleaning and repair. The tracks ran through a corridor, cleaving through the barrio of tiny houses crowded up to the cinder edges of the railroad bed. Children were forever tempted to explore the railyards, and their parents were eternally pressed to keep them away from the danger.

On a baking hot afternoon in the summer of 1935, children playing near the tracks heard the insistent cry of a baby coming from the direction of a Pullman sleeper. Not daring themselves to investigate, they called their bold elder brothers to solve the mystery. Climbing up to the top of the guard fence, the boys could make out through the windows a moving, wailing bundle atop one of the bunks. Moving fast to avoid the guards, the boys dove in and out of the Pullman car and carried home their trophy.

What they had found was a beautiful baby boy with light blue eyes, rosy cheeks, tow-headed with the whitest skin. Only a few months old, he still wore a bead bracelet from the hospital that spelled out OLSON.

Marcella Garcia would not see her husband for another twenty days, because his section gang in Los Lunas had just started up another work period after a two-day rest at home. A combination of her immediate affection for the baby and not knowing exactly what to do with him—other than to give him love and care—kept him from being passed along to the authorities or to the priests. By the time that Alfredo Garcia returned to his family, the baby was firmly in place as the sixth son and ninth child of the family.

From time to time the Garcias talked about speaking to someone "in authority" about the baby, but it never came to pass. As far as the neighbors knew or cared, he was a child left behind with the babysitter, a baby whose mother may or may not return some day. A number of children in the barrio were semipermanent residents after having been abandoned by their mothers. Not a few were gringo children. The baby was named Michael Olson, in expectation that he would be reclaimed one day. The family always called him Miguel, however.

Although he was never to know, Miguel's birth mother was a corn- and milk-fed Wisconsin high school prom queen who was convinced that her future lay in Hollywood, where platinum blondes were prized beyond gold and diamonds. What was more, her albinism was authentic and not the product of the peroxide bottle. An unexpected pregnancy, a sojourn in a home for unwed mothers in Chicago, and her eventual escape on the Super Chief to Los Angeles were but steps on her path to stardom. Baby Olson was left to his fate when she changed trains, equipped only with a blanket, diapers, bracelet reading OLSON and his mother's sincerest, most fervent best wishes.

Miguel grew up as a barrio child fluent in Valley Spanish and mores. When school began, Marcella explained to the staff that his mother would return soon to fill out the rest of the enrollment forms, but in the meantime, *por favor*, this child should start school with the other children, *con su permiso*?

The years stretched by, Miguel never perceiving any real difference between himself and his siblings. When children new to the neighborhood chanced to call him *gabacho*, they soon learned that Michael Olson had five mean brothers and three sisters all named Garcia who were willing to defend his adopted place in the social network. Reaching his teen years, even with his hair darkening, he heard "*gabacho*" said behind his back from time to time when his team played sports with outside barrios. But when he opened his mouth and spoke, when he moved his body, when he reacted to people, it was unmistakable that he was *simpático* and at one with *la gente*.

Miguel Olson's second adoption took place at the Chosen Reservoir in Korea. Plucked from the barrio at eighteen years of age, he was trained to be a killer by the army for eight weeks at

Fort Ord. After five days' leave with his family and friends in Barelas, he proceeded to Fort Campbell for advance infantry training and jump school for ten weeks. Too soon, he found himself in Seoul with the 187th Airborne Regiment.

The day came when, on a combat jump into the Chosen Reservoir area and never even yet having fired his M-1 in anger, he and his whole platoon were struck down. When he swam back up to consciousness, someone was trying to feed him C-ration soup into his mangled face, teeth, and jaws, someone who spoke no English. For a while, flirting with pain and delirium, he thought he had been captured by the North Koreans. He eventually figured out that he was among Turkish soldiers. They treated his wounds and gave him small attentions such as a single Lucky Strike cigarette—which he could not smoke because of his ruined face—or a spare canteen cup. A Turkish officer appeared some days later who explained that Miguel was the sole survivor of his platoon and that he would have to stay with them until arrangements for a transfer could be made.

As with the rescue from the Pullman car, all that he carried was a dogtag reading OLSON with which to enter this strange and unknown culture of the Turkish soldiers. And, as perilous as before, his ability to survive depended on the kindness of persons he did not know and who had no reason to help him.

All he could do was watch and listen. He could not speak nor could he understand a single word of the language being spoken. Yet it came to him powerfully that he was among professional soldiers, in stark contrast to the amateurs with whom he had trained and jumped in the U.S. Army.

He often heard small arms fire overhead and sporadic impact from mortar shells exploding nearby. Outside the region of pain radiating from his destroyed face, he nonetheless felt safe among the Turks. He tried sipping the C-ration soup, and before long felt strong enough to set about cleaning a .30-caliber carbine and looking for ammunition. Within days, he left the bunker and fought shoulder-to-shoulder with the soldier who had given him the cigarette.

From then on it was continuous combat, which he learned to absorb as a routine job but a job in which he could take pride. The Turkish soldiers instructed him in the care of their special knives and how to use them. Beyond that, they taught him how to be a professional soldier in all aspects of the art. Most important of all was what he learned through his eyes having to do with death— that dying was not to be feared.

Then the time came when an American medical supply truck carried Miguel back to the field hospital where he was treated and released. He was reassigned to a regular infantry division next.

With orders for a ten-day leave in Seoul, he began seeing the Korean civilians for the first time. Like his experience with the Turks, he would spot someone who reminded him of a person from Barelas. Once he saw a woman carrying a child who looked so much like Marcella, his adopted mother, if not in face, at least in posture, that he gasped out loud.

Another time at a bar near the post, while picking up change on the counter, he turned to see an altercation between an American sailor and a Korean bar girl. About to turn back, it struck him how much the face of the girl resembled his sister Consuela's dark beauty. He proceeded to get deeply drunk.

Miguel encountered the Turkish officer at the American medical supply center when he returned to duty from his leave. In a flash of insight, he felt that if he were to survive Korea, it would have to be with his new family, the Turks. So he climbed into the back of the supply truck as it was leaving. When he awoke some hours later, he was once again among his Turkish friends, enjoying the special feeling of homecoming. They gave him an ornate knife with an ivory inlaid silver handle to mark the occasion and their friendship.

In the morning, while sharpening the knife, he suddenly realized that it was destined to disembowel a Korean who might in some faint way resemble someone he knew from Barelas. He laid the knife down and walked all the way back to the American regiment. He had made his peace with the Korean people and never fought again. Nor did he ever look back at the so-called Forgotten War in which almost as many American soldiers were killed in three years as in Vietnam in ten years.

■ ■ ■

The afternoon newspaper carried a two-inch item taken directly from the police report.

MAN KILLED NEAR BAR

A man believed to be Michael Olson, 48, of 1213 Bridge Street SW was found burned to death in a car sometime between 2 and 3 a.m. in the parking lot adjacent to La Paloma Blanca bar.

Patrons of the bar said that three Mexican nationals who they could not identify left the bar with Olson earlier in the evening. They thought a scuffle had ensued.

The police spokesman said that an investigation into the incident would continue and that a positive identification would be made later after forensic evidence was made available.

The death is the fifth to occur at La Paloma Blanca Bar in the last four months.

■ ■ ■

That night at La Paloma Blanca, conversations about Miguel Olson's death spun one story after another. One had it that maybe Miguel had been called *gabacho* or gringo just one time too many and had struck out at the nationals who did not know that he was as Chicano as anyone raised in Barelas.

Friends and associates disagreed about that hypothesis. At base they agreed that there must have been some kind of fight over, maybe, a business deal. But reflecting on this, not one of them could honestly say that he had ever cheated on them or on anyone they knew. Truly, in their experience, he had treated everyone fairly. But there was always a lingering question about the source of the tools and appliances he sold. If they were stolen property, he might have gotten in trouble fencing them, or with the ones who had actually committed the burglaries.

A variation on the theme suggested that Miguel had sold a truckload of secondhand television sets, refrigerators, and other appliances in Mexico for a substantial amount of money, and that, upon completion of the deal, the Mexican nationals with whom he was collaborating ganged up and killed him.

Those people closest to Miguel were mindful that he may have maintained connections with longtime Barelas pals who were now very high up in the international drug trade hierarchy. Several lived lavish lives in Mexico. This group of rumor-spinners claimed that they knew for a fact that drug runners in small planes developed a return trade whereby northward flights brought drugs to the United States while southward flights carried small arms to gun dealers who sold them to guerrillas in Chiapas or farther south into Central America. The historical promiscuity of handguns in the United States, a free trade ticket guaranteed under the Constitution, made them a natural age-old "cash on the barrelhead" export.

So maybe they—whoever *they* were—brought Miguel in on parachute drops of small arms. Why not? the tale weavers theorized. Unlike drug drops, which can be done by amateurs with no concern for damaging the goods, precision drops carefully planned and executed were necessary for breakable commodities such as small arms.

One mechanic contributed his know-how by saying that neither Cessnas nor Sky Kings—favorites of the drug trade—were constructed for air drops, and so they needed modification. The skills needed for such air drop operations were at Miguel Olson's fingertips, he said.

As a general rule, another chimed in, if you really knew Miguel, you would know that his political sympathies have always been supportive of indigenous revolutions. Don't overlook that fact.

As the evening wore on, the difficulty the spinners of these explanations for Miguel Olson's demise could not reconcile was the drug-dealing card: it did not fit. He was clean in his dealings, everyone agreed. Close friends often heard him rant about the destruction of Chicano minds by drugs. He was heard to say that law enforcement agents must be deeply involved in the trade for it to be so successful. Maybe, someone suggested, he had said that too many times, too loudly, and in too many ears.

Both friends and not a few enemies were left with the conviction that whatever the treachery, Miguel's death was no mere bar fight. This suspicion deepened when they noted that State Police Officer Jack Spencer was at the scene of the investigation. That was really curious.

The *chismeros* were finally left with the ultimate question: Was the dead man in the car really Miguel Olson?

One dangling rumor suggested that Tony the World Traveler was at La Paloma Blanca Bar that night, but the USSCBD members in attendance quickly dismissed that idea.

Waldo

Jacobo Beserra traveled a path crisscrossing cultures. If he had talent, it was his ability to manipulate just about anything that came his way. He could turn incidental information into gold. He could, if he wished to, give thanks to his mother's quiet determination to make an "American" life for her son.

His mother reflected the Spanish rather than Mexican Indian blood in her light skin and hair color. Yet she was the product of the barrios, a Chicana who held down a job as bar waitress in the old Club Chesterfield out on Highway 66 at the west end of town. The club drew cowboys in the early 1940s, serving up Western and hillbilly music, a storied place where even Gene Autry, Roy Rogers, and Randolph Scott stopped by from time to time when traveling by car across country, leaving autographed pictures of themselves and their horses on the wall behind the bar.

The man she married against her family's wishes, Jacobo's father, was a scab brought in from Mexico to break a strike at the railroad roundhouse. In Mexico, he and other men like himself had been told that Anglo-looking Mexicans could make good money up north helping to bust up the railroad union. Those large young men from Chihuahua with blondish hair and light eyes, descendants of German, Mormon, and Amish colonies, were eager to make a better life for themselves and so signed up with the railroad agents who served the line running south through Mexico. They would provide muscle. They could also glean inside information about the Chicano strike leaders and their strategies to pass back to the agents.

Some months after arriving in El Norte, Jacobo's father and a few scabs visited La Paloma Blanca Bar in the barrio. Near midnight, when he made his way to the men's room, two men followed him in. They were brothers of the union leader of the railroad strike who had been savagely beaten into a coma. Ramón Chávez and his brother moved up behind Beserra while he was taking a piss. Ramón put a choke hold on him and spun him around. His brother shoved a knife in under his ribs and tickled his heart. Unhurriedly but before the body started to bleed they opened the window above the toilet and pushed out the dying Mexican into the back alley. They cleaned up the few drops of blood and walked back into the barroom.

The body of Jacobo Beserra's father was not found until the following morning. It was reported as that of an unidentified Mexican national. This was nothing new, nothing spectacular. The other scabs said nothing.

Jacobo Beserra grew up in the barrio and went to school in the Valley until he was seven. He lived in his grandmother's home and saw his mother less and less often as the years went by.

Barrio life for Jacobo proved difficult. He was often caught in traps caused by inherent suspicion of his Anglo appearance but as much, or even more often, from flaws in his character. He found himself growing to hate the kids around him, resenting their distance, their avoidance of him, and blamed it on his light complexion and not on anything to do with his behavior. The few Anglo teachers treated him differently from the Chicano students.

He developed an ingratiating personality and, combined with an infectious smile, his fortunes changed as the grade school years passed.

Yet he still had to be careful walking to and from school. He had many enemies. Chief among them was another *rubio* like himself, Miguel Olson. Jacobo knew nothing about him save that he could speak Spanish and was, like himself, taller and larger than most of their classmates. Jacobo was never sure why Miguel Olson looked at him only from the corners of his eyes.

The day came when the free-floating hostility between the two boys erupted. How was Jacobo to know that the little Chicana he fondled on the playground after school was the sister of Miguel Olson?

Miguel and a swarm of small, dark children pounced on him from nowhere while screaming, "Waldo, Waldo, take that, Waldo." They beat him bloody.

Jacobo survived the bruises and cuts, but he never survived the nickname Waldo, a name in the barrio denoting white stupidity, or gringo perversity, or simply a maker of mistakes.

■ ■ ■

Sometime earlier, Jacobo Beserra's mother, still working at Club Chesterfield, had married a Texan named Luther Jack Spencer. She lived with him in a trailer home on Route 66 where Spencer repaired car radiators and ran a one-pump filling station servicing Okies, travelers on the migrant auto trains crossing the western deserts to a golden future in California.

Luther Jack Spencer was already far along in accumulating automobiles and trucks when he first met Jacobo's mother. His signs along Route 66 advertised repair work, warning LAST STOP BEFORE DESERT NO RADIATOR REPAIR WORK FOR 500 MILES FREE AIR AND WATER. A giant cowboy doffing his ten-gallon hat held another sign, which said, HOWDY FOLKS. This one let the migrants know that Luther Jack was kin and spoke their language.

Luther Jack Spencer would check out the dilapidated vehicles passing through or choking to a steaming halt at his station and would gauge his bill according to the amount of money he figured they had. He would accept items in trade for any gap between his bill and what they could come up with in cash. The vehicles—the cars and trucks, and things that looked like combinations of both—carried all their owners' possessions. Luther Jack Spencer could tote up their financial worth within seconds. The sum that he offered to take the vehicle off their hands amounted to the price of a bus ticket to Barstow, California. The Greyhound bus made unscheduled stops in front of the station with the wave of Spencer's hand, always willing to pick up stranded wayfarers and a tip from Luther Jack.

Within a few months after opening, Spencer accrued enough furniture and appliances to set up a secondhand store next to the station.

He also captured business coming in from the west. Inside the station he began stocking flour, sugar, Vienna sausages in small cans, beer, cigarettes, and other sundries. These were sold to Navajo, Zuñi, Acoma, and Laguna Indians as they came by on their way into town. Often, they bought what they needed with hand-crafted jewelry and pottery rather than cash. Woven blankets, too. It piled up. On their way back to the reservations they bought kerosene for lamps and snack food for the trip. He joked with his friends that he snagged Indians "a-comin' and a-goin'."

That was about the time he met Jacobo's mother.

It did not take a second look for Luther Jack to see that she could almost be considered a gringa. He admired her ability to deal with the Texans, Okies, and other patrons at the bar. He watched her over the course of several months, perhaps even years. The day that she came into his furniture and appliance store to buy a sewing machine, he offered her a job as his sales lady. Attached to the job was the inducement of living in the small trailer behind the building. She moved in right away but left young Jacobo with her mother in the barrio.

Soon she was managing the secondhand store, doing the books for the service station, and occasionally pumping gas when the press of westward traffic became especially heavy during the summer months. From time to time, once she had gained his full confidence, Luther Jack would leave the filling station and store in her hands while he went off on fishing trips with friends or to visit relatives in Texas. Even though she could match him at his own game of fleecing the Okies, he knew she would never betray him, having saved her from a bleak life either at Club Chesterfield or worse—in the barrio. He also knew she would never tell anyone exactly how he was able to accumulate wealth so quickly. She provided a façade of integrity and honesty and could calm the most outraged, hoodwinked migrant from back east.

Spencer's appearance began changing over time. He wore clean clothes instead of blackened overalls and a hat instead of a cap, a hat that was traded up for ever larger ones until settling on a cowboy hat like the one doffed on his highway sign, a big white ten-gallon Stetson. He wore a bolo tie made of a scorpion sunk into a triangle of clear plastic. His fifth finger was weighted down with a silver ring carrying large saladlike chunks of turquoise and coral.

He no longer lounged around the front of the filling station. Now Chicanos waited on customers and worked on radiators. He was the manager, the one they called to make the final estimates of the cost of repairs or the new tires. He would emerge from the office, greet them with a frank handshake and a loud voice, push the Stetson back on his head, and engage them in sympathetic dialogue.

When the deal was done he shook their hands heartily and waved them off to Barstow, stripped and bewildered.

After years of one success after another, one Easter Sunday Jacobo's mother felt confident enough in her position to bring her son to the trailer for Easter dinner to meet Luther Jack Spencer. Jacobo was dressed in his Sunday best, and she added a special touch to the outfit: she balanced a small white cowboy hat on his head.

When Luther Jack cast eyes upon Jacobo, taking in his Anglo features, he forthrightly stretched out a hand and said, "Come on over here to me, son." At that moment, when Jacobo mirrored the outstretched hand, he became Luther Jack Spencer Junior, although he did not know it for yet awhile.

Luther Jack Spencer now had a presentable family. Maria, Jacobo's mother, was now called Mary, and he had another worker on board—a son and potential heir for his empty loins. Behind him lay an ugly, hidden history in Texas. Ahead of him lay respectability.

■ ■ ■

Luther Jack Spencer Junior, now called Jack Spencer instead of Jacobo Beserra, began attending school where no one spoke Spanish. He could exercise his first language only with the janitors. His name was legally changed to Luther Jack Spencer Junior, no comma. He affected the Texan drawl of his adopted father.

Jack transferred to a private junior high school where the local establishment could afford the tuition and upscale wardrobe for their sons and daughters. Money was not the only doorkeeper for this school. The application process effectively precluded undesirables, starting with name recognition.

Visits to his mother's family in the Barelas barrio became fewer over the years, dwindling to Easter Sunday, and then not at all.

Luther Jack Spencer Junior's language skills did not go unnoticed by the teachers and administrators. He was frequently taken out of class to make sense of a predicament in which, for instance, a non-English-speaking delivery man or a janitor needed interpreting to be understood and dealt with. For his help, he was rewarded with extra recess periods or a second helping of his favorite dessert. In the third year he could come and go at will into the principal's office as though he were the staff's official interpreter and liaison to the Spanish-speaking public. He had full use of the telephone. He had all the makings of an informer. Or a politician. Or a law enforcement officer.

Since his schoolwork was only modestly passing—he could not really read or write, although his basic math was flawless—he went to a public high school some fifteen miles from home instead of the private academy where his former classmates typically matriculated. His parents and teachers felt that the nearest high school would put him together with too many Valley Chicanos and Indians and not afford him adequate opportunity, meaning that it was underfunded, understaffed, and overhoused, thanks to the differential allotment of public school funds within the system. In addition, his teachers in the private school suspected that the informer they had created would not survive in a public school in the Valley. They generously lent a hand in bending the rules requiring students to attend a school in their own districts.

During the summer the private school administrator telephoned Jack's new high school principal to tell him about the case of this nondistrict student who was about to enter. He told him of Luther Jack Spencer Junior's special talents in translating and communicating with maintenance staff. As a favor, he would appreciate Jack's receiving a fair shake, since he had been so very useful to them in the past.

On the first day at the new school Luther Jack Spencer Junior received a penciled notice on his registration card telling him to report to the football coach at the gym. Till then, he had never played any sport more strenuous than Ping-Pong. The message was disquieting. He knew he had grown a lot, thanks to a huge appetite. But he did not like to be hurt.

At the gym the coach sent him to the line coach, who assigned him to managing the football equipment and keeping the locker room in order. To his enormous relief, he would not have to play football after all. He was given a key to the coach's office, to the equipment room and the locker room. He was instructed to fill out his schedule so that each Friday would be free for him to work with the team. His teachers received the message that he should have special treatment because of the athletic department's special needs. He also got a cafeteria card that was color-coded to signify that he, like the football team members, could eat how much and whatever he wanted. And as before, he had use of the telephone.

Throughout his high school years, Jack's passing grades reflected more the tacit understanding between the academic and athletic staff than any effort on his part. His reading ability actually fell for every year of high school. But his math was excellent.

At home, his father's business grew from swindling Okies to defrauding new and used car buyers. He kept the garage and secondhand furniture store going, letting Mary run them, but he had moved east along the main street to set up his used car lot and Chrysler dealership. He sold the turquoise-and-coral ring and bought himself a large diamond set in gold for his fifth finger.

One night after Mary had closed the doors of the secondhand store and retired to the trailer in the back of the business, the butane tank exploded. The store and the station blew up in a great ball of fire. It was believed that a careless individual, hanging around after hours, had unknowingly dropped a lit cigarette onto the spilled coal oil beneath the holding tank. That winter night, flames engulfed the trailer in which Jack's wife had lived alone while he and his son were housed some miles away, guarding the dealership. Mary did not survive the fire.

With the insurance settlement he received from the loss of the businesses and the life of his wife, Luther Jack bought young Jack an aqua green Ford convertible with overhead cams. And he added to his dealership.

Jack Junior was popular in high school. He was able to go into the barrios, where his ability to get what the team members wanted—liquor and drugs—came in handy. He drove an impressive car and wore a spiffy wardrobe. When they played games near the international border, he introduced them to "real women" on the other side of the river, who in turn introduced them to their first serious sex and, sometimes, venereal disease. He could facilitate these escapades without problems with police or authorities because, through his father, he had friends on the Mexican police force. The line coach sometimes went with them.

After one of these trips the high school was flooded with good-quality marijuana. It was then that Jack traded in his Ford for a pink Mercury with a Plexiglas top.

By now, Jacobo Beserra had completely metamorphosed into Luther Jack Spencer Junior, a very big man on campus. In his senior year, when the football team won the state championship, Jack's face and name were on the front page of every paper in the state, sitting in the front row and holding the winning football in the official photograph.

It could have been said that he had won the high school championship for being the key facilitator. His knowledge of Spanish and his ability to gain useful information consistently placed others in his debt.

His crowning achievement, for himself and the team, took place in his senior year. Learning through his sources that the star quarterback on the Valley team, Miguel Olson, used marijuana to alleviate the pain in his damaged knee, a telephone call prompted a raid on the locker room and the playing field just as the game was to begin. Miguel Olson was handcuffed and led away.

Miguel did not go quietly. He turned back and shouted, but all that Jack heard above the roaring fans was, "Strike two, Waldo!"

Miguel Olson never finished high school. In court, he was given the choice of jail or the army. He chose the army and not long after was air-dropped over the Chosen Reservoir in Korea.

The following spring, in response to a personal request from the city police chief looking for tall, well-built, upstanding candidates for the new class at the police academy beginning in early summer, Jack's name was forwarded with an enthusiastic recommendation supplied by the principal. The letter contained the information that Jack was fluent in Spanish and knew his way around the barrios. As it happened, his father, now a prominent businessman, had recently been named to the state police board by a grateful governor for a sizable campaign contribution. Everything fit nicely.

Jack did very well at the police academy. His career got off to a strong start with a major drug bust, through which he reinforced his relations with members of the Mexican police force. He went from uniform duty to detective squad in a matter of months.

Whereas Miguel Olson fought Communists in Asia, Jack Spencer fought Communists on the homefront. In time the vice squad was commonly known as the Red Squad, and Jack was in his element judicially and politically.

During the McCarthy era, when jingoism gave license to hound leftists, suspected leftists, and left-leaning liberals of all stripes, union leaders in Silver City were jailed on charges that they were Communists. Juan Chacón and other leaders and their families suffered harassment and terrorization. New Deal Democrats were hauled up before tribunals of the House Un-American Activities Committee meeting in El Paso, their careers and livelihoods ruined by innuendo and outright lies. Tenured university professors were flushed from the supposed safety of academia on grounds of having taught, nay, fostered, the tenets of communism, the Red Threat.

Those identified as possible subversives sometimes descended to lower-level positions in which to hide. Some ended up teaching on the Indian reservations. Some dove into alcohol and drugs. Some committed suicide. Some did all four. Few really escaped.

Community leaders and precinct politicians, if they did not rage against the Red Peril, often left the state for some Siberia—usually to California, where it was easier to take on protective coloration—for fear of public scourging. Until then, their lives became more and more unbearable in the face of whispered *chisme* campaigns set in motion by undercover police of the supersecret Red Squad. Tax bills on their property could suddenly triple, water bills soared above what the neighbors paid, bank loans were called in and new loans refused. Men in unmarked cars were seen parked a few houses away, staying there for hours on end. These things led the neighbors to believe that something illegal was being done. Community members started to shun them for fear of becoming involved in whatever was happening. Life grew insupportable and they left the state too.

Jack Spencer's career flourished in this climate of repression. He next joined the state police.

As the 1960s advanced, the Vietnam conflict exploded into a full-blown national issue. Those vocally and publicly opposed to the war were added to the list of subversives under surveillance by the police. It was also a time when civil rights issues sharpened ethnic and racial awareness, when community consciousness grew in measure with the burgeoning suspicion that the nation was morally and ethically hurting.

While there were differences in attitudes about these cantankerous issues, in the barrios there was no lack of patriotism. Too many of the people had struggled too hard to get to America to feel estranged toward it now. Too many were inheritors of hundreds of years on this American soil to turn their backs on it now. Too many people had sons and brothers and husbands and fathers filling foxholes in the jungles of Southeast Asia to eschew their loyalty to those who would die for the nation. And, finally, there abided a tradition of the warrior, such as Mangas Coloradas or Emiliano Zapata, which called out the young men with an insistent voice summoning them from out of the gangs, from out of the barrios.

Yet the perception that the nation was going in the wrong direction was pervasive. Why was it that Chicanos and Indians and Blacks were meeting death in that faraway land all out of proportion to their numbers at home? Indians joked that, from their point of view, it was indeed "better red than dead," in counterpoint to the national slogan that it was "better to be dead than Red." The domino theory, which warned of communism's step-by-step conquest of the whole world, had little reality in the community mind. Who played dominos, anyway? No one there had ever met a Communist face to face. No one had ever so much as laid an eye on the dangerous Communist newspaper, the *Daily World*. So where was the threat?

Jack Spencer thrilled to be part of Cointelpro, short for Counter-Intelligence Programs, that involved his office from time to time. The Cointelpros were largely more secret, aggressive and destructive. Their methodology for targeting and destroying suspected subversives of whatever race and political stripe was rated highly effective by their anonymous leaders.

Jack was exceptionally proud of the success gained by a Cointelpro crusade against a local group seeking to establish a citywide citizen's police review board, a panel that would be charged to review specific cases in which the police may have been at fault in the poor outcome of a police matter. Jack and his peers held that civilians should keep out of police affairs; if such a board were established, would a state police civilian review board be far behind?

Although the citizen's committee was clever enough to be acephalous—there was no identifiable group leader—the Cointelpro efforts focused in on a certain few whose names showed up on other lists as antiwar protesters, civil rights demonstrators, or free speech advocates.

One of the people caught in the Cointelpro crosshairs was the Reverend Raul Sena, a Protestant minister of a tiny parish in a northside barrio.

Reverend Sena never understood what happened to his ministry. All he knew was that his church attendance and then membership dropped to nearly nothing overnight. Not long afterward, his national board withdrew its support funds.

He sought answers from among his friends, but they either could contribute nothing toward solving the mystery or they too turned their backs on him. His efforts to establish a citizen's police review board were silently struck down one by one. One day it looked as though the city council would support the plan, and the next day none of the city council members would answer the telephone when he or anyone on the committee called.

On a Thursday night his old car was vandalized. Garbage was thrown at the little church. Cars were parked up the street with watchers in them. His telephone was tapped and sometimes would not work at all. On a Saturday night he heard the scream of tires cornering the block and shots being fired.

It was not his imagination. In the morning he pried out bullets lodged in the face of the adobe chapel.

The harassment planted a seed that was cancerous and that would one day take its toll.

Not long after this, his national board reassigned him to a parish in Idaho.

■ ■ ■

About the time when Reverend Sena agonized over the reassignment letter, Jack Spencer's career path would bifurcate. As opportunities arose through the years, he had always dabbled in the illicit. But now, upon the death of Luther Jack Spencer Senior, his father's business interests would fall into his lap.

On a hot Sunday afternoon, Jack Junior was called to the Piggly Wiggly supermarket. In the parking lot he found a swarm of police and shoppers standing around his father's long pink Cadillac. As he pushed through the crowd, he could see his father at the trunk, standing but leaning in as though to reach for something. Going closer, he registered a strange imbalance in his father's posture, something not quite natural. His Stetson was oddly askew.

Then he saw the small black hole at the nape of his neck showing through the fringe of hair that was all that was left of his balding head. Jack recognized the bullet hole, absorbed the information, paused for one brief moment of human emotion, and then became a police officer on a routine call once again. Except that there was nothing routine about this situation.

Jack knew he had to make some fast moves to divert the other officers away from catching on that this was an execution. He must ever so lightly lead them to the conclusion that this was a simple case of an attempted mugging gone bad. All his years in the police force gave him the ability to be steely calm and then play on the sympathies of the other officers to attain that goal.

By the time the ambulance and the coroner arrived to take the body away, the police on the case had penciled into their casebooks that Luther Jack Spencer Senior was killed by unknown assailant or assailants whose objective was simple robbery.

Jack Junior, who normally steered clear of his father's modest sideline in the drug business except to do small favors for him now and again, suddenly had to decide how he would deal with this developing situation. He could launch a vendetta, or, on the other hand, he could cut himself in where his father had been selected out. Given his keen business acumen, his understanding of the art of negotiation in the netherworld, and a respect for diversification of investments, he decided to buy into his father's former partnership. His own portfolio at that point carried no more than bluff, the threat that he might know the perpetrators and what police and judicial connections he might command to enforce his will.

It was enough. In time, Jack Spencer managed two careers, one with the police and one in the drug trade. Both careers made excellent use of his manipulative and linguistic skills, a pure synergism in which each supported the other. The final effect was much more profitable than what either of the two careers could achieve separately.

Goodwill

Joanie, white and poor, born and raised in the barrio, was as Chicana as many of the girls she grew up with. No other life or other way of living was know to her. She wore her hair the way the others did, experimenting with long lavish froths. Black was her color of choice, and even with jeans her blouses and T-shirts were usually black, emblazoned with local *taquería* or tortilla factory slogans. Her front teeth were missing as she approached her twenties. An unguarded face, drained of animation, carved too early by the poverty, misery, and pain that had been a constant companion through her years, was what she greeted others with.

Joanie and Miguel Olson were blessed with a daughter of angelic beauty whom they named Soon Young, a name that caught Miguel's fancy in Korea. Now four years old, people often looking inquiringly at her parents, having difficulty believing that they could produce such a comely child. Miguel's face, so battered by an M-1 rifle butt at the Chosen Reservoir, and Joanie's prematurely ruined looks gave little clue that they, too, were once considered handsome. The toll taken by the Reservoir and the Valley was equally high.

In Miguel's absence, El Indio Jesús saw to Joanie's housing, food, and protection, assuming the care and responsibilities of the wife and child of his *hermano*.

El Indio Jesús' visits to Joanie's home, never predictable but nonetheless frequent, served warning upon the neighbors and watchers that she was under his protection. As hyenas follow behind the wounded, anyone who thought to stalk Joanie and her daughter would have to think twice with El Indio Jesús as their champion. He came and went at all hours. It was neither unusual nor unstudied that he showed up sometimes very late at night to unload, say, a hundred sheets of used corrugated tin into her back-yard, or find it necessary to pound out a dent in his *caro troquita* at eleven o'clock at night.

El Indio Jesús used this Tuesday afternoon to help Joanie hack through the bureaucratic jungle to secure Miguel's social security benefits. They had been legally married, and Soon Young was legitimately their own. Miguel had earned those benefits.

This day El Indio Jesús brought Joanie a used hot plate and then drove her and Soon Young to the welfare office, located not where the poor of the city resided but in the middle-class neighborhood of the Heights.

Like threading one's way through a cactus patch, Joanie wove through the eligibility criteria and was in sight of success when a technicality came up that could defeat all prior effort. El Indio Jesús had anticipated it, however, and was ready for battle.

To obtain food stamps it was necessary to produce a rent receipt to prove residence, as opposed to being a transient or under another jurisdiction's responsibility. But since her landlord was renting property already sold to the urban renewal program, her lessor could not give her a receipt disclosing his name, address, and the address of the property in question. As part of the terrorism practiced on the poor, they were told that a case worker would visit the homesite they claimed within a few days of processing. Although this was pure bluff—there were never enough caseworkers to carry that out—the barrio poor believed the lie and would not enroll without a valid rent receipt.

El Indio Jesús solved this problem for Joanie by producing a receipt book, a pad with carbons and lines to be filled out saying, "in receipt of . . ." Having found an old water bill at the apartment with the name of the last *gabacho* renter on it, he filled out the form in his fine script and signed it with a flourish. Joanie then had two pieces of evidence testifying to valid residency.

Joanie thus obtained food stamps but still needed hard cash for nonfood items such as soap, detergent, toothpaste, and insect spray, which were exempt under the Department of Agriculture's definition of covered groceries. El Indio Jesús gave her a few dollars in exchange for an equal amount of food stamps, which he could use elsewhere.

Joanie needed no additional clothing for herself and Soon Young because, in fact, their prior career with Miguel brought her to one of the highest standards of dress in the Valley, although her devotion to the color black would have seemed unimaginative. Even so, other women and girls looked to her to interpret the changing national trends into Chicana haute couture.

■ ■ ■

The system that Miguel had devised some years before began at sunup each Saturday and Sunday, when Miguel's 1961 sun-bleached lime green Chrysler Imperial with Hemi motor reached a central staging area in the Heights. From there they would visit the most fecund Goodwill boxes within a few miles' radius. Miguel kept the car in perfect mechanical shape, replete with continental rear deck kit, protruding head- and taillights, push-button gears, and an automatic light dimmer on the dashboard that looked like a miniature periscope. The battered exterior gave no hint of its internal integrity. It was, in fact, the most powerful of all the

Chryslers. It was the one bought by police departments, which they equipped with siren, lights, turbocharging, and fuel injection.

Miguel would sit in the wide front seat with Joanie and Soon Young next to him, all three dressed up as though on their way to church. He would pull in to a parking lot having a visibly laden Goodwill box.

As a general rule, America cleanses itself on Saturdays, purging itself of the obsolete. Sundays were therefore usually more profitable for Joanie and Miguel's efforts than Saturday mornings. But since Friday nights as well as Saturday nights could witness the expulsion of the man of the house, landing his tools and equipment into the Goodwill box before the dust settled behind him, Saturdays could not be overlooked in the Olsons' scheme.

It was important that they be in the Heights between sunrise and eight-thirty on either morning. Miguel checked the newspapers and television news as a double check for the sunrise calculation. In the Heights, the police did not care what kind of car was on its streets when the morning sun was up. Since crime was rare during those early morning hours, the Heights police routinely ate breakfast at the pancake houses, gratis.

At the first Goodwill box Miguel parked nearby, got out, and surveyed the accumulation of cast-off clothing and miscellaneous items. He did not touch anything. He returned to the car.

As it happened, this gringo-appearing family in the Chrysler always brought with them an article from home that could then be discarded into a Goodwill box for redistribution to the needy. Joanie then got out with the piece—a lamp, a broken iron—and placed it on the pile. With consummate speed, she extracted the best of the clothing inside the box and returned with it to the car. Then Miguel got out again, snatched up tools, small furniture pieces, and other items, put them into the trunk, got back in the Chrysler, and drove off to the next Goodwill box. Unless they were watched closely, one could not tell exactly what happened in the short amount of time taken.

Pickings on Sunday mornings in the summertime were especially profitable. Not only did the disposableness of America's material possessions fill the Goodwill boxes with regularity, but the quality of the throwaway also rose along with the Dow Jones averages. Most Goodwill boxes stood in a sea of items on weekends in the Heights.

Miguel not infrequently came across whole collections of tools in perfect condition. Men hoping to outflank the car repair shops bought equipment to patch up their vehicles, tools and materials that lay about impotently until the garage was finally cleaned up and the stuff thrown into the Heights Goodwill box. Or the breakup of a couple could precipitate a windfall of sentimental and practical goods for selection.

Trends in hobbyism could be read by what found its way into the boxes, too: leather working, rock hounding, stained glass construction. When sets of uncommon tools were discarded, it was important to look around for the instruction manual or missing component parts. The price doubled in resale value in the Valley if the manual accompanied the set, particularly if the instructions were also in Spanish as well as English.

After systematically culling the better class of Goodwill box treasures, it was important to head home between eight and nine o'clock while the morning traffic was still light. The powerful Chrysler would not stand out for questioning in such traffic until they passed the freeway. Then they might face the danger of being stopped by the police. Passing out of the Heights and dropping across the border into the Valley, there was the inherent risk that the county sheriff's patrolmen would stop vehicles containing anything that protruded beyond the back seat, particularly large household goods and furniture, triggering their suspicion that a burglary had been committed.

If Miguel and Joanie escaped notice, they were back in the Valley by nine o'clock, the winnings stored by nine-thirty. By ten o'clock, the three of them were spruced up again and off to the pancake house on Central, where they always ordered Swedish pancakes.

During the week to come, mostly in the evening hours, Miguel bartered two or three items to supplement his day jobs. Joanie sold clothes during the day. It was not haphazard, however, in the sense that there were often orders to be filled from the inventory: a toaster oven, a particular kind of saw. Miguel filled the standing orders first. He was a reliable, dependable dealer whose warranty was more respected than General Electric's. If he sold a tool that did not work, he would replace it even two or three times until the customer was satisfied with the product. Time was no object: he had his good name to protect.

Piecemeal, then, their gleanings would ultimately be converted, sold, exchanged, and traded for labor and services, bringing to the young, resourceful Olson family a profitable sideline, making use of weekends when the rest of the country believed that only play and rest were acceptable occupations.

The Art of Lowrider Maintenance

Whenever possible of an evening, El Indio Jesús dropped in on the newstand across the street from the university. He made an effort to take along a *vato* having trouble in school, especially one with reading problems blocked by conversion from Spanish to English or from barrio patois to the written page. The magical transformation, a kind of birthing, that consistently took place at the magazine shelves never failed to thrill El Indio Jesús as he covertly watched a youth's sullen face light up with interest when paging for the first time through *Popular Mechanics* or *Popular Science* or, more enchantingly, *Hot VWs*. The automotive magazines always spun their webs, unerringly capturing the boys' imagination with just a few minutes of visuals. Next to snag them were the slick-covered issues on the latest developments in technology, aviation magazines with home-built butterfly-like craft to ponder, and the range of solar- and wind-driven experiments.

This evening, however, El Indio Jesús was alone when he left the store at the nine o'clock closing. He glanced at the median splitting the four lanes of traffic, remembering that not long before it was tastefully landscaped in native shrubs and cobblestones from the river. Since then, in the interest of safety from politically driven hurlers, the university and local commercial establishments had prevailed upon the city government to cement over those islands of opportunity.

He turned up the street toward his *caro troquita* at the "time expired" parking meter (no pay after 6 P.M.) only to find a very large young man, perhaps a student, down on one knee examining its undercarriage.

"Wow," said the man, shaking his head and addressing El Indio Jesús, "who built this? It's great, absolutely great!" Standing up, he said, "This is exactly what the Third World needs." He returned to his examination, walking all around the vehicle, going "um-hm, um-hm" as new things caught his attention.

El Indio Jesús watched his progress, to his own surprise thinking, "this *pinche* gringo can actually think! But is he a cop? *La chota* focusing in on me again? He could be a cop; he has the profile. He seems taken with the technology, though . . . but is he checking out the numbers on the pan? No . . ."

In fact, the young man was enjoying himself enormously with what he perceived as a marvelous puzzle. He looked at how the body was cut to make a pickup, how the rear shock absorbers were strengthened, reinforced, and clearly fit to carry more than just two passengers.

The young man paused in his survey and asked, "Why did you change the shock absorbers?"

"Don't you know?" responded El Indio Jesús. "The German engineers in the Fatherland made the car to carry only two or three people, or at the most four hundred to five hundred pounds of weight. But what is needed here is something to carry a thousand pounds, twice the weight of what Dr. Porsche had designed."

El Indio Jesús paused, then continued, smiling slightly with a touch of humor mixed with pride. "Our engineers—even though none of them attended the University of Stuttgart—modified this insect's carrying capacity. Now it can easily transport a thousand pounds to anywhere in the city and in a pinch might even be capable of carrying a ton for short distances."

The young man by now was standing next to El Indio Jesús looking clearly impressed, even dumbfounded.

"You know," he said thoughtfully, "this is exactly what I need at home. I live close to the border. Lots of sand. I've got projects this would be perfect for . . . How can I learn? Where can I go to learn how to construct something like this?"

El Indio Jesús mentally drew back, wondering again whether or not he was talking to the police. He decided to check this guy out.

To the young man he said, "I will get in contact with you." In his mind, he determined to call on an ex-*grafitero* now a lieutenant in the police department who could run off a complete printout on this guy, whoever he is, if he has a record of any kind.

"I will get in contact with you," he repeated. "Who has known you for the last fifteen years?"

"What?" reacted the young man, "I'm only twenty-five years old! Fifteen years? I was just a baby then!"

El Indio Jesús quietly regarded him, saying nothing, forcing him to think and thus testing his intelligence. If he was unable or unwilling to supply that much of his history, El Indio Jesús would not be interested in him further. There were plenty of others who could use his time and skills.

In effect, El Indio Jesús required three things from this young man to determine whether or not he was worthy of attention: first, inquisitiveness (already proven by asking the right questions); second, floating his name among the ROTC, the USSCBD, and the Valley; and third, the printout.

■ ■ ■

In time, El Indio Jesús learned a great deal about the young man whose name was William Haywood Williams, called by many "Big Bill." Their friendship began while Big Bill was a student at the university, where he learned just about nothing, and continued through the years during which he interned in the Department of Labor library, where he learned just about everything he wanted to know concerning labor and unionism in America. In time, his life in Rio Abajo placed him temporarily in the Immigration and Naturalization Service.

It was those first few years that held special texture for their friendship. El Indio Jesús was, of course, the teacher and Big Bill the pupil.

The first long trip they shared took place when Big Bill caught a ride with El Indio Jesús, who was on his way to Mexico. Big Bill invited him to stop by his home in Rio Abajo, near the border, to meet his family and to take a look at his various projects. On that ride down the Jornada del Muerto, much of the discussion was about "lowriders," the why and wherefore of the automobiles converted by so many Chicanos in the north of the state into specialty vehicles.

Big Bill, while observing the passing traffic, started the conversation off by asking, "Where do you suppose all the gas guzzlers have gone? Stolen? Chopped? Below the border? How in the world did hundreds of thousands of Detroit's automotive dinosaurs disappear from the face of the earth virtually overnight?" Big Bill chuckled. "Maybe, like with the dinosaurs, some iridium-soaked comet destroyed their food source—what do you think?—causing a catastrophic die-off?"

El Indio Jesús thought there was a lot to consider in this last conjecture. He shared his reasoning with Big Bill, surprising himself with what turned out to be an impromptu lecture.

"It all started in the 1970s when OPEC—the Consortium of Oil-Producing Nations—shook Americans down to their wheel lugs when its oil embargo struck. Till then, our shamelessly promiscuous use of gas and oil seemed really to be a right guaranteed by the Constitution or Congress to everyone falling beneath the American flag. The American people were insulted, outraged. Americans blamed Arabs up and down, left and right. How dare they slow down our God-given right to petroleum consumption! Arabs took the political hit, but OPEC also—as you know—includes Venezuelans, Ecuadorians, Mexicans, Nigerians, Angolans, Cameroonians, and many others as well. Maybe you are fully aware that Americans are chronically and endemically short on historical and geographic grasp. That's why it's easy for them to choose to blame 'Arabs' for threatening their driving ease, to say nothing of indoor ambient temperature.

"Are you with me so far?"

Big Bill had been grinning during this exposition and nodded his head in understanding. "Don't stop now, amigo. I suspect I opened up one of your favorite topics."

El Indio Jesús laughed. Then he continued.

"It didn't take long for Americans to feel the effects of that gasoline shortage. Lines to the pump snaked down the blocks, and the cost of household heating soared. I already told you that their outrage centered on the 'Arabs' but also on the president who had long since warned the country about its profligate ways.

"You could probably go as far as saying that more than just economics and politics were involved here: the embargo attacked American culture, hitting it below the belt, really.

"You see, there are only three conditions under which American citizens will tolerate standing in line: for sports events, rock concerts, and unemployment compensation. Anything else is un-American and a threat to our way of life. An intolerable offense. So is the imperative to turn the thermostat down to sixty-eight degrees."

"And so that was the end of the sitting president, wasn't it." Big Bill responded rather than asked. "Look, though, there goes one of those massive cars. Seems to me that everywhere I go, there are two old guys driving around in a two-tone white-above-yellow Cadillac. Have you ever noticed that?"

El Indio Jesús just laughed.

"Want to stop here in Socorro for something to eat and get the tank filled?" He looked over to the huge young man stuffed into the passenger side of the *caro troquita*. He was not obese, just tall and solidly built, energetic with vibrant good health and a constant pleasant disposition.

"No," he responded, "I'm okay. I can last till we get to the Owl Cafe. I'll just keep my mind off the Owl's green chili cheeseburgers best I can. Just get gas here and keep on with the lecture."

Back on the road again, El Indio Jesús was in no hurry to resume his dissertation on where America's big cars had disappeared to, especially when he knew the story had other, longer, and more fascinating chapters. He knew the fate of many of the petroleum monsters now vanished from driveways across the country. And he had played a modest part from time to time in assisting the process by which automobiles of the Oligocene fell into the hands of the most enthusiastic, inventive recyclers present in the Southwest.

"Okay. Just remember that you asked for all of this." He paused for a moment and then continued.

"Those most cherished chariots—that's hard to say—were among the first casualties of the dried-up fossil fuel supply. Detroit's obsession with vehicles big and fast began to lose ground to foreign gas-efficient cars. So what do you do with the gas burners lined two deep in middle-class neighborhood driveways which no one would buy anymore? What do you do about payments and repairs and insurance for these baby behemoths?

"Here's how some of it happened. First, sometimes a big-car owner would approach a *vato* who was working on the car in a service station. He'd say, 'Look, just take my car and burn it or strip it. Do whatever you want with it. I just don't want it anymore. I just can't afford it, what with insurance, payments, the whole thing. Just get rid of it for me. *¡Hasta la vista!*' The guy would be pretty pleased with himself for throwing out the Spanish." El Indio Jesús chuckled.

"But the deep structure of the monologue was, 'Look, take this car away and I'll give you a few weeks to dispose of it however you want to. Then I'll call the police and my insurance agent and report it stolen. By the time they find what's left of it, you'll have totaled it one way or another so I'll be able to get full Blue Book value for it and not just the cost of repair. Then I'll be shut of the stupid thing.'

"A simpler way of getting rid of it, though, was when an owner would just abandon his car in the Valley somewhere, like on a dirt road in the *bosque* near the river. This solution was so popular that the *bosque* became a virtual parking lot of orphaned cars that stretched for miles from north to south of the city.

"And then the same reporting procedure would go on—a call to the police and to the insurance company after a waiting period sufficient to guarantee that the car had been properly scavenged. Sometimes you could see the owner cruising by the place where he had abandoned his car. That was to cheek out the progress of the dismantlement in order to gauge when he should make his reporting calls.

"And then there was another element or maybe a couple of elements to add here.

"There was also a brisk towing business run by good old boys who were also in on the scam. That operation started at city hall. The city authorized certain towing companies, insured and bonded, to be on call when the police reported the abandoned vehicles. Each company received a schedule specifying which days of the week it would be on duty.

"The police always played favorites with the companies, cultivating one or another through the years. They still do, of course. When a policeman spotted what looked like an abandoned vehicle on, say, a side street, he had the option of reporting it right away or waiting until the day of the week when his towing company of choice was on duty. By throwing the business to his buddies, he could then ask them for favors. That could be for parts he needed for his own vehicles or maybe a tip-off when a good quality pickup fell into their hands which he could bid on at a silent auction.

"Still with me? This goes on."

Big Bill smiled back at him. "I'm still with you. I'll leap right out of here when you hit my saturation point."

"All right. Next, reporting the recovery of lost vehicles took time, searching out the license number if the plate was still there, recording the engine serial number, and making all the calls and paperwork this entailed. Meanwhile, the recyclers were at work. By recyclers I mean not only the usual scavengers like junk collectors and the kids who wanted chrome or whatever; it included also the police and the towing company people, too. By the time the owner was reunited with his brontosaurus—whether he wanted to be reunited or not—typically only its basic skeleton remained. That's what he was counting on. And certainly the insurance agent surveying the carcass would agree that the car was a total loss and that full compensation was appropriate. Such a shame.

"This is where the story gets really interesting to me.

"What was left of the vehicle might then find its way for a mere one hundred fifty dollars into the hands of a Chicano in the *barrio* with a plan for its resurrection and many of the necessary resources to revive it.

"Before I get into the plans: Not infrequently, a gas guzzler would become available through a more direct approach. Here's how it works out.

"It is always easy to identify unused cars when you drive through residential areas of the city. Just look for weeds springing up through the pavement below the car or behind it, or see one or more flat tires, or broken windows or a lot of accumulated dirt on the windows, or police tags on it warning of impending towing and fines. Or if it's still in the driveway and not on the street, look for any and all of the above plus or minus its being up on blocks.

"A dinosaur hunter need only list the license plate number, adding it to a list of those he had spotted, and for a few dollars the motor vehicle department will give out the names and addresses of the owners. If the motor vehicle clerks got sticky about giving out the information, well, the department was always heavily staffed by Chicanos and surely there'd be a *primo* or two to dig out the information.

"Often a telephone call during the day to the home of the owner would land a sale. During the day was a preferable time since the man of the house was probably at work. The deal could be struck with the woman of the house who is just sick and tired of seeing that messy eyesore taking up space in the driveway or parked permanently in front of the house. (She would handle the man of the house later, after the done deal and the car towed away.) You can imagine that the would-be buyer would have to be ready to tow it away right now before Dad arrived home."

"Right," said Big Bill. "To get it out of there fast."

"Um-hm." El Indio Jesús drank from his thermos.

"If it was at all possible, it was wiser to make your approach by telephone first: the sudden appearance of a young Hispanic male at the front door in those neighborhoods more than once has been known to cause knee-jerk 911 calls.

"Really," he concluded, "coming into possession of the large Buicks, Oldsmobiles, Chryslers, Monte Carlos, or whatever was never any problem at all. What took time was the next part: turning them into their next manifestation."

"The lowrider," Big Bill inserted.

"Right. The lowrider. And we have just arrived at the Owl Cafe in the nick of time for us both to take a break from this peroration."

The Owl Cafe never failed to live up to its splendid reputation. It was always filled with customers, impossibly busy for such a remote location. The two men had to wait until a table was cleared before ordering and working out the remainder of their plans for the trip.

Big Bill savored the opportunity to spend this time with El Indio Jesús. He was enthusiastic about what he was creating in the south and hoped to earn this man's approval and maybe get some good ideas about what else could be done. There wouldn't be much time left in the summer, though, before he was due to go east for his internship in the Department of Labor.

They were going south again on the Jornada del Muerto within the hour, sated with memorable Owl meal. This time, Big Bill was at the wheel, squeezed in as best he could, since the little *caro troquita's* seats were not only narrow in the beam but also short on the front-to-back slide. Sometimes El Indio Jesús removed the passenger seat altogether and left just the back seat area for his riders. This trip, however, required a pickup area for today's version of the vehicle, precluding the loungelike back row seating.

The radio kept losing the signal for National Public Radio. Finally, Big Bill clicked it off and with a smile said, "Well, I guess you might as well finish up your lecture on the origin and evolution of lowriders."

"*Bueno*, if you want the whole recitation?"

Big Bill said something about being a captive audience, and El Indio Jesús continued.

"Before lunch, I tried to emphasize that coming into possession of the Buicks, Oldsmobiles, Chryslers, Monte Carlos, or whatever big car they wanted was never a big problem once the gas shortage changed people's attitudes about things. What took time, what required careful planning and great patience, was the process of assembling and converting all the many parts into a single entity— a custom-built, low-to-the-ground dream machine capable of hopping and dancing on hydraulic pumps: the lowrider.

"The process of consolidation is truly amazing," said El Indio Jesús. "Say a Ford, a Lincoln, and a Mercury—all three—were discarded and recovered one way or another. In most cases the motors will be interchangeable, transmissions and rear ends as well. Or at the very least, many of their component parts are interchangeable depending on the year the vehicle was manufactured. Let's say just the shells or bodies would remain whole. Or essentially so.

"The challenge then for the lowrider design engineer is to develop a completely conceptualized plan for his car, detailing every step of the process. He must recreate from all kinds of parts—bodies, fenders, hoods, rear decks, drivetrains, and the two thousand associated pieces—a mechanical and aesthetic wonder.

"Three vital elements are essential to bring forth the lowrider miracle: time, trade, and vision."

"Time, trade, and vision," Big Bill repeated. "Makes sense. Go on."

"But there is a fourth element that is the oil to lubricate the whole process. Can you guess what that is?"

"Well," Big Bill mused, "if trade is a primary element, then it has to be relationships, *¿que no?*"

"*Que sí, mijo.* From the skeleton on up to the finished product, the relationships between *carnales*, one to another, are the key to success or failure. What they trade extends well beyond pieces of motor or frame. A more important exchange is advice, on the one hand, and on the other, the trade in expert physical labor. The exchange of information about how to do a task, or the willingness of one *vato* to work on another's project in exchange for a part or labor of a different kind is always essential in every single case.

"So there you have it, the primary elements: time, trade made possible by relationships, and first and foremost, vision."

"That's pretty fascinating stuff," commented Big Bill. "If wanted to build me a lowrider (although what I really need down here is a VW dune buggy), tell me how to go about it, step by step."

"Okay, but remember that you asked for this. I am not forcing this on you, *¿correcto?*"

"*Sí, es correcto. ¡Adelante, profesor!*"

El Indio Jesús was silent for a few minutes, gathering his thoughts. Taking a drink from the thermos, he drew a deep breath and returned to the topic.

"Okay, start with, say, a derelict 1977 General Motors Monte Carlo, once fully equipped and beautiful, now bought for one hundred fifty dollars from a junk yard in stripped-down condition and 110,000 miles registering on the odometer. A friend or relative tows it home in exchange for labor or parts that he may have collected during his years of facination with that particular model of American car. The Monte Carlo's transmission leaks oil and is seriously slipping, the passenger-side window is broken as the result of a break-in, headlights and taillights are missing, upholstery is torn and dirty, the radiator has never been flushed, cleaned, or recored and is now full of pinhole leaks, the suspension system is sagging, there are different-sized tires in the front and in the rear, there is no gas cap, the radio is missing with wires dangling down the dashboard, and the license plate is held on with coat hanger wire. There are dents and scrapes everywhere on the body.

"After reviewing his plan, the next thing the young man does is to send out word along his network of friends and relatives on whose cars he may have worked in the past. They in return will now advise their contacts of his needs for parts or assistance. Mostly by word of mouth. It gets out that he is looking for help with his transmission, or a replacement window, or radiator work, a left front fender, advice on the suspension system or on any number of things.

"Let's consider for a moment that if General Motors can be considered the species of a vehicle, certain members of its subspecies can accept interchangeable parts without displaying sterility. I know that's stretching a point a bit, but what I'm trying to get across is something like that, like compatible blood typing. This is how, for instance, a 1977 Monte Carlo can receive transfusions from Oldsmobiles, Cadillacs, Buicks, and even some General Motors truck parts. He will look for subspecies matches to create his lowrider.

"If all goes as planned, soon good replacements will begin to roll in for which he will trade parts he has in his collection or offer labor, labor that is not necessarily automotive. He might plaster a wall for a set of headlights. He may clean out a sewer for something else, either a part or someone else's labor. He may work on another's same model for parts, or he will seek out someone skilled in specific competencies such as drive train, suspension, upholstery, bodywork, or painting for which he will swap parts or his own special talents.

"In no time at all, the hunt for parts and skills becomes absorbing. If he has a job, he will work hard to hang on to it for day-to-day living expenses. The emerging lowrider becomes his recreation. He does not ski. He doesn't play golf. During the years—and I do mean years—that the process takes, very little cash actually changes hands throughout the entire operation. It's really amazing. Furthermore—and this is very important to always remember—thievery, stealing, is definitely and simply not a cost-effective method for obtaining what is needed. I guess we could say that in the whole of the process, the only criminals in the scenario may have been the original owners who deliberately deserted their giant uneconomical autos and then reported them stolen for insurance reimbursement." El Indio Jesús drew another sip from the thermos. "For the lowrider builders, no one ever needs to risk a jail sentence for what can be gotten for virtually nothing, thanks to the perfection of the system."

"What I mean by the 'system' is this: that the miracle of recycling, the lowrider, will eventually emerge loaded with sociological implications, something the sociologists may be figuring out at last. The elements of trade, barter, imagination, labor, restoration and re-creation over time has transmuted into a significant, unique social movement centered on the concept and practice of *la familia*. *La familia* integrates males and females of all ages involved in one way or another with the lowrider wave into new patterns of interaction, into new extended *familias* based on shared interests, exchange systems, and mutual support. Community sense not only grows from functioning nuclear and extended *familias* but also involves migrants, the displaced, and those from fragmented homes. In turn, these communities became affiliated with other such communities from state to state across the nation.

You've seen the lowrider magazines at the newsstand. It's nation-wide, now, and growing. It's a major sociological phenomenon with very far-reaching implications.

"I am about to wind this up. And we're almost there, aren't we?"

"Yes," Big Bill said, "I'll use the next exit. So finish up."

El Indio Jesús shook the thermos and drew out the last of the ice water.

"In this way," he summarized, "what started out as the sharing of unwanted automobiles jettisoned by OPEC-offended American middle-class owners became an information network and then the basis for the births of this dynamic, creative subculture made up of *Las familias* united in the cult of the lowrider vehicle. Thus, hundreds of thousands of cast-off cars became reincarnated into hundreds of thousands of refrigerators made of scrap metal—and a few thousand lowrider creations, which gave birth to a new day in the Chicano communities in the United States."

"Amen," says Big Bill. And both laugh in appreciation *y con respecto*.

The Columbus Air Force

Miguel Olson, like so many others in the barrio, was a man of multiple skills and interests. One of those talents was his ability to wield a paintbrush on automobiles and airplanes. He had learned from the lowrider crafters new techniques and about products for producing top quality fine-line pinstriping and ghost patterns, illustrations sunk deep beneath several lacquer coats barely visible to the untrained eye.

When some of his work was seen by an alert visitor walking through a parking lot, opportunity opened up for him: he would take occasional jobs detailing, decorating, and in general customizing exteriors and interiors of private airplanes.

His first big success was the 'southwesternizing' of a Lear Jet owned a major rock star. Tony the World Traveler helped him with the symbols: zigzags, coyotes, cactus, Zia sun designs, boots, and Stetsons. Word spread to the Sangre de Cristo smart set in the north of the state, and jobs, very high paying jobs, were there for the taking. He accepted few of them, however, since there were many other projects he would rather spend his time on.

Late one afternoon, he and Tony the World Traveler were playing cards with two other men at a small private airstrip's hangar south of the city when a classic summer monsoon storm strode over the mesas from the west and bore down on the valley pushing violet thunderheads before it.

"Looks like this storm might drop its load," commented one of the men at the card table.

"Yeah," a second added, "but sometimes they just growl and threaten. Like guard dogs. And those virgas just move over the land and don't drop nothing."

The four men squinted against the afternoon sun's glare coming through the dusty window at the end of the large Quonset hut that served as a hangar for a number of small planes. The Cessna they were customizing gleamed in the dusk.

"That's what the Navajos call a male rain," said Tony the World Traveler. "Those big loud storms, they call them male because they hit with a lot of noise, drop a lot of water and cause damage, and then they go off fast without being helpful. Then they call the soft warm rainstorms that last a long time female rain because they slowly water the earth and help the crops to grow.

"Yup, this is a male rain for sure," he concluded.

They returned to the game, which they frequently interrupted for one reason or another.

"Got a new Texan joke for you," one of the men offered.

"Is it as bad as the last one?"

"Naw, well . . ." He would not be put off. "Seems these three men, a Californian, a Texan, and a New Mexican, were drinking together in a bar . . ."

Someone groaned.

"They're drinking, see. The Californian is drinking this wine thing, and when he's done, he throws the glass against the wall, where it crashes.

"'How come you did that?' asks the New Mexican.

"'Well,' says the Californian, 'the standard of living is so high in California, we never drink from the same glass twice.'

"Then the Texan drinks his margarita and he also throws his glass against the back wall, just like the Californian.

"'How come you did that?' the New Mexican asks.

"'Well,' says the Texan, "we're not only rich in oil in Texas; we've got so much sand that glass is cheap, so we never have to drink out of the same glass twice.'

"The New Mexican then finishes his Dos Equis beer, draws his six-shooter, and shoots the Californian and the Texan dead right there.

"'How come you did that?' asked the bartender.

"'Well,' says the New Mexican, 'we have so many Californians and Texans in New Mexico, we never have to drink with the same ones twice!'"

They laughed and one redealt the cards. He looked up and said, "I know for a fact that you got that joke out of the *East Mountain Telegraph*. So tell us the other one you read."

The jokester smiled. "Okay, you guys want to hear it?"

They all assented.

"Okay, it goes like this. See, a guy from Nebraska, one from Texas, and one from New Mexico were walking along, when one of them kicks up this metal lamp thing. He picks it up, and when he starts dusting off the sand, a genie comes out, poof!

"'Thank you for letting me out,' says the genie. 'For that, I will give each of you one wish.'

"They're real happy about that. First the Nebraskan tells the genie his wish. 'I have a farm in Nebraska and I would like all the land in Nebraska to be fertile forever.'

"'Fine,' says the genie, and he snaps his fingers. 'Done!'

"Next came the Texan's wish. 'What I wish for is that there is this real big wall all around Texas to keep out everyone who doesn't belong there, like Mexicans and Easterners and such.'

"'Fine,' says the genie, and he snaps his fingers. 'Done!'

"Last comes the New Mexican. 'Genie,' he says, 'tell me about the wall you just made for the Texan.'

"'Okay,' says the genie, 'it's about two hundred feet high, fifty feet thick, and it goes entirely around the whole state of Texas.

"'Fine,' says the New Mexican, 'and here's my wish: fill it with water!'"

Tony the World Traveler slapped him on the back while they all laughed at the joke.

They played a few hands more as the clouds darkened and the hanging lamp was switched on.

"What's the word on the Columbus Air Force these days?" one of the men asked.

"Yeah," added another. "We haven't heard much since that forced landing over near Willard. What's the real story, Miguel?"

"What makes you think I know anything about it? I just paint pretty pictures for *los ricos*."

They all laughed at this weak evasion.

"So what really happened over there? Come on, Miguel. We all know you and Maxey Houltin are *compadres* . . ."

"Hey, let's get this straight: I'll never be *compadres* with those guys. You ought to know by now how I feel about them. Don't make me start preaching again . . ."

"Okay, okay," surrendered the man across the table, "but give us the story anyway."

Miguel shifted in his chair. Laying down his cards, he leaned back on two metal legs and smiled at his friends as he began his story.

"Well, you know it wasn't Houlton who ditched over in Willard. He's too good a flier for that. Besides which, he almost never penetrates this far north in the Cessna. Mostly he stays east of the mountains and south of Cloudcroft. The Willard thing was pure amateur night. You should know that for sure, Tony."

"Okay," the man interrupted again, "but he did have a forced landing over at Claunch one time. You gotta remember that . . ."

Miguel, chuckling, leaned back onto the chair's two legs. "You heard about that? Who told you? Never mind. I don't want to know. But I'll fill you in on that one."

He paused. "It was really rare."

He took a sip of his Coke and continued.

"You know that one of the papers called Houlton the 'Flying Ace of the Dope Air Force.' Well, the truth is that he did a lot of other stuff, too. It wasn't all just marijuana. He did a lot of other things between here and his pickup points south of the border. As long as he got paid: paid up front—money on the barrelhead. Like all of them in the Columbus Air Force. Make no mistake: it's ninety-nine percent money and one percent the thrills of it that motivates those guys . . ."

"Awright, awright! Get on with the story. Whew! save the lecture."

Miguel grabbed another Coke from the cooler nearby.

"Okay," he gave in. He tipped up the drink, then drew in his breath. "Anyway, this great story was about one time when a professor of snakes and such at the university gave him a small contract to bring in a bunch of rattle-less rattlesnakes—"

"What?" interrupted the man to his left. "There's no such thing as a rattle-less rattlesnake."

"Sure there is," rejoined Tony the World Traveler. "They have them down on the Gray Ranch near Columbus. I seen them."

"He's right," added Miguel. "But there aren't very many, and the beer company that owns the ranch won't let anyone harvest them, even professors. Like it's just too much trouble.

"And so the snake professor wanted Houlton to pick up a load of them in Chihauhua, where they're all over the place, like the *lobos* the animal huggers want to restock in the Gila. Real pests. But you're not allowed to bring them in without going through a whole lot of trouble with Customs and all that.

"So in comes Houlton with his bales of *ganja* and a crate full of these snakes. It's bad weather, see, and very bumpy on the run-in.

Also, he plans to land on a dirt road alongside some fields over there. He didn't know the rain left potholes full of water and mud which, because of the heat, the mud dried out on the top and it *looked* like solid surface.

"So he lands and, sure enough, real hard—and you already know what I'm going to say—the box full of snakes crashes down on the floor of the Cessna and there are snakes wiggling all over the place. But Houlton has to come to a stop into the wind on that bad road and can't do a thing about the snakes just yet. He's got his hands full . . ."

The men are laughing now.

Miguel winds up his tale.

"Well, he comes to a halt and turns around real slow, lifting up his feet from the pedals slowly, slowly. He sees snakes all around and they're not happy snakes. They're really pissed-off!"

"How could he see them with the partition in the way?"

"Oh, he took that out a long time ago, to lighten the weight and give him more space for cargo."

"So how could he get out without getting hit?"

"He slowly stood up, bent over, on the two seats up front, and carefully reached over to the door latch, all the time hearing hissing like dozens of teakettles going off at once.

"Then he got the door open and dove headfirst right through it. He said he nearly broke his neck when he landed in a deep mud hole."

They were laughing and picking up their cards again.

"But wait," prompted Tony the World Traveler. "So how did he get rid of the snakes?"

"Very carefully," answered Miguel.

They laughed.

"That's not the whole of it, though," Miguel added, "after he got rid of them one way or another—maybe the professor helped him, I don't know—a lot of them got away and I'll bet you there's a whole new crop of these rare rattle-less rattlesnakes living over there at Claunch even today. Maybe mating with the locals, producing a whole bunch of *culebras mestizas* never before seen on the face of the earth!"

As an afterthought, he added, "And you'll never catch *me* in Claunch after dark ever again!"

■ ■ ■

The light decreased with the coming clouds and the evening hour. Not more than thirty minutes later, the rain smashed down against the curved ceiling of the hangar, pounding so hard with a mixture of hail that the men had to shout to be heard. Lightning cracked closer and closer. In minutes, the light dangling from the ceiling blinked out. They were left surrounded by thick hot humid blackness.

"Must've hit a transformer," one remarked.

They listened to the clatter and roar above them. They listened for leaks to begin dripping from the old rusty roof.

Miguel left his chair to walk over to the paler darkness of the window facing the airstrip. The street and house lights in the neighborhood were knocked out too. The lightning was fearsome. Miguel could see the trees swaying and bucking in the light of the flashes.

And then he saw something unexpected. At the end of the airstrip he could make out a row of vehicles lined up side by side, facing the runway, headlights turned on.

"Hey guys, look at this."

The other three crowded him at the window.

"Okay, look down to the end of the runway. See those lights? Wait for the next lightning flash. There! Did you see them? The vans at the end of the strip? Look again. There! See?"

The next bolt clearly showed the row of vans parked far to the right, at the end of the runway.

"What the hell are they . . . ?" began Tony the World Traveler.

"What's going on? Miguel, you know of anything coming in tonight? Houlton? The Columbus boys?" one of the men asked.

"Nope. Nothing." He kept staring at the vehicle lights, which seemed to be crying through the rain on the window. "Nope, not a thing."

"You hear anything? Listen. Hear that?" asked another of the men.

They strained to hear it above the sound of the rain and hail clattering on the roof. Some long seconds passed.

Then Tony the World Traveler heard it. "It's a plane coming in. It's taking a turn over the runway. It's low. Real low . . ."

They listened intently. They couldn't see anything over the field. The rain continued hammering but no lightning flashed for longer and longer intervals as the storm moved on toward the east.

"Look!" cried Miguel, pointing toward the south end of the runway.

A plane was attempting to land, its landing lights nearly useless in the liquid dark. A moment of light showed it skewed over on its left wing and then jolting to the right. Dark was complete again except for the plane's wing lights.

And then it was down, cruising past them in a rush of sound. They watched it slow down as it neared the end of the field. It came to a jerky stop and then taxied farther on up the runway to the place where the vans were waiting, lights glaring.

A flash of lightning lit up the faces of the four men at the window as they turned to look at each other, puzzled.

"What the hell?" asked one of them. "What's going on?"

"Want to go take a look?" asked Tony the World Traveler, always interested in a possible adventure.

"Not me. Are you serious?" responded the first man. "You and me, we both know what we think's going on, and I want no part of it."

"Naw," seconded another. "Who needs trouble? Besides, I don't want to get wet." He laughed weakly.

"Let's go," said Miguel to Tony the World Traveler. "Let these old guys play with their cards."

The rain continued, but now it contained no hail, although the drops were fat and falling thickly. Miguel and Tony made their way along the hurricane fence toward where the plane and the vans were, still shrouded in dark and wetness, with patternless glimmers of lights from one place or another. The minutes seemed long.

Where the fence took a turn at the far end of the runway, Miguel reached back and stopped Tony the World Traveler with an outstretched hand against his chest.

"Stop. Wait a minute. Let me catch my breath. Let's think about this."

The two of them hunkered down in a puddle of mud that they could not see, now that their flashlights were off, but could feel sliding against their shoes.

"Let's think about this again," Miguel repeated, panting.

"Yeah," Tony responded. "Yeah."

They tried to make out the scene taking place several yards away, but could not pull out enough detail to give them much information.

"How about using the culvert?" suggested Tony.

"The culvert?"

"Yeah, the culvert. There," he pointed.

"Are you serious?" asked Miguel. "It's full of water. We'll drown. And snakes."

"Nah," said Tony, "there's not all that much runoff, and besides, the rain's letting up."

"Well, I don't know . . ." began Miguel.

Tony the World Traveler was already running, hunched over, toward the black hole. Miguel followed.

The drainage culvert was covered by a grill to sieve out debris. Tony pulled it open and immediately entered the darkness, water reaching nearly to his waist.

"Hey," Miguel whispered harshly, "wait up. Do you know what you're doing?" He bumped into Tony.

"Take it easy," said Tony. "Look. You can see the end right there, that light area. There's plenty air. Come on."

They stooped their way along the tunnel, Miguel more cramped than the shorter Tony. Nearing the end of the culvert, Miguel choked on a wave of panic: the end was covered with a grill like the entrance, but he realized that the grill could not be opened from the inside.

"We're trapped!" he rasped into Tony's ear.

"Shh. Quiet. Look!" Tony moved aside so that Miguel could look out through the grill also. The rain had stopped.

Within a few yards of them, they could discern an ancient DC-3 being off-loaded. Men hustled from the cargo door to the waiting vans, which had now doused their lights. The cargo was in small bales wrapped in shiny material.

There was no question in the minds of Miguel and Tony the World Traveler: the cargo was drugs from Latin America.

They crouched in the culvert, water now receding to knee level. The darkness in the culvert still kept them invisible to anyone outside. Yet the rush of water through the grate hindered them from hearing the conversation that was taking place very near them.

For at that moment, three men walked from the plane. They approached the edge of the tarmack closest to the culvert. There they continued an intense dialogue, the tallest of the three doing most of the talking. He was nearly yelling at them in barrio Spanish, as though they were hard of hearing.

". . . weather reports. Why don't you check with my man in El Paso? Where you come from, maybe there's no such thing as weather reports, but here, they're accurate and free. This is a modern world up here, not some backward banana republic. We're not hotshot amateurs here. This isn't an amateur operation we're running here. McDonald's burgers are served up with more efficiency than what you guys did today. And this stuff's worth a lot more than hamburgers!

"You guys screwed up three ways. One, you missed the time window by more than an hour. Two hours. Two, you failed to call in for the weather report. And three, you landed at the wrong end of this airstrip. I'm fed to the teeth with this kind of . . ."

As he enumerated his complaints, the two victims of his outrage slowly, casually, reached up to their left sides and removed Uzi automatic machine guns from their shoulder holsters. Languidly, they directed the muzzles toward the tall man.

"Hey? What's this? What's the matter with you guys?"

In careful Latin American Spanish, as though the tall man could only minimally comprehend, one of the two spoke to him, holding the barrel of his Uzi downward.

"Señor Beserra." He paused and sighed. "We are serious people. We have a serious purpose. What you have arbitrarily termed 'inefficiency' may have reasons behind it about which you are unaware, and which are, in truth, none of your concern. Suffice it to say that if you are in any way dissatisfied with our service, there are many others who would be willing to put up with our 'inefficiency,' as you judge it, and who would receive us with the courtesy that we expect. If—"

At that moment, one of the van drivers approached and whispered to Beserra. Then, spotting the Uzis, he backed away, looking back and forth between the Latinos and Beserra.

Beserra smiled broadly at the Latinos.

The driver lifted his hands at shoulder level, palms out.

"What the hell's going on here'? What's the deal?"

Beserra continued smiling at the Latinos, not looking at the driver. In English, he said, "Nothing, nothing at all." In Spanish he said, "We are totally in agreement, señores, that this is a serious business. I will continue to respect your judgment. Forgive me if I spoke somewhat roughly, but that is how the American businessmen taught me. It was only to make a point about our mutual need for continued vigilance and attention to detail.

"*Entonces*, my man informs me that all is in readiness for your return to your country. Please assure your people that we are pleased, as always, with their continued cooperation."

The Latinos, just as slowly as before, reholstered their weapons. The spokesman responded, "*Bien, bien, Señor Beserra, hasta la vista.*" The two men turned and strode back to the airplane.

Beserra watched them go, hands on hips.

"What was going down?" asked the driver.

"Nothing," replied Beserra, "Nothing at all. Just a little culture conflict is all. Not to worry. I can handle it."

"Did he call you Beserra? I thought he called you Beserra. What's that all about?"

"Oh, nothing. That's just a code name."

They walked to the waiting van, the only one with its head-lights lit. In seconds, it sped past the culvert, dousing Miguel and Tony with a sheet of muddy water.

The two men in the culvert waited for several minutes more, maybe fifteen or so, until the remaining vehicles had also gone. They punctuated their departures, one by one, so as perhaps to avoid looking like the convoy they were.

■ ■ ■

Miguel and Tony the World Traveler sloshed into the hangar some time later. It was still dark inside.

"Any light in here yet?" yelled Miguel.

"Hey, hey. Sure. Wait a sec," came a voice.

The lights went on. Their two friends rushed over to them, full of questions.

"Wait, wait, wait!" Miguel begged. "We're freezing to death. Full of mud, too. Where are those overalls I've been using? Tony, I've got overalls for you, too, though you'll have to roll up the cuffs a foot or two." Everyone laughed.

"Let's get cleaned up. Then we all have to talk, okay? The four of us."

"Look," one of the young men tried again, "look, just tell us if it was *carga*, okay?"

Miguel drew in a deep breath. "Yeah. It was *carga*, all right. And more. We'll talk. Just wait."

It took only a few minutes for a shower to warm up the filthy, shivering men. They returned to the other two back at the card table.

"Yeah, well, it was *carga*. Probably two or three tons of the usual assortment of Colombian Gold for the ski crowd and the artsy-craftsy *tipos*, cocaine for the yuppies, and a new supply of really bad stuff for the barrios and the off-rez Indians. That would be my guess. Right, Tony?"

Tony nodded.

The four were silent for a while, weighing the matter.

Then one of the young men asked, "But who was it? Who's bringing it in? Could you see who it was?"

Miguel and Tony looked at each other, agreeing silently.

"Yeah, we saw who it was. We saw it all, Roberto," Tony replied. "It was Beserra."

Tony added, "Yeah, it was Beserra, alias Jack Spencer, alias Jacobo Beserra. Of the State Police."

Again there was a long pause.

"So what are you going to do about it?" Miguel asked the two young men.

"Us?" asked Roberto.

"What do you mean by 'us'?" asked Chuco.

"Well," began Miguel, stroking the remaining water off his beard, "we just witnessed another load of poison come down, which'll burn out the brains of our people, or get them in jail for dealing, or both. Yeah, it's been coming in for years, but we've never known for sure who's behind this particular operation, and how it's run and all.

"The word has to get out to the people. Tony plans to talk to the leaders on the reservations, at the pueblos, mainly to get the message to the off-rez Indians. Those are the ones who need to know—the most vulnerable to the poison, more apt to get hooked away from their communities. That's what Tony'll do.

"For me, the Hollywood hero whose plane I'm painting isn't due back in town for a while and, even so, won't miss one or two howling coyotes in the interior. I'll pass along the message to *la gente* around the barrios about what we've seen go down here tonight, so they can decide what to do about it.

"So my question to you, Roberto, I repeat: What are you going to do about it?" Miguel paused, looking back and forth between the two young men. Then resuming, he pointed out, "You have your lowrider organization and an information network covering the whole Southwest, maybe even farther. You could put the word out on Beserra and what this is all about, if you wanted to. Call it technical advice, or whatever. You can use your system already in place to alert your members. And their associates. If you want to.

"And you, Chuco. What do you think you can do?"

Chuco thought about the question, glanced at Roberto and back again to Miguel and Tony.

"Hey, man," he leaned forward in his chair, "you know we've been onto this guy for a long time. Remember when we did that graffiti campaign on Waldo? The first Waldo by our older guys, and then later they did the Waldo II?"

"Right," Miguel smiled, thinking back to his football days. "A lot of places, you can still see Waldo II. I guess the question is, whether this is big enough for Waldo III. It's not a decision I can make. Or anyone here tonight. It's a decision that has to come from the barrios, a community decision, before you *grafiteros* get busy for Waldo III to hit the walls from here to East L.A. But it's your call. Tony and I will do whatever, in our own ways. But this evil business has got to stop. As Malcom X said, 'Whatever it takes.' And for however long it takes, too."

Two of the men collected their belongings, bade good-bye, and left Miguel and Tony the World Traveler alone in the hangar.

Sitting again at the card table beneath the dangling bulb, they were silent for some time, contemplating the situation. At last, Miguel spoke.

"How do you think this'll affect Houltin and the rest? This is really the hard stuff. A very rough crowd. He said he'd never get into that. Never. But we need him. You know that."

"Yeah. We do." Tony the World Traveler looked troubled. "This has bothered me all along, Houltin's sideline coming up against what we're trying to do. Well, let's be honest: the pot's not his sideline, it's the whole game to him. For us, doing business with him is a matter of necessary evils, maybe, but I don't know."

"He's been talking about getting out of the business."

"On account of the Latino mafia."

"They play too rough."

"And pot's one thing, the hard stuff is another."

Miguel shifted in his chair.

"Well, for me, it's all the same shit. Ugly. I can't speak for you, but dogs carry fleas. And pot carries the next level and the next level and the next. It's all rotten.

"But we still need Houltin and the others right now—especially now."

Tony the World Traveler thought about this for a long minute, then concluded, "Okay, let's do this: let's let this play out a while longer, let the community in on what we know, and they'll decide. But for us, this is a really bad time to divorce ourselves from the Columbus Air Force. Like you say, especially now."

Miguel looked at him thoughtfully. Then agreed. "Okay. Yes. For a while."

WEDNESDAY

Grafitismo

Wednesday afternoons presented El Indio Jesús with a most plea-
surable challenge: to nurture the graffiti arts of the Valley. At no
time in the long history of this art form had it been under such
relentless attack. Indeed, in the centuries of its artists' growth and
development, the *grafitero* could expect praise and honor in more
enlightened times and places. But here and now, an implacable
campaign to search out and destroy this ancient mode of artistic
and political expression had been launched by the mayor and the
city council. If their mission could prevail, *grafitismo* would be
wiped from the face of the city, if not the state and the rest of the
world.

Amply funded by the federal government's summer youth
work program and staffed at the top by triple dippers, veterans
of several wars and conflicts, the Valley was viewed as the focus
of a new Phoenix Program in general and the barrios as the
strategic hamlets to be pacified in specific.

The summer offensive began with hiring the sons and daughters of lowest-echelon city workers, who still lived in the barrios
and not yet in the nirvana of the Heights. Their job was to identify

the *grafiteros* and try to lure them into socially acceptable modes of expression. Those *grafiteros* able to read and write English would be enrolled in the summer arts program. Those not functionally literate in English would be signed up with the Police Athletic League or the Boys Club summer camp set in the wilderness atop a hazardous waste dump.

A small number of especially intelligent *grafiteros*, the cream of the crop, would be skimmed off and placed in the technical vocational school or, in rarest cases, in the university. The rare university survivors might eventually land grants-in-aid leading to a master's degree in fine arts, which essentially guaranteed future unemployment in academia.

Should actual employment come about for any of the corralled *grafiteros*, it was then but a short step to full articulation with the *gabacho* world with its Trans Ams, La Blondi, and house payments—the ultimate tamers.

What was left in the barrios would be the incorrigibles who, under siege, would face juvenile authorities and detention facilities or seek asylum in friendlier, more benevolent cities.

Phase Two of the pacification program was the rebeautification of the city. But while neutralizing the *grafiteros* was one thing, purging their existing artwork was another. Certain chemical companies once in the defoliant business now came forward with "vandalism mark removers" in aerosol cans looking not unlike the spray paint cans used by the *grafiteros*.

Modern spray paint was employed by the *grafiteros* only because the natural materials used by countless generations were no longer available. The original paint pigments still resided in deposits around the area but could no longer be reached.

The top-quality white *caliche*, for example, is found only in the midrange of the Manzano Atomic Bomb Storage Depot, and the most popular red—between a rust and a flamingo pink—is nearby. Barring access to this Abó Red, as it is called, the second-quality red is some one hundred fifty miles further. This one does not have the lasting quality of the other, having a life expectancy of less than a hundred years. The choice greens and purples lie in arroyos within the White Sands Proving Grounds, where malfunctioning Pershing missiles make pigment hunting hazardous not only to the health of the *grafiteros* but to the survival of the many endangered species residing there as well.

Phase Two also had to contend with the varying surfaces that the *grafiteros* needed to use for their messages, murals, and designs. Their artist ancestors had free access to volcanic walls and rock palisades, as attested to by the Southwest's abundance of petroglyphs and pictographs. Now the best sites have been caged up in state parks and federal historic sites such as the West Mesa, La Cienega, Chaco Canyon, and around the Farmington area. Park rangers and summer field school university professors lecture to rapt audiences about the rock canvases of the pre-Columbian past, yet they fail to bring their topic up to date while, at the same time, the art form is being forcibly suppressed in the city.

In short, with regard to the hardware of the *grafitero*, neither the original pigments nor the canvases are currently available, so that the Phase Two task force must cope with inspiration that is now expressed with materials at hand: spray paint and public surfaces.

El Indio Jesús held the art of the *grafitero* in high esteem, for it spoke the soul and mind of the community throughout the centuries. With or without writing.

Like Altamira in the Old World, the Valley once carried the purest expression of the medium. Later on, it experienced a florescence born of the cross-fertilization of Olmec with Arab Spanish traditions. Hybrid vigor came about when the Mexican *pochteca* merchants traveled from the south, when Spanish colonists arrived, and when the continuing flow upriver of Mexican *campesinos* and *intelectuales* met and intermarried with the Tiwa, Towa, Tewa, Athabaskan, and Piro populations.

It was no accident that the Valley soared to the heights of the art form then.

Later, however, in the twentieth century, public education became the enemy of *grafitismo*. In no time at all, the few high school graduates who were also the best wall artists found themselves seduced into the world of politics. Uniquely, this part of the country has always allowed its oppressed classes to have nominal participation in elective and appointive politics. Chicano *políticos* with Indian faces and gingo pretentions were encouraged to cut each others' throats in full equality of opportunity with Anglo politicians.

However, the quality and quantity of graffiti as an art form suffered proportionately to the political successes of the natives. El Indio Jesús mulled over the sad possibility that more than one sitting governor may once have been a promising *grafitero*.

With regard to the development of the art form elsewhere, cousins who moved to Los Angeles to build ships in the 1940s and to pack tomatoes for Del Monte in later years reported back the news that the land of Orozco and Rivera was contributing wonderful practitioners to the land of Andy Warhol.

He recognized that San Antonio and Los Angeles had long since surpassed the lead that the Valley once commanded and held for hundreds of years. Even Denver. In Texas, the cognoscenti no longer viewed Valley graffiti as competitive.

Most humiliating was the word from Chicago brought by Mexican nationals who reported as they passed through, "Your work isn't worth *mierda, manito*. You should see what's in the Windy City. Your stuff *no vale una chingada*." When they pulled out their snapshots showing the Chicago murals and messages, the Valley *grafiteros* had to concede their inferiority.

El Indio Jesús, mindful of the eclipse, sought to stem the decline by identifying the potential Mirós and Picassos in each of the twenty barrios. He then set up a training program for each of them, depending upon their current skills. In view of the climate of fear and hostility that prevailed, it would be dangerous to convene them as a group for seminars at the D. H. Lawrence or

Ghost ranches. Not long ago, a *compadre*'s ranch had been arsoned for just that sort of thing. No, the educating must be done one by one.

■ ■ ■

On Wednesday mornings, El Indio Jesús picked up that week's student and took him along to his current ROTC project site. This afforded the student an opportunity to learn a few basic construction skills, to make a little paint money, and often enough, a chance to try out some new ideas.

In the afternoon, El Indio Jesús conducted a tour for him through some of the other barrios, those with the best murals and universal messages. Since a typical *grafitero* does not leave his own territorial limits, such anonymous visits presented rare opportunities for contrast and comparison. In this way, as in the past, cross-fertilization accelerated the creative process by many years in just one afternoon—a great evolutionary leap forward, demonstrating the effectiveness of punctuated equilibria.

On the rear shelf of the *caro troquita* were books and folios presenting the works of the giants: Orozco, Miró, Picasso, Rivera, Dalí, and Siquieros. Driving around the Valley gave opportunity to thumb through them, to discuss relative merits of materials and styles, to analyze techniques, and to develop more universal themes in the messages yet to be born. When the student was returned to his barrio, a rapid radiation of *grafitismo* theory and practice was set in motion, peer interaction always being the most effective vehicle for education.

Although he contributed in this way to the educational process, El Indio Jesús recognized that there existed current challenges to the growth and development of *grafitismo*. These still needed to be met. The art was only as good as its theoretical underpinnings.

He noted that almost all of the *grafiteros* were male. Female practitioners of the art seemed to confine their efforts mainly to bathroom stalls, where they were rarely seen and seldom appreciated. Yet he perceived that they had something very special, something currently lacking, which needed to be restored to Chicano art.

Female influence and contribution to graffiti as an art and communication medium had to have harkened back to its very origins, he was certain. It was the exclusive division of the sexes, El Indio Jesús believed, that spelled the doom for many civilizations and their arts, including graffiti. In his view, the rigid, unrelenting segregation of the sexes was the most insidious yet ingenious method of control ever devised by oppressor nations in the history of the world. He theorized that the downfall of benevolent democratic cultures and the rise of fascistic governments throughout the millennia could be traced to the deliberate pitting of men and women against each other as classes. He believed, furthermore, that whenever the ruling class placed power into the hands of male priesthoods, whenever a priestly class claiming divine authority captured significant strength over the common people who then became voiceless, men and women competed for diminishing benefits. Soon came war of all against all. And cultural collapse and extinction. He saw history walking the same road now.

El Indio Jesús felt that if the female principle could be restored to *grafitismo*, a florescence surpassing all past achievements could be won. The isolation of the sexes one from another, producing warring entities and subsequent loss of male-female synergy, meant the loss of contact between body and soul, flesh and spirit. The Toltecs followed the Mayas, and the Aztecs stood ripe for conquest because of this severing of the male and female principles, from the loss of the feminine in all its special genius. Malinche and all the other female enablers of the conquerors— Pocahontas, Sacajawea, Katherine Ortega, Linda Chavez, for example—despised their loss of role and status in their own right, he believed, and they recognized that they had nothing to lose in the wars of males versus females. The oppressors, if they could keep the sexes fighting each other, could bank on the fact that the natives would be unable to discern who the real enemies were, *los autores intelectuales*.

El Indio Jesús came near to reaching his dream of bringing a viable feminine synthesis to Valley *grafitismo* some years earlier when, for a brief moment, a truly special artist suddenly appeared. Their meeting was pure happenstance.

Driving down Twelfth Street long after midnight on a May evening his eye caught a fleeting movement on the Indian School grounds that struck him as strange. He pulled his *caro troquita* over to the curb and killed the motor and lights. He watched through the side mirror.

There was no moon, but the streetlights gave an angled illumination that picked out the next movement when it came. A figure separated itself from the sparse bushes near a dormitory and sped to the fence at the verge of the street. Something was thrown over the ten-foot-high chain link fence. The figure then clambered up and over, dropping to the sidewalk.

For a while, El Indio Jesús thought he was seeing just another of the countless cases of runaway students, another homesick Indian child who could no longer bear the Bureau of Indian Affairs' indoctrination centers. But the figure crossed the street diagonally to the Horn service station and disappeared behind it.

Curiosity battled with discretion in him over whether to go or stay, or perhaps go behind the building to find out what was going on. At last, remembering Rumsfeld's Law—"When in doubt about the correctness of an act, do nothing"—he simply stretched out as best he could in the VW seat and waited for the next thing to happen.

He had the priceless ability to nap anywhere, at any time, day or night, and so dozed off only to be awakened by a passing car on the nearly deserted street just in time to catch the shadowy figure slide back over the fence and into the school dormitory.

The next day, being in the general area, he thought he would see what he would find behind the gas station. And there was indeed something for his eyes to feast on. On the wall was an outline of a large-scale figure, rather madonna-ish, laid out and awaiting further treatment.

Over the next several weeks, El Indio Jesús stopped by there from time to time as his travels allowed. Each time there was progress made on the work. As it became more defined, the shape of a woman appeared more clearly. The artist must be using milk crates to stand on, for the figure was nearly eight feet tall. It was not a stick figure like a Navajo Yei but rounded and naturalistic. The female figure wore a manta-style robe with one shoulder bared while the rest of her body was draped with a colorful rebozo. The muralist was using both aerosol spray paint and paint in cans, and in a variety of colors.

El Indio Jesús was torn between the wish to learn who the *grafitero* was and the fear that rooting out the artist would impede or completely stop the completion of the labor.

He decided to take up the night watch again. Perhaps there was more to learn this way.

And there was. While this evening was a simple repeat of the first, his alertness this time picked up something he had completely missed before, something important: the *grafitero* was a *grafitera*. The object of his attention was a young woman.

What he failed to notice before now became so obvious as to be embarrassing. Now he could detect femininity from the grace of the form, the gait, and the posture as she made her way to and from the Horn service station. He loved the intrigue.

It was time for him to call in a consultant. The obvious choice would have to be Tony the World Traveler. He, above all the others, had entry into the Indian School, even the girls wing. He would know how to identify the midnight artist without exposing her to the wardens.

Tony the World Traveler reveled in this assignment, holding as it did opportunities for confounding the school authorities while plotting with the clever children. Besides, in his days as a student there, sneaking into the girls wing at night was one of the few joys of his incarceration.

It took two weeks. In two weeks' time the mural was essentially completed.

On a misty early morning near the end of June, El Indio Jesús and Tony the World Traveler stood together before the finished painting. The woman's eyes reached out and held the viewers in place, restraining for a long moment further examination of the rest of her. Then one noticed that she was clearly a madonna, but more: she seemed to personify the ancient Diné Spider Woman and the Pueblo Katçina women and Mother Earth and all the women who composed the lacings of life. Her aura of colors was reminiscent of La Virgen de Guadalupe but lacked the baroque quality of the more Spanish-influenced *santos* of the Catholic Church. She was elemental and eternal, but most of all, she was the soul of the *indigena*.

The men stood in silence, appreciating something special that had not yet been brushed by countless pairs of eyes. It was a little like being the first to walk on new snow.

Then Tony the World Traveler broke the spell by saying it was time to meet the artist.

At a nearby coffee shop El Indio Jesús met Desbah Peshlikai, after having known her in a peculiar way for the past two months. She exhibited a natural shyness, but at the same time she was amused and curious about the discoverers of her secret.

The meeting, at first awkward, changed into one of mutual appreciation. They shared from the start a strong camaraderie that was to last for years.

Tony the World Traveler merely sat watching the two with a smirk.

El Indio Jesús was taken aback when he learned that she was already aware of the *mujeres muralistas* in the San Francisco Bay area and had, in fact, been inspired to do her own mural from their example. Art for her would be public and political, she averred.

She would continue to seek ways to make that happen. In the meantime, being older than many of her classmates but needing a high school diploma to go forward with her life's plans, she was about to graduate from Indian School. Her next step would be entering the life of a religious. She had learned all she could about the work of Maryknoll nuns in Latin America. In the fall, she would begin her own training.

As if answering questions that the men did not ask her but which she anticipated, she acknowledged that for a Navajo woman from south of Oljato, she was taking an unlikely step out of her own world and into one that held a mixed record with native people.

"Look," she said, "at this point in my life, I am not prepared to make judgments about what's right or wrong with the way that the Maryknolls think. Coming from a very traditional clan and being brought up in a medicine way, I have always been pretty skeptical about the Christianity that we see out on the rez. But I like the solid work that they do. They really help people. And they are not afraid to get their hands dirty over political issues. I like that. I like that a lot.

"I don't know how much you are aware of our government's meddling in Guatemala. I don't mean to talk down to you. You probably know more about it than I do.

"I see the work that the Maryknolls are doing in Guatemala with the terrorized native people as a valid contribution to their well-being. It is an example of what I would like to do, too, to be of real help." She paused here, but then finished her thought.

"I guess you could say that I am more of a pragmatist—I just learned that word—than a theo . . . theo . . . how do you say that?"

"Theologian?" Tony the World Traveler helped.

"Yes. One of these days when I'm a little old lady sitting high up in the Manzanos, maybe I'll sort out my personal theology—did I say that right?—and fancy it up. Till then, though, there's work to be done. I want to help . . ."

She trailed off, suddenly flushed. The men could see the wave of shyness that overcame her, a young woman unused to sharing her innermost thoughts. And with strangers, even.

"Let me ask you a question, if I may," ventured El Indio Jesús, "and I don't mean to be intruding, but what about your own people? Don't they need help, too?"

"Yes, you are right, they do. I have thought a lot about this, and that is why I have come to the conclusion that I should go to Guatemala."

El Indio Jesús and Tony the World Traveler both appeared confused by her response, and she saw that.

"What I mean is this. Right now the Navajo Nation has the very best leadership it can get, led by Peterson Zah. The people around him are excellent, too, like Vivian Arvizu and Claudeen Bates Arthur.

"So I have confidence that while this administration is in Window Rock, well, I think things are on the right track. And that's reason number one.

"Reason number two is that I am not ready. I am not prepared to contribute much to helping my people yet. That's why I picked up on the idea of getting training and learning from the Mary-knolls while assisting them day to day in Guatemala, where life is so fragile.

"When I feel I have something to offer the Diné, I'll be back . . . if I'm still alive!" She laughed, but then again looked taken aback at the confidences she was sharing with these two men, secrets she had shared with no one until now.

Sensing this, El Indio Jesús reached across the table and took her hand in his. Tony the World Traveler did the same. For a long tender moment, the three held hands in appreciation of her and the new friendship that had just been created.

Tony the World Traveler was fascinated with Desbah and saw her often during the summer months. When time permitted, she spent a few hours with El Indio Jesús, too, occasionally joining him and his current *grafitero* as they toured. In time, she felt confident enough to share with them her special insight about the political possibilities of the art of *grafitismo*.

El Indio Jesús and Tony the World Traveler heard from her that when she took her vows, she took the name Sister Lupe in honor of the Indian woman respected throughout the New World: La Virgen de Guadalupe.

She wrote *adiós* when she left for Central America.

■ ■ ■

Today's budding *grafitero* fairly quivered with excitement over the variety and quality of the spray-painted messages and drawings that El Indio Jesús showed him on the tour through the city's *barrios*. One special mural was saved as the high point of the day. It was a collage of faces. On the left were the stately portraits in vivid colors of Mexican and Indian leaders. The left half displayed cartoonish faces of Chicano *vendidos*—politicians and priests who traded on their heritage for places of stature in the gringo world.

"Sometime you should see this mural in the moonlight, *amiguito*. In that kind of light, the whites of the eyes come alive. They seem to look right at you and make you think. Which is, of course, what they are meant to do."

Still looking at the mural, the youth spoke thoughtfully. "I would like to ask you a question, Don Jesús.

"We saw many things today, but there is something I don't understand. In many places in the barrios we saw markings that said 'Waldo.' And then after the name, there were numbers like 'I' or 'II.' There were many like that. I don't understand."

"Ah, *sí*," El Indio Jesús nodded. "Yes, it is a message of great power. I think you are old enough and cautious enough to learn its meaning.

"The name Waldo has come down to us through the years to mean a person who has committed an offense against *la gente*. It is not the real name of anyone, yet everyone knows who is meant by it. The person may perhaps not have actually broken a law but has hurt someone in the barrio. Or maybe the person has broken a law and has not been punished. Usually, the one who is called Waldo has broken the unwritten laws of *la gente* and he is being warned. The grafitti with 'Waldo' and a number after it means that he is being watched and *la gente* are counting his mistakes. *La gente* have a long memory for things like this. The paint may wash off but the memory remains."

"But why is he called Waldo?" asked the boy.

"I can't tell you what I don't know. I only know that this name has been used among us for a long time, and we all know it means someone who has harmed us."

"And the numbers?"

"They tell how many times this person has done something terribly wrong. It means *la gente* are counting. At first, it will just say 'Waldo,' or 'Waldo I.' The second time, it will be 'Waldo II.'"

"I saw only 'Waldo' or 'Waldo I' or 'Waldo II.' Are there any 'Waldo IIIs'?"

El Indio Jesús laughed without humor. "If, or when, there is a 'Waldo III,' that person had better get right with his god, if he has one, because he will not be in this world much longer."

"You mean someone will kill him?" The boy was stunned.

"You are old enough to ask these questions of your fine grandfather. This you should do. I am answering only your first questions. The rest you must find out from your own family. They know as much or more than I do. All I will say now is that there are two kinds of law in the Chicano and Indian communities: one that the Anglo has imposed on us and another that governs our lives with a special code as old as our time on earth, I would guess. Sometimes the two systems of laws overlap. Many times they do not. Our system has as its foundation the concepts of honor and dignity. Too often the code of the gringos sacrifices honor and dignity so that it becomes a game of cleverness between opposing lawyers and even among the judges themselves. It is not where right and correctness triumphs, but where the fastest dog gets the bone. Peace cannot be found in this way.

"But for us, when someone violates the code of the people, when honor and dignity have been compromised, it is our responsibility to see that peace and correctness are reinstated. That can take many forms. The peacemaking courts are in our homes. The jury is made up of all the people who have something to ask or who have something to say. And the punishment also is in the hands of the people. All of our people are responsible to see that justice, our justice, is carried out and peace renewed.

"What you saw today was 'Waldo II,' which means that someone whom *la gente* are watching has done a second act against the sanctity of the community, or has done something against someone that the people feel should be protected."

"And do you know who this person is?" persisted the youth.

"Oh, I think that almost everyone in the barrio knows who that particular Waldo is. And why his name is there, and why he is being counted."

"That is not an answer," reproached the young man.

"No, that is not a direct answer. But it is the answer that you will receive from me. If you are at one with your barrio, then the people will share their knowledge with you. But you must learn to listen. You must learn to see. And to learn.

"And now I will take you home. There have been two kinds of lessons for you today. Both lessons come from the wisdom of the people. One lesson is the system of informal information. When the newspapers and radio and television are in the hands of the powerful outsiders, other systems of passing information among the people are needed. Grafitti serves one small but important part of the informal sharing of information in the barrios.

"The second lesson for today is that of our informal justice system. And really, it is not all that informal. It is not seen on the surface, but it has a code, procedures, and results. It is peacemaking. The Waldo thing is one small but important part of this, a tool, I might say.

"These things I tell you so that your interest will cause you to find answers from your family, and from those answers, you will become more aware of the strength that the barrio holds. And you will, with this understanding, become a better, stronger trustee of the heritage of your people."

El Indio Jesús paused thoughtfully. Then he added, "There is also an important caution I would leave with you, and that has to do with self-aggrandizement."

"What?" asked the youth.

"What I mean by the term 'self-aggrandizement' is the trap of falling in love with seeing your own name or initials on the walls you use. Or your own very personal messages. The true charge for the *grafitero* is to serve the community, as I have already said. To splash your own identity, your name or nickname or initials, or that of your girlfriend serves no purpose except to make useless noise. The same goes for inscribing your barrio's name on walls, or worse, engaging in marking out the work of others with silly things like 'so-and-so rules.' That is only unjustifiable defacing of walls. It serves no community purpose, just self-aggrandizement.

"Whenever I see names that do no more than shout the *grafitero*'s own identification, I know that the mission of the *grafitero* was either not clearly taught, or else it was not understood. I am reminded of a poem, or part of a poem, that I read in a Caracas newspaper some time ago. It is much like our *dichos*:

> *Cantar bien o cantar mal*
> *Puede ser indiferente;*
> *Pero estando entre la gente*
> *Cantar bien o no cantar.*

"It is my every hope that your art will serve the people of your community, and not your own ego."

Not long after those lessons, the young man left the *caro troquita* and disappeared into the heart of Five Points. El Indio Jesús continued on to a meeting with a group of young radio station managers and directors near the university.

1 2 3
4 5 6
THURSDAY
7

¿Quién Ganó?

On Thursday afternoon El Indio Jesús gassed up his *caro troquita*, checked the oil and the tires, and made sure the spare was in good shape. He proceeded to the upper region of the North Valley. There he paid a visit to his *amigo* Armando Salazár.

Armando was one of the very few Chicanos who graduated from high school in the 1940s. He was voted most likely to succeed and best looking of the senior class. He also made the National Honor Society.

Because of an asthmatic condition, Armando did not serve in the military after high school but rather packed up and drove out to Los Angeles, where his natural industriousness won him high-paying jobs. He usually held down two jobs at a time, such as working in a shipyard for one shift and in an aircraft plant for a second shift.

Sometime around 1955 Armando returned to the North Valley behind the wheel of a bright red '55 Thunderbird exuding success from head to toe. He made a big splash up and down the valley. Nearly all of his friends were married by now. They each had two children to show him. They questioned Armando about his love life and his bachelorhood. He informed them that the key to his success was a matter of staying single and not marrying any of the females here in the United States. He said that *las chicas* here are no more than dark gringas who had been Anglicized and corrupted, that all they thought about was refrigerators, Elvis Presley records, and wall-to-wall shag carpets.

Armando became eloquent over his solution to the problem of wife selection. And at the age of forty, he actually carried it out. When his business was going well and he had put money aside, he went deep into the interior of Mexico and returned with a four-teen-year-old virgin Indian child-woman of surpassing beauty. Those who had laughed at him at La Paloma Blanca saying that he was full of bullshit scratched their heads at his wedding and wondered over his good fortune.

Armando and his wife Margarita produced a girl baby the first year, the second year, the third year, and the fourth year. Armando was now forty-four years old and Margarita was eighteen.

His grocery store was branching out into a filling station, a feed store, and a construction materials complex. He sold groceries, gas, oil, tires, feed, alfalfa, peeled *vigas*, *adobes*, red flagstone, corrugated tin, and a pile each of *caliche* and red clay. Traditional building materials were his specialty. It was this outlet for the materials that brought El Indio Jesús back at frequent intervals through the years.

The four little girls presented rare beauty as they played around the store. Margarita was the cause of admiration and envy among the neighbors, male and female. She rose before dawn each day to present her husband with hand-ground corn tortillas to eat with his *huevos rancheros*. No one in the Valley, north or south, had seen such a sight in more than sixty years. So extraordinary was it that people pointed him out on the street, saying, "There goes the man who gets real hot corn tortillas with his *huevos* every morning. All he has to say is *otra calientita*, and she puts another one into his hand."

Each year Armando bought a new Chevy pickup, and he took great pleasure in driving to the shopping center with his four little girls crisp in white pinafores. He bought up parcels of land one after another until he owned more than twenty acres of prime river bottomland where he grew vegetables, orchards, and alfalfa.

With great pains he constructed a home so beautiful that cars would park across the street on Sunday afternoons, their occupants discussing its merits. It was a two-story adobe with John Adams windows and doors imported at great expense from somewhere back east. It was spanned by a front porch with white pillars. Most amazing of all, if they could but see it, was a spectacular staircase cascading down from the second floor to the landing in the main entryway. Armando hired master carpenters from Missouri to fashion them. They produced in wood the content of his most precious fantasy—that of his four girls and their mother descending the stairway in a cloud of white lace.

Margarita became more beautiful with each child and with each year. Now, at twenty-two, men turned their heads to watch her pass by and looked at the graying Armando with questions in their eyes.

The youngest daughter, Angelita, stood closest to Armando's heart. She was referred to as his *consentida*, his favorite. Even when she became a teenager and her older sisters busied themselves with high school activities, Angelita stayed home to help her father or to read books sitting on a stool in the store.

Before long, the eldest daughter was enrolled as a history major at the University of Missouri, the second daughter was in Denver at Regis College, and the third daughter had employment and glamour as administrative assistant to a Chicano *político*. The three daughters came home only on holidays and special occasions: their lives were now elsewhere.

Through the years El Indio Jesús made use of his trips for construction materials to keep current with his friend's life. Recently word had reached him that his friend was being called Ya No Las Puedes, which translates roughly to "you can't do it," "you can't make it anymore," implying that a man was no longer a man. El Indio Jesús, contemptuous of *chisme*, refused to acknowledge rumor, attributing it to jealousy of his friend who had figured everything out and was so successful.

But the *chismes* continued.

One day when El Indio Jesús went for *vigas* with which to construct a roof, Margarita stepped into a jet black TransAm and drove off in a hail of gravel, waving back to Armando and shouting, "See you later, Armie." She wore designer jeans and held her hair in place with sunglasses perched atop her head like Jackie O.

Noting how beautiful she looked, El Indio Jesús was especially surprised to hear her speak English.

Angelita came out of the house with green chili and tortillas— tortillas not freshly made nor homemade, but warm. Armando's *consentida* performed duties like her mother before her, except that the art of making corn tortillas did not survive into this generation. Her green chili was excellent, however. She fed Armando's friends graciously in her mother's absence.

Although El Indio Jesús visits were irregular and based on his need for materials and not for socializing, nonetheless he began to witness a kind of slow deterioration in the condition of the house and of his friend Armando. There were dishes in the sink. Dust coated the furniture. Armando was unshaven, his clothes rumpled. His eyeglasses were taped together where they had broken at the hinge. El Indio Jesús thought he could smell liquor.

If El Indio Jesús were a more frequent visitor, he would have been able to see that Armando was making mistakes—little mistakes, but mistakes nevertheless. He forgot to put oil in one of his trucks. He left water in the radiator instead of replacing it with antifreeze. The store inventory grew smaller and older. The house began falling apart.

Margarita traded the TransAm for a Continental Mark VII. She said that she needed it to go to the university for evening classes. Every evening she dressed up and went to classes.

Angelita stayed close to her father. She did not go to school. She did not date.

Armando began selling off small parcels of land to keep things going, since the store was no longer as productive. More and more land was sold—but not the bottomland.

He began drinking. He sometimes asked the young men to go get him a bottle of wine.

One winter, Angelita began leaving the store. At first it was just overnight, but the time stretched out longer and longer.

Margarita bought a condominium in the city to be near the university.

Angelita came back home on weekends to make green chili and to do the laundry. Even so, Armando began looking *como un trampe* and living like a hermit.

The gas station closed. He was drunk so often that people stopped buying materials from him. The store inventory now included only bread, Cokes, bologna, sandwich meat, two kinds of soap, Tabasco sauce, candy, cigarettes, and Ortega chili, whole and chopped, in four-ounce cans. Few people shopped in the store any more.

Before, no one dared to call him his nickname to his face, but now, even little boys and girls knew it and in their ignorance would ask, "*¿un* Milky Way, *por favor*, Ya No Las Puedes?"

One day when El Indio Jesús stopped by to help his friend remove corrugated tin from the roof of a burned building nearby, a Cadillac drove up to the store. The driver, an Anglo, stayed behind wheel while Margarita got out. She called the soot-covered Armando down from the roof. Outside the store, the two took turns talking to him, but he did not respond. In only a few minutes they drove off again, leaving him standing in the driveway.

He stood there for a long time. When El Indio Jesús climbed back down to the ground, he asked, "*¿Estas bien?*"

After a protracted silence, Armando responded, "*Bien.*"

The next time El Indio Jesús saw Armando he was sitting on his porch in a derelict upholstered chair in which he seemed to be a habitual inhabitant. He told El Indio Jesús that Margarita wanted a divorce and half of everything he owned. Appraisers said that he was worth a quarter of a million dollars. He would have to sell the land and house to give her and his daughters their share of that amount of money.

But that did not happen. Armando, *a.k.a.* Ya No Las Puedes, continued to sit on the porch as he approached his sixtieth birthday. Angelita, he said, came home from the city to make sure he had green chili and tortillas from time to time. He was thinking about making a will that would give her his half of the property.

The last time El Indio Jesús drove up the Valley to get materials and look in on his friend, no one was at the house or the store. A neighbor told him that Ya No Las Puedes was in *la casa de los locos* in Las Vegas. He was making bigger and bigger mistakes, she said, and he nearly burned the house down one time with him still in it. He shot all his chickens. She said that his *consentida* Angelita was the one who decided he must be put away because he was dangerous to himself now and to everyone else. The *abogados* put her in charge of all his money and property, she said.

Before he left, Margarita, Angelita, and a dark man drove up in a large late-model car. The neighbor, ever lurking nearby, told him that Margarita, only now in her early thirties, recently remarried. The man was from her native village, the son of the hacienda owner for whom her mother had worked as a cook. They played together as children. Someone had written to her saying that he was at the university. She found him doing graduate work at the Robert O. Anderson School of Business. He was studying international banking.

He watched the three enter the house, which was again as beautiful as it had once been. A spotted, wrinkled hand plucked at his sleeve. He turned around to face the probing eyes of the omnipresent *vieja*.

"*¿Quién ganó? Quién ganó?*" she demanded.

El Indio Jesús only shrugged his shoulders. He did not know who the winners were in this game of life.

FRIDAY

El Rancho En El Bosque

It was Friday noon. El Indio Jesús packed up some leftover materials that he then stored in the box of his *caro troquita*. Leaving the church parking lot he drove up the Valley to Corrales. At its northern reaches, he turned off Highway 46 onto a dirt road. Past alfalfa fields and horse pastures, over *la acequia madre* and a smaller irrigation channel and into a *bosque* with ancient cottonwoods, he arrived at a *ranchito* looking as though it had been painted into the scene a hundred years ago. He drove through the dooryard and directly to a barn in the rear of the house. He dismounted to open the barn doors and then drove his vehicle in, closing the doors behind him and hitching the padlock. As he walked along the red flagstones to the house, the early summer dust swirled past. Two dogs bounded toward him, tails whipping back and forth. Rapping on the door in the enduring rhythm of shave-and-a-haircut-two-bits, and without waiting for an answer, he entered.

"Where are you, *mujer*?"

"Aha. That must be our friendly neighborhood handyman, I'd guess." A small, energetic woman entered the kitchen and walked into his outstretched arms.

"Is she here?" he asked.

"Yes," she replied, her head tucked under his chin.

"*¿Estas bien?*"

"*Bien.*" After a few more minutes savoring the embrace, she moved back, looked up at him, and said, "Come have something to eat. *Sientate.*"

She turned to the stove and spoke over her shoulder. "Big Bill called a little while ago. He picked up the message. He says everything's go, no problem."

"*Perfecto,*" he responded.

A tired young woman then entered the room, favoring one leg. El Indio Jesús rose from the table and embraced her.

"Sister Kateri," he said. "Safe."

"Yes," she smiled. She sighed.

"Come. Sit," he ordered. Both sat at the oil-clothed table where freshly made flour tortillas and steaming green chili stew were placed before them by Pilar, who, returning, worked at the wood stove and talked over her shoulder.

"Which would you like to hear first, *compadre*, the plan of action or the list of chores?"

"Oh," he groaned, "give me the list of chores now. I can wait till this evening for your next *movidas.*" Turning to the visibly fatigued woman at the table, he put a hand on her arm.

"How long have you been on the road?"

"Six days. Hard ones."

"You must rest now, as much as you can."

She expelled a long breath.

"Yes."

Placing a large bowl of frijoles in the center of the table, Pilar spoke to El Indio Jesús.

"That fence fell down again. That *cabrito* you like so much, I think he eats through it. Next time, bring me llamas. They have pride. It's beneath their dignity to knock down fences."

"Maybe I'll butcher him today. Do you need the meat?"

"Well, no, and really, I'm not *that* mad at him."

He laughed. "What else needs to be done?"

"The usual: drainage ditches need cleaning. The roof on the shack is leaking again. You might want to take a look at the bridges, just to make sure they're okay."

He laughed. "So I have even you believing that they're about to fall into the *acequias*! I'll look them over, but I used enough steel and concrete underneath that they'll probably see the year two thousand fifty without needing repair." He reached out to take the cup of coffee she handed him. "I brought signs to put up. I thought I'd print just one at the church, and then I became creative—or so I thought—and I ended up with a bunch. How do you like 'Danger: Magonistas Ahead,' or 'Do Not Feed the Snakes,' or 'Welcome Ayatollah Khomeini'?"

"Well, those should certainly chill out *turistas* looking for adventure along my shady lane!"

They laughed and enjoyed the good feelings the room held.

Sitting down at the table with the other two, Pilar continued with the list. "That storm Tuesday night stood right overhead long enough to soak through the mud on the shack's roof. It got the feed a little wet. It probably has high priority if you have the time and the materials. Do we have any tar paper left? I think there is still a bucket of tar in the barn somewhere."

"The holy fathers are donating materials for the roof this week. Even though they don't know it, I am certain that they would approve of this use of their extra materials." He looked searchingly at the nun.

"Shall we wait until dinner to talk? How would you like it?"

"Yes," she replied, "I'll catch my strength by then and we can work up the plans. Thanks."

"No problem."

■ ■ ■

El Indio Jesús left the women in the kitchen and walked back up the dusty car track to the first of the two bridges over the ditches. He brought with him a sign he had nailed to a stake. On the approach side of the bridge, he hammered the sign into the ground. Then he walked to the other bridge, the first one that a driver would see coming in from the main road. This one he nailed directly to the bridge, on the face of the railing. The railing on the other side of the bridge was torn out and dangling over the *acequia* in places.

El Indio Jesús visualized the approach to the *casita* from the viewpoint of a curious driver who had never been there before but wanted to look around the area.

As the driver would make his way for the last half mile or so, he would have to slow down for more and more dips and bumps in the unpaved road. Rain and drying had left the way muddied and caked, with ruts that grabbed at the car tires. El Indio Jesús had put in a few turnaround places for those easily discouraged. The next obstacle for the driver would be the larger bridge over the main ditch. Its sign read, DANGER: UNSAFE BRIDGE. Planks of different heights and not quite meeting gave the impression on instability. The broken railing leaning out over the water also said disrepair.

If the driver were intrepid still, the second bridge, shorter and without railings, should look even more precarious. His new sign read, DEAD END / PRIVATE PROPERTY / KEEP OUT. Past that, not within view of the second bridge but facing the driver, who would now be weaving through the *bosque* on the wooded drive up to the house, a final sign in red paint on black background read, GRINGOS STAY OUT.

El Indio Jesús wondered if his hypothetical driver could have even the faintest idea of how much danger he actually faced if he proceeded on further toward the *casita*. For his sake, El Indio Jesús hoped that the driver took heed of the warnings.

He walked back to the barn and busied himself with the fence of the goat pen. He thought about Pilar on her *ranchito* in the *bosque*.

■ ■ ■

Pilar Valles y Martínez was the great granddaughter of the legendary Solomón Valles, a man revered as a patriot throughout the villages of the mountains and the valleys. Those who were still linked to the cultural chain had heard of the family that had been sold twice, *la familia que vendieron dos veces*, and although they might not have heard the whole or the accurate story, there was no mistaking the honor of his memory and the deference even now paid to his descendants.

And so it was that Solomón's rigid commitment to an ancient code of honor in turn committed his offspring and their offspring to a political consciousness that seemed to have been genetically passed on.

Not that some in his line did not try to ignore the family code: Pilar, surrounded by keen political concern while growing up in Mesilla, expected that her new life in Rio Arriba would be different among her husband's people. But she was wrong.

Pablo Martínez was an heir to the Maria Elena Land Grant, which ran from the mountain crests to the river north of the city. The *casita* of his family and in which they now lived sat upon one of the last pieces of land still occupied by original heirs to the grant.

Although the climate in the state had never been healthy for land grant activists, the 1960s were especially repressive. Pablo worked long and hard against the sale of the Maria Elena Land Grant. Pilar found herself making coffee for an endless stream of nameless confederates, and against her will she heard and understood what was going on around her. Yet she did not speak and she took no active role other than maintenance.

But that changed in 1963. Pablo's body was found on the West Mesa, one leg pinned under the rear left tire of his car. His death was long and cruel. And anonymous.

Left with a nine-year-old daughter, Lucia, and the *ranchito*, Pilar's anger rose to heights rivaling that of her great-grandfather Solomón.

Running the farm and caring for Lucia was exhausting, depleting. The task of getting the girl to school each day was nearly insurmountable. Finally, she made arrangements for her to stay at a school run by a religious organization. She returned home on school holidays and for the summer. But they grew apart. Lucia's lessons at school took her from one world and put her into another. It may have been true that her problem was intelligence. She was identified early as something special, a Chicana who fell into the category of educable for those who would excite her toward different paths, even if it meant on some levels a betrayal of her own background.

Lucia became a chemistry major at the university, where she met people working toward a future at Sandia Laboratories and Los Alamos National Laboratories.

As the estrangement between Pilar and her daughter, Lucia, grew, starting as early as high school, Pilar found herself drawn once again into the political network in which her brother Carlos in Mesilla remained an important link. Contact was renewed with Tio Augustín as well, a man who left for Nicaragua in the 1920s, who became a colleague of Sandino and witnessed the assassination of Sandino at the airport, and who found refuge in El Salvador, where he built up a *ranchito* sufficient to his needs.

Pilar kept the small farm going while serving those causes that centered on the convictions of old Solomon: the primacy of cultural integrity and its linkage to the ancestral lands from which it had sprung. From time to time, she would drive north to La Bajada, where, in a sand-blasted box canyon, melting remains of the Valles homestead were still visible. Recognizing the nearness of the pueblos of Santo Domingo and Cochiti and San Felipe, she felt strong as an inheritor of a tradition built not on Spanish conquest but on *genízaro* partnership with the native communities. The pulse of this partnership never ceased to throb in the veins of their descendants, either Indian or *genízaro*, Pilar acknowledged, and from time to time she wondered when the time would come for those symbiotic partners to stand together again against a surrounding world no longer tolerable.

Conversation

El Indio Jesús stored the ancient sickle among the tools hanging and leaning on the walls of the shed. Many of the hand tools bore rough handles, fashioned perhaps by the father or grandfather of Pilar's dead husband. The grip areas showed dark sheens. In the slant of the setting sun's light he could see past the doorway old saddles and harnesses mossy with dust, strung beneath the eaves by rusty hand-hewn nails and hooks. A scythe leaned against a corner, the ripples in its metal blade speaking of hand forging and yesterday.

Walking out to the barn, he removed the charged six-volt battery of his *caro troquita* and replaced it with Pilar's, with which she powered her radios and television set. During the afternoon he was able to prune some of the many fruit trees, sharpened hoes, shovels, and an ax, and chopped down part of the first growth of summer weeds in the irrigation ditch. He now looked forward to a good meal with good people.

At the house he found Sister Kateri again sitting at the kitchen table, but now she looked rested and was wearing freshly laundered clothes.

"*¿Estas bien?*" he asked.

"*Bien,*" she replied, a smile crossing her face that never really reached her eyes. "Just fine. This is such a lovely place to recover in, a good place."

"Yes, it is. Nothing bad has ever happened in this house. You can feel it, can't you?"

"Yes, that must be it. It's the first time I've felt truly safe in a very long time."

He got up from the table and walked to the stove. "Coffee?" He poured one cup and reached for another.

"Yes. Please."

He passed a steaming cup to her where she sat, but he leaned back against the wooden drainboard and stood there to sip his coffee.

"And how is that old scoundrel Augustín?" he asked with a smile dancing around his mouth.

"'Scoundrel' is right," agreed Pilar, now entering the room. "Kateri told me that there is an important señora there on her way out with her grandson, and there Augustín is, breaking out his best homemade wine for her! Can you believe it? *¡Que caballero!*"

El Indio Jesús laughed with the women.

"Yes, well, it's kind of hard to believe, really. I have great trouble picturing him at ease, taking 'leisure time,' as we are calling it these days."

"'Leisure time'? What a concept! The Michelob weekend!" Pilar's laugh was derisive. "Only in America could the free enterprise system come up with another money-making scheme to get dollars from people who're just resting up from a week's work!"

"Convincing people to buy all kinds of things in order to relax," added El Indio Jesús. "Like appropriate attire, uniforms of all kinds, expensive 'complicated' sneakers—that's Kingsolver's term— designer sweatsuits. You do understand, don't you, Sister, that you aren't supposed to sweat in inappropriate clothing any longer?" Addressing Pilar, he asked, "By the way, while I'm thinking about it, have you seen where I put that article by John Mohawk on the concepts of 'leisure time' and 'the weekend'? I'm sure it was in *Akwesasne Notes* somewhere."

Pilar shrugged. "You'll have to rummage through the boxes of newsclips you call your library. I haven't seen it lately. But that one by Richard Wilk floated to the top recently when I was rearranging the dust in your *oficina*. You know, the one about the coevolution of leisure time and the recliner chair?"

"What?" asked the nun.

El Indio Jesús explained. "He lays out the thesis that the recliner transformed the parlor into a living room, and with the addition of the television set, he says, leisure became a project for the whole family requiring more and more time, energy, and of course, financial resources. He goes on, but it's a brilliant analysis."

"Capitalism's genius for inventing ways to take back earnings never ceases to amaze me," commented Sister Kateri.

"Well, how about this: the garment industry is digging deep into my personal crusade for freedom of speech."

The nun looked intently at him. "What do you mean?"

"I'm sorry to have to tell you this, but the textile and clothing industries are capturing the graffiti market, and in a much bigger way than I could ever have imagined." He returned to the table, tipped back in his chair, and warmed to his topic.

"Here for centuries, *grafitismo* has been the voice, the conscience, the vehicle for free speech in culture after culture. Literacy has had only a little to do with its value and spread: all over the world pictographs have carried vital information when other means have not been available or have been suppressed by power holders. It has always spoken with the voice of the people."

"And well I know your point of view, *compadre*, since Sister Lupe has drummed it into my head often enough at the orphanage!" Kateri injected.

"What I am getting at is the printed T-shirt. The walking graffiti of the present."

He leaned his chair back on its hind legs and continued.

"With the explosion of printed T-shirts, the garment industry has suppressed free speech by peddling its own graffiti, each shirt a message, each shirt a slogan, a commercial ad. Adults and children, males and females alike are strutting around with messages on their chests that they didn't invent, unlike a true graffiti statement, but with what the garment industry and its—you'll pardon the expression—artists have divined will sell. The messages replace wall graffiti, replace billboards, replace picket signs. You get dressed and your opinion is walking along with you, loud and clear. If you want to insult, there are insulting T-shirts. If you want to make a political statement, the industry will dish up any kind of statement you want: it has no biases, only pragmatism. It'll do whatever will make money. You name it: philosophy, politics, feelings, sports, sex, consumer goods, rock groups, geography, all the -isms: racism, sexism, polemics and prejudices of all kinds."

He paused to sip some coffee and then continued.

"In 1978 about five hundred million T-shirts were sold in the United States. A number of the plain ones ended up silk screened by small concerns contracted to add additional sentiments of one kind of another. But of course they had to buy the shirts from the industry in the first place. I read an article by J. D. Reed that said, 'The T-shirt, whether promoting Budweiser or Bloomingdale's, became one of the great advertising mediums in the history of hype.' Another writer, Paul Fussell, has the idea that if you wear a brand name, for just that moment you become a 'somebody' who is linked to some successful commercial commodity like a rock group or a hot designer.

"But I'm straying from my point. I feel that while printed T-shirts give voice to the voiceless, they also inhibit expression among those who would otherwise speak out, write more boldly, attack windmills, do graffiti on the courthouse walls. And in that inhibition, I smell suppression and channeling of opinion, I sense the dulling of involvement when you can parade around all day with your chest trumpeting your message, offending some, coalescing with others, as you strut along. It comes to a point where nobody cares what your T-shirt says and the whole thing becomes meaningless. But all the while, the amateur public writers, the graffiti artists, feel they cannot compete any longer with the clever sayings and pretty pictures that are walking down the street . . . or rather, through the shopping malls (except for lunch time, nobody walks down the streets of America anymore). Worse has even come to worse: a number of *grafiteros* are copying T-shirts!

"And so my point is that the invasion of the printed T-shirt has seriously cut into the exercising of the people's informal expression, and in that way it is a serious threat to the transferral of important information among those who do not control radio, television, and print media either in this country or elsewhere."

He got up from the table to pour himself more coffee. "Anyone else?" he asked, waving the pot. The women both shook their heads no.

"Can you really say that graffiti can handle the range of T-shirt messages you describe?" Sister Katori asked.

"Right," Pilar added. "Can you make the case? Give examples. Present-day examples."

"Yes," the nun chimed in. "Examples!"

Walking back to the table and sitting down again, El Indio Jesús thought about the challenge.

"Okay, I'll give you some examples from this week's crop of graffiti, as best I can remember them. What were those categories I threw out just now?"

Pilar said, "You started out with philosophy, politics, and sentiments, I recall."

"Philosophy. That's an easy one. So many of the messages are philosophic in one way or another. A new one this week was, '*Muchas cosas son arenas en el reloj de la vida.*' Terrific, eh?"

"Terrific. Now politics, although I know that's a giveaway," said Pilar.

"Well, there are always the 'get outs,' like '*EE.UU. fuera de America Central*,' but Tuesday I saw one that said, '*EE.UU. Fuera de America del Norte*'!"

"More," demanded Pilar.

"Let's see, what was the next category?"

"Feelings, sentiment."

"Easiest of all. Those are all over the place. Add sex to that and they'll account for eighty percent of the messages!

"How do you like this one, Sister? It's for you. '*¿Kati, un viejo? ¡Que Triste!*'"

The three laughed together.

"And, of course, there is always the code, '*T.Q.M.*,' which stands for '*Te quiero mucho*.' Sometimes they add other letters, but they are more graphically sexual and not fit for present company." He smiled coyly at the women.

Pilar groaned while the nun smiled.

"Ah, here's another one for you," he continued. '*Entre una pasión y una locura estas tu.*'"

"Maybe that one should go under the heading of psychological disorders'!" offered the sister.

"Sure, and under utilities disorders, how about, '*¡Fati, me electrizas*'!"

"Geography needs no examples. Go to your local car wash and you'll get the social organization of the barrio youth groups spread out on the wall. You'll even be able to see levels of dominance by what group has written over another or has defaced other groups' logos. Near the Plaza you'll see 'XVIII' everywhere, done up in black, silver, or gold spray paint. What it signifies is that it is the home ground of the Eighteenth Street Gang. It can best be explained through the study of ethnology, probably, and how various groups mark their territories and home ranges. They recently spray-painted one of my *caro troquitas* with a gold XVIII, but it wasn't a hostile gesture. In fact, it was more like a sign indicating that I am under the protection of the Eighteenth Street Gang.

"And that's fine with me," he added. "They're a really great, creative bunch. I'm looking forward to the time when they are old enough to get into building low rider cars."

"Lowriders? The ones that go up and down? Painted in all those incredible designs?" asked Sister Kateri.

"Right. And sideways, too. The genius that goes into the mechanics as well as the artwork is unbelievable!" El Indio Jesús exclaimed, striking his forehead.

"You are getting away from the topic, Butch," Pilar warned with a smile. "Give us one more example for us to contemplate, and then I need some more work out of you."

"All right, Sundance. One final example for today. Ah yes: here's an all-purpose, serve-any-situation kind of statement. I haven't a clue about what it was there for, but it's great to contemplate on. Ready? *'Lastima que seas pura bulla.'* That one can almost make me sad.

"But finally," he said, rising from his chair, "on a more optimistic note," brightening as he put down his coffee mug. "As long as there are walls and substances to mark them with, the graffiti art and information form will continue, T-shirt and Dow be damned!"

The three laughed together.

Pilar left the table then to continue preparations. When the nun moved as though to get up and help her, Pilar gestured for her to stay resting. "I hope you can tolerate green chili, Sister. It's mother's milk in these parts."

"Tell me, Sister, do things go well for Tio Augustín?" El Indio Jesús inquired.

"If you are asking is he still working with our friends, the answer is yes, of course. And he is as careful as ever. But he is changing. There are still plenty of the usual kinds of people who seek and get his help. But there is a new kind we haven't seen much of before. I've been talking to Pilar about it. Tell him what I mean, Pilar."

"Apparently, he is going beyond the family's traditional conditions for helping others. He's helping those who are actively taking part in the struggle, not just those escaping."

"And things grow hotter for him by the day. I tried to get him to come along this time, you know, to see Carlos and Pilar and old Ándres, but no. He went on eloquently at great lengths to explain that his ancestor Solomón Valles was 'sold twice' and that he, Augustín Valles, had been pushed out of Nicaragua by the Somozistas and he'd be damned if he would be pushed out a second time, and so on and so forth." Sister Kateri smiled wryly, shrugged her shoulders, and raised her palms in a gesture that said, "I did what I could; I tried."

Pilar, placing a bowl of green chili stew on the table, leaned over and kissed Sister Kateri's cheek. "We know, and we are grateful. Do you ever hear from Sister Lupe?"

"She is in contact with Tio Augustín from time to time, and has helped us on occasion. She does most of her work in the city with the teenagers." She turned to grin at El Indio Jesús. "With the *grafiteros*."

They all laughed.

"Tell us what you see for the future," he asked. "I don't know how much longer the people can stand the constant siege. Day after day. They are afraid to talk to each other. They don't know whom to trust and whom not to. And then they see all the goodies the United States is larding out to its friends in the cities, and the Catholic Church is caught in the meat grinder between Bishop Romero's memory and the pope, who was once himself a freedom fighter and now threatens anyone who does the same with excommunication or worse. If there is a worse. I don't know. I guess I really need a rest. After this trip."

"We have tried to keep up with the Maryknoll newsletter and Moises Sandoval. It helps us understand a little better, I think. I am proud to know you, Sister Kateri. Give our love to Sister Lupe if you see her, please." He squeezed her arm affectionately.

"Be careful," she warned, smiling, looking at his hand on her arm. "I'm told that liberation theology is a communicable disease."

Amusement swirled among the three.

"I've kept a clipping here somewhere," said, Pilar, indicating with her chin a cluttered bulletin board. "A clipping that quotes Dr. Gustavo Gutierrez saying that 'class struggle is a fact and neutrality in this matter is impossible.'" She thumbed through newsclippings like leaves stuck together with thumb tacks. "Yes, here it is. Dateline Peru."

"Then old Solomón would have had to come around to Augustín's activist support of the poor and oppressed, don't you think?" El Indio Jesús asked Pilar. "Isn't Augustín merely going the next logical step that many of the Third World activist priests are taking and that so upsets the pope?" he directed this question to the nun.

Sister Kateri answered first. "We liberation theologians, otherwise known as 'radical religious,' can't help but see the class struggle going on around us: the unjust laws and unjust social and economic systems. What we can no longer support is that old-time reconciliation line, dishing out soup until the bad guys have found conversion. That day is just too far away to be of any help to the people who are suffering. If you could only see what we face . . . but you have. I'm sorry. I forgot for a minute. Any chance for me to stand on a podium and there I go," she smiled ruefully.

"Old Solomón and Pope John Paul would have been soul brothers, I think," Pilar agreed. "I can hear it in my mind as though it were yesterday, my dad saying to me and my brother, 'Now, don't you run off to the wars like your uncle Augustín. Our job is to preserve people, not to kill them.' So I guess the answer would be no, I don't think old Solomón would ever agree with Augustín. He was a fervent believer in nonengagement or perhaps disengagement. Sort of 'if you hate 'em, leave 'em, but don't fight 'em.'"

"You can't fight with your feet forever, though," El Indio Jesús reminded them.

"Yes, that's true." Pilar reflected a moment. "That is where the conflict lies in some of our hearts, the conflict of active passive resistance and the apparent uselessness of the boycott. I've never been able to reconcile those concepts when it comes down to actual situations."

"After boycotting Coors all those years, we now have black and brown people on the TV commercials guzzling booze just like real folks," chuckled El Indio Jesús. "But us, we're . . ." He paused. "Oh," he continued, "let's not get into our plans for the weekend. We can just think of ourselves as red-blooded Americans at play in leisure time, okay?"

They all laughed.

"There, I guess that's everything," Pilar said as she looked over the still-steaming food just placed on the table. "Please eat. What would you like to drink? We have coffee, tea, juice." She moved back to the refrigerator and continued serving the meal.

"Tell me, Pilar, what should I know about current events, just in case anyone asks me?" Sister Kateri had been out of the country for more than three months.

"Well, let's see," began Pilar, "I guess the continuing saga of males versus females and females versus males is the most insistent issue. Every day, all day, all night. Read anything. It's everywhere: *Time, Newsweek*, especially *Cosmopolitan*—oh, I guess I should say *Cosmo*—the magazines and the scandal sheets at the checkout stands at the supermarket. Sometimes I think there must be something really wrong with me, waiting for Fridays to come so maybe I'll see this *vato* here!" She smiled with visible affection at El Indio Jesús, whose smile matched hers.

He shoved back his chair. "So, that's about it," he agreed. "The media blitz is very pervasive. The Sunday newspaper supplements in the last year have pushed the joys of singlehood, single motherhood, single fatherhood, single foster parenthood—it goes on—and then the joys of second families, of May and December marriages, 'parenting,' whatever that is, and how great it is to start up a new family if you're a guy of fifty or so. This gives younger women who missed the baby boat another chance for mother-hood. So what if dad's seventy years old and having to shell out for college tuition.

"People are being bounced all around and they haven't figured it out. But to the extent that families are broken up by whichever inducement, more workers become available for needy industry, mainly low-paying service workers and the whole pink collar scenario. The entry-level office workers are typically female heads of households, the poorest class of people in the country—except for their children."

"Well," mused the nun, "becoming aware of propaganda in this environment of crushing media messages, do you find that the younger people are more immune to the impact of television as time goes on?"

"No," he answered. "In a word, no. In addition, the television programming is doubling up on the messages bringing even more separation of the sexes. Internecine warfare is sharpened with evening as well as daytime programming. The nighttime soaps compete with Monday night football or whatever. The consumer family doesn't even watch TV together. Dad has his set, mom has hers, the kids have theirs—even one to a kid. Add that to what we've already said about the breakup of nuclear families and you end up with two of everything: two houses, two fridges, two barbecue pits, TVs for everyone . . . It goes on, all to the benefit of the marketplace, while kids and adults suffer in confusion and dislocation. Well, it goes on . . ." he ended lamely.

They ate in silence for a while. Pilar had made a meal identical to those eaten in homes along the river for hundreds of years: *maiz, chili rojo, chili verde, frijoles, tortillas.*

"Your daughter, Pilar: how is she?" Sister Kateri wanted to know.

Pilar put down her fork and reached for the pitcher of lemonade. Filling her glass slowly, she spoke carefully, picking her way through her thoughts.

"Sister, we have a sad development these days. Maybe it's not all that new, come to think of it. Maybe it has just become more pronounced, what with the fracturing of communities.

"Too often, it seems, the educated young men and women turn away from *la gente*, following career paths that are irrelevant to helping the communities. More than that, they become helpers, intentionally or not, to the forces that are destructive.

"Oh, I am not making myself clear, I know. But this really distresses me." She took a sip of her lemonade, then continued.

"Are you aware of the concept of *malinchismo*? It comes from Mexico, but we use it, too. It refers to a woman who sides with the powerful, aiding them against her own people. She might even be unwilling, but accedes to the situation anyway. For whatever reason.

"The term comes from Cortez's Doña Marina, also known as Malinche. Whatever her rationale—and this we may never know— she facilitated the Spanish conquest of the Aztecs and the loss of native hegemony in the New World. Thus the term *malinchismo*."

She pushed her plate aside and clasped her hands at her place at the table.

"In short, Sister, Lucía seems to be this family's very own Malinche."

She took a deep breath.

"It's not just a matter of having a career that doesn't relate to the community. You see, she majored in physics and chemistry, and did very, very well. It was her next choice that we find unacceptable. She is up at the Los Alamos National Laboratories helping the madmen—and it is mostly men—who are trying to figure out how to destroy the whole world."

Looking for words that they could see were painful, she continued. "Do you remember what Tom Banyacya said about the

Hopi prophecies? About the foretelling of a time when men would invent a gourd containing ashes that would wipe out all people, all plants, all animals? Well, Lucía is helping them to make the gourd."

She paused, then completed her thoughts. "We fight a lot whenever we get together, so we don't get together much anymore . . ."

El Indio Jesús and Sister Kateri left her to her silence for a few minutes. El Indio Jesús reached over and squeezed her hands. Then he arose. Looking at the nun, he said, "It's time."

She nodded.

■ ■ ■

An hour later a white, windowless 1965 Ford Econoline panel van pulled out of the barn. On its sides were professionally painted ads in red, white, and blue reading, MA EXPRESS / 24-HOUR SERVICE / YOUR WISH IS OUR COMMAND / TELEPHONE 247-8143.

Pilar met the truck at the gate.

"Did you get the portable generator?"

"Yes," he replied, "and I've filled the extra tank. It will give us six hundred miles, more or less."

"*Vaya con Dios.* Come back soon, Sister. Safely."

Leaning into the cab window, she asked El Indio Jesús, "You're sure you have enough food there, Butch?"

"We're fine," he assured her. "I'll be back by Sunday, if all goes well."

"*Cuidadito.*"

They kissed briefly through the open window.

"Not to worry, Sundance. There will always be a Zorro."

Then he backed out the van and looped it out the driveway, Pilar watching it retreat into the darkness of the *bosque*.

■ ■ ■

El Indio Jesús centered a red magnetic lamp on the roof of the van just above the windshield, giving it the appearance of an official vehicle of some kind. Back in the driver's seat, he asked, "Where will we pick up the telephone number?"

"Unitarian Church in the Heights, on the wall facing the parking lot," Sister Kateri replied.

"Good. The Quakers can use some Unitarian help, I'm sure. They're really stretched to the breaking point."

"There are some Episcopalians involved, too," she added, "but not enough, still too few . . ." She sighed.

"The Presbyterians have certainly kept their lead in the sanctuary movement, haven't they? Fife and Corbett in Tucson, especially."

He paused, his thoughts winding along with the pavement under the van. He continued the theme. "I remember back several years ago when that first call came in from Arizona letting us know how La Migra was getting around the 'political refugee' status and rejecting people fleeing from El Salvador and Guatemala. They told us that in Los Angeles—and elsewhere, I guess—after the routine interrogation of someone, the agent would close up the folder, put it away in the desk, and then get up and walk them to the door, all friendship and *simpático*. Then, in the most casual way possible, he would say off-handedly something like, 'I'll bet you'd like to find a job, right?' and when the refugee answered *sí*, the agent would pounce and say, 'Aha! You're an economic refugee, not a political refugee! Back you go. Good-bye and good luck. The next plane leaves first thing in the morning. Be on it.'"

The nun chuckled with a note of bitterness. "Yes," she said, "I remember some of those planes. They were met by security trucks. No one was ever seen alive again."

The van stopped at the light at Lomas and University, then proceeded eastward. El Indio Jesús picked up the thread of thought again.

"Are you old enough to remember the open-armed reception the Hungarian refugees received, or for that matter, the welcome anyone from a Soviet bloc country got when looking for asylum?

And in contrast to that, the reception that the Haitians got in their flight from Baby Doc and starvation? Not only were they the wrong color, they were illiterate, low class, and spoke weird French. The U.S. just can't absorb them into the mainstream digestive tract."

She interjected, "And then Castro opened up the prisons and sent us all the ones who were caught for participating in the U.S. drug trade. Plus a few other undesirables. What irony, eh?" she asked, not really looking for a contradiction.

He continued. "The Asian refugees were something that couldn't be ignored, even though we tried to for as long as we could. The boat people just couldn't be passed over, the outcry was so loud all over the world. But the screening process has kept most out, letting in only a fraction of those who ought to be given asylum here and in Australia and New Zealand and France, and all over the world. But we are afraid of the wrong color again. Most are ethnic Chinese. History repeating itself with our closed door to the Chinese who built our railroads and most of the West. We wouldn't let them bring in their wives and daughters for fear they'd reproduce, swamping our own industrious citizens who were the correct color. The fear of the Yellow Peril is still alive and thriving in this country even today. We just can't quite grasp the idea that race and geographical origins are not legitimate criteria for denying asylum.

"So here we have Latinos and Haitians and Southeast Asians willing to do the work that the majority of whites scorn—the stoop labor, the monotonous jobs, the ugly jobs. The jobs that don't pay the hourly minimum. Our politicians jump up and down about how jobs are supposedly being taken away from deserving Americans by all this sneaky foreign infiltration, but the fact is, while it always makes a lot of political hay, there's not a grain of truth in it. The so-called illegal aliens or undocumented workers or refugees are in no way threatening American workers, making them idle. These are simply the latest cannon fodder for the system, the latest underclass to keep the industrial machine running."

El Indio Jesús pulled into the driveway of the church, dark now except for a few spotlights illuminating the lot and doorways. Driving slowly, he gave the nun a flashlight, which she played along the wall.

"There," she said quickly, breathlessly. She pointed to the message in graffiti.

He drove close to the wall. While she held the light steady, he whispered the translation. She pulled out a small pad and scribbled on it in the dim reflected light.

"Got it," she said. "Let's go."

Sister Kateri

This dark tube of the van reminds me of the iron lung, thought Sister Kateri as she lay on the padded floor, working toward sleep while El Indio Jesús drove south. Her turn to drive would come soon enough. She should sleep. But as she looked up into the dark interior of the van, its swaying motion recalled the pulsations of the iron lung in which she had lain for so many months as a child.

The horror occurred on a perfect day. The pond water was warm but not too tepid. She and all the children that could be rounded up in the reserve community were driven to the picnic grounds for a day's outing. Every boy and girl dashed to the beach and into the water. They steered clear of the water grass and reeds where the boys said bloodsuckers would get on your skin and suck and suck and would have to be taken off with a knife or a burning match. They also kept away from the water lilies: the boys said some girl had "drownded" there and nobody ever found the body because the roots held her down and she was still there.

They played water tag for the longest time, starting with all the players and It on the raft. When It started counting, all the rest dove off and hung underneath among the pontoons or else swam some distance away, too far to be tagged if It lunged at them from a running start off the raft. To get in free, it was a matter of climbing up and tagging in while It was off the raft or distracted by someone else, not seeing your approach. The first one caught would be the next It. Those that were caught just lounged in the sun on the raft while the others were tagged out, one by one. They hoped the last one still out would sneak back, yell, "Allie allie in free," to set them all free, and make It start all over again. They repeated the game tirelessly.

Each of the various mothers from time to time would try to bring her child in to rest or eat, but all were delicately ignored. One mother persisted.

"Joanna, it's time to come in now. Come in."

Her best pal, Joanna, pretended not to hear. She dove off the raft and swam a long distance under water.

Her own mother was calling now, too. The mothers were ganging up. Too much swimming in pond water was thought to be unhealthy, not as healthful as river water.

The boys were running and wrestling on the raft when she looked up from the water. They were slipping and scraping their knees on the rough surface, laughing and pushing each other off, crashing into the pond at funny angles, coming up sputtering. They were then cannonballed by the few left on the raft.

She slid herself up onto the raft again just as Joanna climbed up nearby. As she stood, expecting the last boy to push her off, too—deliciously hoping he would—Joanna lurched off balance into her. They crashed down together onto the canvas cover. Feeling no injuries, she laughed for a moment, but then the most intense pain seared her from waist to ankle on the left side. She screamed and screamed and screamed. And remembered no more until days later in a hospital far from home.

■ ■ ■

The van's interior was like the iron lung she loved and hated for all the long time it took to come back from the worst part of poliomyelitis, what was called infantile paralysis then. The lung breathed for her when her chest nerves refused to function. It forced air in and out of her lungs with rhythmic pulsations performing a mechanical artificial respiration. With it, she lived an unreal life, but it was still a life.

She underwent operation after operation on her leg until the leg looked as though it carried its own ladder, a scar running from ankle to thigh showing the crossbarred stitch marks. The leg stopped growing. In time, the therapy sessions of endless laps in the swimming pool provided by the March of Dimes strengthened her arms, shoulders, and right leg, but the left leg could not be coaxed into matching the right. It never matched again.

The hospital stay from iron lung to therapy to discharge took her out of what would have been her normal life for several years. As the time lengthened, she grew to be a different person, someone alien from the one she ought to have been, someone becoming more and more removed from her large family back home on the reserve.

She lost contact with her friends, as well. Joanna at first begged to come to see her, but children were not allowed in the polio wards. Her mother said that Joanna believed she was somehow to blame for the fall and the polio and would not be dissuaded, no matter what anyone said. Joanna was haunted by guilt and woke up screaming sometimes, her mother reported.

At first, a number of family members came: mother, father, uncles, aunts, older cousins. They fretted and smiled morosely. It was always uncomfortable. Then, after a while, it was really only her father and mother who made the long drive down from the reserve. Even so, she began to secretly wish they would not come, to save them from the long trip down the peninsula—especially in bad weather—but more so because of the strain the visits caused everyone, herself included.

It was easier to lie in the iron lung in the early days and just read. Someone had to turn the pages for her, though, since she was enclosed from neck down, the book clamped in a frame over her head. An attendant would brush her straight dark hair and turn the pages as she read along. She remembered how she astonished and alarmed the attendant one day by dropping into deep painful wails of sorrow over John Steinbeck's *The Red Pony*. It was a gift from someone back home who must have thought it was a book about a cute little animal just right for a twelve-year-old. Instead, she learned agonizing lessons from it about sex and procreation, life and death.

She made many friends in the hospital, staff and patients. There were nurses and doctors she loved and others she hated. Some of her friends recovered enough to leave; some died.

Her special friend, however, was someone who had come in as a tuberculosis patient years ago and had stayed on to work as handyman and friend to the children. He had lost what might have been a life at home, much as she had. Now the hospital became his community.

His name was Billy, Billy Whiskey. He was an Ottawa-Chippewa originally from L'Anse. He told her stories. He told her about his childhood, his trapping, fishing, and hunting way of life along Lake Superior. It was a rugged but beautiful way to live, so far away from his youth now that it seemed like ancient history.

World War II snatched him away from that world and thrust him overnight into noise and regimentation utterly unlike the quiet, solitude, and seasonal turns he had known. When the opportunity arose, he volunteered for the Tenth Mountain Division out of Fort Carson. So much of his winter trapping was done on skis and snowshoes that it was a natural choice. And it was quiet there, high in the Rockies.

He was vague about fighting in Europe. He pointed to his left canine tooth. "See?" he asked. "You see it's missing the tip? Well, that's the only part of me the Germans ever got—shot it clean off. Don't know to this day how my head managed to stay on!"

"Tell us again about when you were in jail, Billy," she asked. She never tired of imagining the saga as he related his story to the children lined up in their pulmonic casts.

Billy placed himself where they could see him best and commenced.

The story began while he was still in mountaineering school above Pueblo. Being high in the thin air sometimes made him dizzy, but he loved the cold, the quiet. Life in the forests and on the frozen Lake Superior prepared him to be comfortable with that.

One weekend, though, his army buddies insisted he go with them into town on a pass and would not take no for an answer. After all, someone with the name Whiskey ought to be great fun on leave.

Their group attacked a bar near the train tracks straightaway, and before long his companions were rowdy and happily drunk. Billy did not like the taste of beer or liquor. Instead, he downed soft drink after soft drink as the night wore on while his friends enjoyed themselves ever more loudly. When it seemed that they were on the brink of destroying the bar, wheeling around the room, charging into each other, knocking patrons and furniture about, Billy decided to leave before the worst came. Out in the dark street, however, he realized that he had forgotten his campaign hat. And coat. There he was, in uniform but coatless, hatless, disheveled, and smelling like a barroom.

He had just cleared the corner when two military police caught him up by each elbow and hoisted him off the icy sidewalk and into their van. He started to talk, but they told him to shut up and not to move a muscle.

When the van stopped at the police station, Billy was not booked but led directly into a cell at the end of a line of empty cells. No one would listen to his protests. They continued to shut him up.

He was held there for two nights and three days. They started their interrogation the first morning. The questions were odd. The

MPs kept repeating them over and over again, asking things like: Who is Babe Ruth? Who has the best batting average in the American League? What was the name of Lindberg's airplane? Who freed the slaves? Recite the Preamble to the Constitution . . .

That third day, he was rescued by his commanding officer, who lost all composure, screaming at the MPs at full volume.

"Are you all *crazy*? Have you lost your (Billy edited out the descriptive cuss words) minds? Haven't you ever seen an American Indian before? *Look* at this man: does he *really* look like a Jap to you?"

He raged on, hardly pausing for breath.

"Well, if *he* looks like a Jap, we're gonna have one heck (Billy's edit) of a war, because you idiots can't tell the difference between a redskin and a yellowskin."

He drew a breath.

"Now, get this man out of here, *pronto*. You haven't heard the end of this, you (Billy's edit again)."

"That's when I finally found out what had happened to me," Billy told the children. "They thought I was an escaped Japanese prisoner!"

What Billy did not go into was why they thought he might be Japanese, other than his bronze skin and dark hair and eyes. The full story could have told them that near Pueblo two major internment camps held thousands of Japanese Americans, men, women, and children, imprisoned for the duration of the war "for the sake of the safety of the American people," the administration said. Anger caused some to call them the first wave of the enemy, the "fifth column," infiltrating California and the West Coast all the way into Canada in a long-term covert invasion. Even the beautiful San Luis Valley was seeded by the emperor of Japan's clandestine agents, it was claimed by those who may have wanted the fields for themselves.

Yet, all the while, Japanese Americans fought valiantly overseas as members of the U.S. forces, protecting all Americans from their mutual enemies.

As could be expected, from time to time, some of the Japanese Americans in the internment camps fled the crush of captivity. Sometimes they were intercepted around Pueblo, just north of the two camps.

With his crewcut, his face darkened by skiing in the high mountain sunlight—in those days, people were not sure whether Japanese really had yellow skin or something just darker than American whites—and being out of uniform, the MPs believed they had caught another "Jap" escapee, a terrific coup on their record, possibly a promotion.

Billy loved to tell that story. He called it "The Three Days I Was a Jap."

She learned that his unit participated in the battle of Montecasino, up against the famed Italian Alpinieri troops. She listened while he told her father in a joking offhand manner about the Battle of the Bulge and hiding out along hedgerows, scared nearly to death, trying to become invisible to the crews of the German Tiger tanks. He received a few minor injuries—that was when the missing tip of the canine tooth was described—but otherwise made it safely back to the northern forests after the war.

But Billy said that things on the reservation and in the Upper Peninsula were tough then, and there was no way to make a living from muskrat skins.

"And after Paris," he joked, "you can't eat muskrats as a steady diet anymore."

So he moved to Detroit to work in the Ford plant on night shifts. That was, until he was felled by tuberculosis.

Another story he liked to tell the children was about his name: it was not really Whiskey, he said.

"One of my ancestors had the name Oui-Ouesh-Quet. He put his X mark next to that name on the Treaty of 1835. That must have been the French spelling, although it was an American treaty with us. Then the name got spelled like We-Wish-Kay and then became Whiskey, maybe as sort of a joke by the English and American fur trappers working the Saginaw Bay area and farther north."

Billy would laugh, then say with pride, "But old Oui-Ouesh-Quet refused to let them have the headwaters, because that's were the beavers live.

"My family still lives up north, still hunting, fishing, and trapping. It's a good life as long as you don't want too many things.

"I keep thinking I want to go back, but I still feel tired. I don't think I could run a trapline anymore. Besides, who are you going to sell the pelts to? It's all done by companies now, and they have their own people. There's no money in it for freelancers."

Her father taught school on their reserve when she was stricken with disease, a history teacher who worked steadily on a book about what he called "The Oneida Diaspora." When he came down from the reserve to see her, he and Billy swapped stories, trying to top one another tale for tale. Their discussions of the War of 1812 sounded like they had been there themselves, she thought.

"Look, look here, out the window, Billy." To her, "Can you see the bridge from your bed?"

She nodded. "Not far from here are the routes Tecumseh and his people, including some of your people, Billy, were traveling to and from Canada and the United States when he tried to stem the flow of Americans and British into this part of the country. Shawnees, Senecas, Ottawas, Potawatomis, Chippewas, Miamis, a whole lot of others got mixed into the whole bloody mess."

"Pontiac?" she queried.

"No, the Pontiac War happened long before that, in the mid-1700s.

"No, it was the War of 1812 that landed a lot of our people and Billy's on Walpole Island, right out there in the middle of the water. Tecumseh and the rest of the patriots were batted back and forth across this very river, leaving behind entire families and communities smashed to shreds on either side."

While she dozed, Billy and her father argued—not once, but many times during her bedridden months—about where Tecumseh's body was buried, or even if it had been buried or burned. Each of them was completely sure they knew the exact spot of his interment. Each had an entirely different site in mind, miles and miles apart in time, space, and continuity.

The discussions picked up where they laid off each time the two men met at her bedstead. She loved to hear their banter even if repetitious.

In time, her father was hired to teach history in a Catholic parochial school nearby. Although most of her family members were traditionalists first and Episcopalian second, she enjoyed attending that school once she was discharged from the hospital. As with the nurses and the doctors, she liked some of the nuns and priests and was offended by others. It did not impair her thirst to learn and excel in classes despite her obvious physical disability. Her body was strong now, maybe stronger than others her age in school because of her swim therapy all those years. Yet one leg would forever be shorter, and she never grew to full height, remaining small, strong, and wiry.

Although she spent each summer on the reserve, more and more she became focused on healing and rehabilitation for children like herself. Her mother's mother had been a midwife for two generations of children, and even saved lives nursing neighbors struck by the 1917–18 influenza epidemic. So it seemed natural that she would seek to learn skills and get the training that would lead her to healing as a profession.

At the age of twenty-two she became a medical missionary attached to a convent in Pennsylvania. She took the name Kateri in honor of the Mohawk woman who devoted herself to tending smallpox victims in the seventeenth century.

Sister Kateri went first to West Africa as part of a survey team investigating rumors that polio was far more common than had been reported. That experience crystallized her dedication first to the child victims, but also to working to overcome the poverty that opened the door to this and other diseases.

This latter, wider agenda fell full-blown upon her late one afternoon outside a tent near Kinshasa when she raised the possibility of returning to the States to get a medical degree.

The exhausted doctor sitting there with her raised his palm up and said, "Look, I can spend every day of my life working to cure the physical problems of my patients, but every day I have to send the more-or-less cured ones back to where they became ill in the first place. Cure the social ills there and I wouldn't have to send them back only to get reinfected again or contract something else.

"We don't need more doctors. We need more people who can solve the problems of injustice, inequality. And all that."

He paused. "That is what can really take care of the long-term health needs of communities like this and all the others."

So Sister Kateri stayed with the Catholic order, working in Africa and then later in Central America. It was natural for her to get involved in the social side of things in the communities in which she worked. She could not keep her head down to what was going on around her modest care facilities.

Even so, in Central America she found it difficult to fix on the true "bad guys," what the papers would call the *auto intelectual*, when all the country seemed to have gone to war with itself. It was too facile to pin all the power imbalance on the *ricos*, especially when they were on both sides of a civil war.

Driving through the barrios in the cities or up along the mountainsides in her battered once-white Volkswagon bus, she became reconciled to the simple truths that worked for her: whatever contributed to the health and welfare of the children was good; whatever was deleterious was bad. She would concentrate on the immediate and the expedient.

Her days were full and compressed. If a child suffered from marasmus or whatever, she browbeat and harassed the next possible source of food and money for the child and the family. She made a lot of enemies while she made a lot of friends.

Her bus was cheered at times, and at times it was shot at by gunmen in and out of government. If she drove over thirty-five miles per hour, the bullet holes set up piercing screams, but the mountain terrain and the barrio potholes seldom allowed that speed anyway. The bus was giving out, too: too many miles, too many drivers.

The day came when she acknowledged to herself that her medical work made little headway against the greed and poverty tearing up the people where she toiled with the other medical sisters. Staff members were constantly under suspicion as subversives, accused of trying to undermine the government, as spies for revolutionaries, to bend the will of the people to traitorous thinking, and on and on. On the other hand, the enemies of the government viewed them as imperialists at best and as meddlers at the least. Both elements were heavily armed with the same makes and models of weaponry, all manufactured elsewhere.

Finally, she and her coworkers determined that what must be saved out of the chaos of a society bent on self-immolation was to preserve the best of the minds and the best of the souls.

■ ■ ■

Now, tonight, she lay in a van that reminded her of the unfair loss of her childhood and of the many childhoods that hunger and pain have denied to others, and how this trip, like so many others before it, might bring promise of a future to some whose hopes for justice were dimming.

1 2 3

4 5 6

SATURDAY

7

La Familia Que Vendieron Dos Veces

He picked up the Interstate highway near the airport and drove south into the night. The nun fell asleep by the time they skirted Isleta Pueblo.

El Indio Jesús' mind wandered over the last week's accomplishments and shortfalls as the miles churned by beneath him. He thought about the women and their words. He thought about Tío Augustín.

Tío Augustín, grandson of old Solomón Valles of La Bajada, the descending place, the slope down which the Camino Real—the Royal Road—plunged from the high plateau to the bed of the Rio Grande.

Before it was called La Bajada for the steep incline it presented, it was known as La Majada, the sheepfold or sheep corral area. Old Solomón was but one of those who kept sheep and goat pens at the base of the meandering slope. Somehow over time the word became corrupted after the gringo's arrival. In this case, the corruption was not without its accuracy, however: it truly was a descent that even yet defied the most expensive highway architecture. The smell of death never left La Bajada after the Valles family left.

And now Tío Augustín. How like him to settle in a distant country beneath a mountain that was named La Majada!

■ ■ ■

At Hobo Joe's in Socorro they stopped for pie and coffee. Sister Kateri drove from there to the roadside rest stop near Elephant Butte Reservoir, so beautiful in the moonlight.

El Indio Jesús remarked on the cheerful twinkling of the lights from the Texan recreational vehicles, the Texans who had come to see a mountain. And water.

In good restful spirits, they slept in the van for a couple of hours.

El Indio Jesús drove again as the sun began its struggle up the east side of the Organ Mountains. The nun greeted "Our Elder Brother the Sun" and reflected on how the serrated mountaintops looked as though cut out of black construction paper pasted onto an orange background.

By five o'clock the sun rose, peering over the sierra and down upon the city of Las Cruces in full splendor. To the west a highway streaked up a plateau, where it vanished on its way to Deming. Behind them, mesas of mauve and purple faced the morning shoulder to shoulder.

The van left the Interstate highway for a suburban road approaching the ancient village of Mesilla. Close to the church, within three blocks of it, they found a little unpaved road that seemed to take them from the twentieth-century United States to eighteenth-century Mexico.

But their destination said both. There was a long garage containing the latest in farm machinery, a small Japanese diesel tractor, and an array of other pieces of equipment standing polished despite visible use. A windmill of advanced design supplied electricity and worked the water supply. There were solar panels to heat the animal stalls and the house. Everything bespoke the newest and most up-to-date farm practices, and indeed, it looked like the model farm it was.

Except for the house. The house and surrounding outbuildings standing at the sheltered edge of the property breathed of the past. When El Indio Jesús and Sister Kateri entered the low rambling structure, the sounds of the outside world were instantly cut off. The air of the rooms seemed not to move even though fresh and smelling like old pink cabbage roses. The light was different, too, a slightly out-of-focus dimness that could not truly be described as dark.

"Carlos doesn't allow television and the newspapers to bring their lethal vibrations into the house," El Indio Jesús told the nun. "Books are fine, although he checks them over, too. And radio, if civilized stations are chosen—and that's getting harder and harder to do. And, of course, there are all the farm journals he reads, stacks of them. In several languages."

They entered an area at the back of the house used for cooking. It opened out onto a patio where the remains of breakfast could be seen on a table.

A dark, graying man looking like a larger, masculine version of Pilar rose quickly from his chair to exchange *abrazos* with El Indio Jesús.

"*¡Hola! ¡Hola!*" Beaming with affection for his guest, Carlos thumped his back a few times as they held each other in manly embrace.

"So you are still alive, *amigo! ¿Que estas haciendo? ¿Que hay de nuevo?* All goes well with Pilar?"

"*Sí, esta bien, bien. ¿Y tu? ¿Rosa? ¿Sus niños?*"

"Everyone is fine, *compadre*." Carlos's arm still gripped El Indio Jesús' shoulder as he turned toward the nun. "And you must be Sister Kateri."

She shook his hand, responding immediately to his warmth. Formally she replied, "*Tengo gusto en conocerle*, Señor Valles."

"*Por favor*," he reacted, "please call me Carlos. May I call you just 'Sister'? I know about your Mohawk namesake, Kateri . . . Kateri Te . . ."

"Kateri Tekakwitha."

"Right. Never could pronounce it. Have they sainted her yet?"

"No, not yet. But with the growing numbers of missions in Indian country being named after her, I'd give you five-to-one odds that it's coming. The Vatican has always responded to vocal constituencies."

They enjoyed the humor together.

"Come now, *un poco de café*?" Turning toward the woman now entering the room, Carlos introduced his wife, Rosa, to the nun. Rosa then embraced El Indio Jesús, who lifted her off the floor and did a pirouette before gracefully putting her down.

Soon they had arranged themselves around the table while Rosa poured coffee. A thin voice was then heard coming from the veranda.

Carlos leaned toward Sister Kateri. "That's Papa. He'll want to say hello and tell you the story of our family."

"Fine," she replied, "good people, good coffee, and a good story is heaven on earth—forgive the religious reference, please."

Rosa brought into the room an old man who stood erect even in his frailty. His face was long and narrow and was covered with the thinnest tissue of shiny skin. Though his hands and legs trembled, his eyes reached out from a faraway time where one knew what one knew.

Carlos introduced him to the nun. He reached out a delicate hand and made a small gesture of seventeenth-century courtesy with his head. He recognized El Indio Jesús and allowed a small smile to grace his mouth while they shook hands.

Then the old man, Ándres Valles, sat in his customary chair, looked into a distant place in time and space, and in measured archaic Spanish told the story of his family, *la familia que vendieron dos veces*, the family that was sold twice.

■ ■ ■

More than a century and a quarter ago, Ándres Valles recounted, the American brigadier general Stephen Watts Kearny came into the land known to us as Rio Arriba uninvited and unwanted. At least by us. Some European merchants begged them to come for their own commercial designs, we understood. The land that had once been inhabited by free Native Americans and then claimed by the crown of Spain had recently been seized from Mexico by the United States of America by means of Kearny's brash entry. The piece of paper ratifying the seizure was known as the Treaty of Guadalupe Hidalgo. It amputated half of old Mexico.

In the new expansion of empire, General Kearny's advance men convened curious crowds of local inhabitants wherever he went so he could tell them that the beneficent American nation had only our best interests in mind, and that life would go on for us as it had in the past. Or even better.

The messages that the people still remember today contain some of his words. They quote him as saying, "We come among you for your benefit, not for your injury." They remember that he assured them of this. "We come as friends, to better your conditions," they recall. "You are now American citizens. I am your governor. Henceforth, look to me for protection."

This is how the people remember those meetings where the English words were turned into Spanish words.

At one such meeting, the small assembly of Indians, Mestizos, and *genízaros*—as the Hispanicized Indians were called—contained a young farmer named Solomón Valles, whose small *rancho* was situated near La Bajada. Solomón stood with the others listening to the translation of Kearny's words. The Hispanic making the translation sweated profusely as he struggled to change the rapid English into Spanish that would not offend the listeners. He feared for his own hide and was therefore very careful to make everything sound *muy suave, muy suave*. But neither he nor Kearny nor his retinue had reckoned on the clear vision of the listeners. As they stood in the dusty street of Las Vegas to hear Kearny's pronouncements, they heard through the interpreter that all would be well under the jurisdiction of the United States of America and that under no circumstances would their lands and property be taken from them.

Other platitudes were flung out to the crowd by the interpreter, but Solomón Valles had fastened his mind upon that promise, that their lands and properties would not be taken from them. Why, he asked himself, would someone even think such a thing, and then say that this would not happen? In another way of thinking about it, if they were not planning to take the lands and properties, then why say it at all? It must be that they are indeed thinking about doing this very thing, and now are trying to put us off our guard. It will then be just a matter of time before they do what it is in their mind to do—take everything we have.

Concluding thus, the young father thought about his little home and family, and as the interpreter once again assured the listeners that their lands were theirs forever, he determined that he would not stand by helplessly until the day came when they threw him off his property. No. He wanted to remove his family from the double-speaking gringos, to take them from the poisonous atmosphere he feared would kill them all—Indians, native Spanish, Mestizos, *genízaros*—all. Now the translation drew to a close, General Kearny turning away from the meeting even while the translator struggled to deliver the last sentiments. In the silence that followed, instead of applause, the general and everyone there heard but one word.

"*Mierda.*"

The general turned back, looking at the rows of dark faces and blank eyes, scanning the crowd, looking for the one who spoke.

"*Mierda.*"

No one in the assembly turned to look at the one who had spoken, although they all knew who it was. He said what was on their minds as well. They suspected that their worst fears of loss of land and all the hard work put into it throughout the years would come to an end.

Solomón Valles also knew that his safety was in jeopardy, his and that of his little *familia*. So after reaching his home again after two days' travel, he spoke quietly to his Tewa wife. Together they and their two sons packed up the essentials of their meager property, put them into the *carreta* yoked with two old oxen, and returned down the Jornada del Muerto by which his grandfather had come in years past.

They traveled at night, ever fearful that they would be molested, not by the general or his military so much as by those who would like to gain favor with the new people by rooting out a troublemaker. Evil often grows out of the smallest seed planted in fertile soil.

They had relatives or *compadres* in La Plaza Vieja, Isleta, Belen, Socorro. Along the Jornada del Muerto, which had seen so many deaths through the centuries, they were told again and again that they were *locos*, that the gringos coming in from the East were only interested in commerce and not farming. So why would they want the *ranchitos*? It did not make sense.

"*Ya verán. Ya verán,*" repeated Solomón Valles, "you will see that I say only the truth to you. My family has now been sold, and without even asking our permission. I cannot live where I can be bought and sold *como una vaca*. We shall continue south to Las Cruces, which is still part of Mexico."

After some weeks and many hardships they reached Mesilla. A cousin there loaned them four acres of good bottomland, where they built a *casita* and farmed.

But fate has a way of catching humans who escape its first grasp. In only five years' time the family of Solomón Valles was sold once again. The Gadsden Purchase turned the soil they labored over into U.S. soil. Unable for a number of reasons to uproot his family and go further south into Mexico again, Solomón Valles remained in the Mesilla Valley. But for the rest of his life he maintained the implacable anger of one who has been toyed with by political forces bent only upon their own aggrandizement, caring nothing for the people whom they affect. It was with anger that Solomón would say *a mi familia la vendieron dos veces*, an unquenchable anger for being sold twice without a voice.

This anger against mindless authority passed from Solomón to his surviving son, Fermín, and then on to grandsons Ándres and Augustín, and now to Ándres' children Carlos and Pilar. For more than a hundred years the family homes served as places of safety for those persecuted by authorities who had no regard for the individual. Political refugees were fed, clothes, and transferred north, south, east, and west. But no evils were allowed to come beneath the roof: no alcohol, no drugs, no weapons, no plots to cause harm to another person.

Through the years, if a list would have been kept of those who had truly or supposedly found refuge there—no such list would ever be drawn up—it would have continued to grow, a list that would have been merely whispered among only the closest kin and allies in the community. Such a list might name the early so-called renegade Indians of Rio Arriba, the patriot Domingo Valles, some would say the great Gerónimo hid out there, and Billy the Kid, Marino Leyba, the Magón brothers, Pancho Villa, Elfego Baca, and Pete Garcia.

But none of these rumors could or would be substantiated, because no one wanted to evoke a protective reaction from the community in which the family had become legendary, *la familia que vendieron dos veces*.

Fly by Night Company

At the start of Ándres Valles' recitation of the *historia* of his family, Carlos excused himself to check out the van. When El Indio Jesús joined him a while later, he cautioned him.

"Next time through, *compadre*, I'll need to install a new clutch and pressure plate, okay? The van's still safe, but they need to be replaced. You still have, oh, thirty thousand miles, I'd guess. More or less. Oh, and I've set up a little *regalo* for you, a nothing gift on the visor. It's a fuzz buster, to find the *chotas* before they find you. You'll grow to love it."

"And when do we see you again? Approximately? I really need enough time to do the job right."

"I'll get word to you. By one of the other transporters." He paused, than said, "And now we go. *Muchas gracias, amigo. Hasta la vista.*" They embraced.

After loading up various items, Carlos and Rosa watched El Indio Jesús and Sister Kateri drive away, Carlos from the doorway of his machine shop and Rosa standing under the adobe patio

arch constructed by El Chewy Jiménez. Neither was smiling, nor
did they wave good-bye.

■ ■ ■

They skirted El Paso, eventually sliding down the Yarborough
off-ramp. On the back wall of a convenience store, they picked up
another encoded graffiti message. It indicated that he should be at
the designated point at nine o'clock that night. In the meantime, El
Indio Jesús would conduct his other business in Zaragosa. Sister
Kateri would visit at the group home of some nuns with whom she
worked from time to time until she continued southward, alone.

After letting her off, El Indio Jesús made his way through
Ysleta's slow traffic and over the bridge into Mexico. In that seg-
ment of the trip, he never failed to think of Carlos Fuentes' words:

> The long spans and vast spaces on both sides of the
> wound that to the north opened like the Rio Grande
> itself rushing down from steep canyons, as far up as
> the Sangre de Cristo Mountains, islands in the deserts
> of the north, ancient lands of the Pueblos, the Navajos
> and Apaches, hunter and peasants only half subdued
> by Spain's adventure in the New World, they, from the
> lands of Chihuahua and the Rio Grande, both seemed
> to die here, on this high plain.

The rest escaped him for the moment except for the part where a
colonel quotes Ambrose Bierce, "To be a gringo in Mexico, . . . Ah,
that is euthanasia."

He chuckled to himself and turned his thoughts to the Fly By
Night Company and its various subsidiaries, the means by which
he made the money to pay for the trips.

During the next several hours, he converted various items of
his cargo into *pesos*. In the van he had carried secondhand portable
generators that were very valuable in Third World countries but

were not worth much north of the border. Their primary users were campers who played with them a few times on vacation trips and eventually sold them through the local *Thrifty Nickle* sales papers. They felt they were not worth the money or effort to repair if broken. But in the *sierras* where these would end up, they could be fixed efficiently to generate an electrical source for the high villages and remote haciendas.

Also in the van were one-foot by two-feet boxes holding four-speed one-ton heavy-duty truck transmissions. These could be installed in half-ton pickups for mountain duty. They fit compactly into boxes for transporting when the shifters were removed.

And finally, there were several battery radios of the tube type rather than transistorized. In the back country, these radios would last thirty or forty years. Replacing the tubes was no major problem, whereas when a transistor radio broke down, there was no fixing it with the available technology.

Everything El Indio Jesús carried with him was legitimate. Nothing he transported was embargoed in either direction. There was never a need for the Fly By Night Company to deal in illegal commodities of any sort whatsoever. It was a matter of understanding the markets.

El Indio Jesús drove through the back gate of a *yonke* lot in Waterfill, a lot in no way different from any of the other dozens of junk and salvage yards lining the street. Instantly, as he pulled to a stop, two grinning men joined him with happy greetings, handshakes, and *abrazos*. Just as quickly, they emptied the van of its load, stowing the items in a battered truck with Frontera Chihuahua plates. The transfer completed, they stood together for a few brief words.

"El Chewy sends his respectful best wishes, and hopes that this load is adequate," he told the older of the two Indian-faced men in Spanish. "He desires to fill your order fully and well."

The man answered in formal language matching that used by El Indio Jesús. "Please thank our *primo* for his labor on our behalf.

These few *pesos* we give for his effort cannot express our feelings. Tell him for us that our village has been too long without his hands of magic with the adobe. But also tell him that his mother is well and all his kin."

"But of course I will carry your good words to our friend. And tell me, *por favor*, how go things with Angelica—*perdón*, La Señorita Nidia?"

"Ah, yes. We bring you word from her. She says to say that she fares well but is in need of reassurance that all goes well with her father."

"You many return to her with word that his health remains stable and that I hope to move him from Las Vegas to Barelas soon. All is being prepared. She need not worry herself, but tend to her own safety."

They then told El Indio Jesús what was needed when he made the trip again. The list was once again things that El Chewy Jimenez could glean with Joanie, now that he filled Miguel Olson's place in exploiting the Goodwill boxes, or things that could be gotten through trade.

With mutual respect, the men shook hands and drove their vehicles out of the lot and into the vibrant streets of the city suburb.

El Indio Jesús picked his way along past the *carne al carbón* stalls and the countless junk lots, past pottery sheds featuring rows of plaster cobras along with the pots. After passing the RCA plant, the street lanes went from two to four and then four and a half or some indeterminate number of lanes, which made driving all the more hazardous. Fleet *ruteras*, passenger vans, slipped through the traffic like silver minnows.

He recalled his visit with her that first time in the mountains. His mind faded pleasantly into thoughts of Angelica, now called Nidia by her comrades, and her answer to the world in which she found herself. There was Pilar, Pilar of the Valles family, with a daughter so far removed from the soul of her people that she may never be saved. And yet that was what everyone thought about Angelica, too.

When Ya No Las Puedes was carted off to Las Vegas and his wife, the former Indian maiden from the ancient mountains of Mexico, moved into the liberal academic world of the city, there was much talk about how this sad—some said outfoxed—old man had been abandoned by his last hope, his youngest daughter, Angelica. But there are strengths that run deep and in places that are hard to detect.

He was not perhaps surprised so much as he was intrigued when he met the mysterious Nidia, *co-comandante* of a rebel army in the foothills overlooking small villages far below in the yellow dusk. For the fabulous, fabled Nidia, under the tan fatigues, was none other than the shy beauty Angelica, Ya No Las Puedes' *consentida*.

Now, under these changed circumstances, even though he had tossed her into the air as a child, he was stunned by his own reserve toward the soldier now standing before him, she looking confident, even a shade defiant, it seemed. And that made him recall moments in the past when he let a shadow of doubt pass through his mind about the condition of her soul as his friend, her father, sank past any reality into the black sea of despair.

Beneath the cautious mask, the face of her mother flickered in and out. Yet, in the canny eyes of this younger woman, he suddenly realized that this new person had seen much that was evil and ugly in her new life in the *sierras*. She had aged.

But fleetingly, her initial coolness evaporated as she rounded the desk and flung her arms around his neck.

"*Ay, tanto tiempo*, you old bear! I can't believe you are really here! Quick, quick, tell me about my father. Is he okay, are they—my sisters, my mother—visiting him enough? Tell me everything . . ." and she paused here, "tell me everything about them," and more slowly, ". . . and tell me what we should be doing here that we're not. I need your opinion . . . and your continuing help, dear friend."

She drew back. She seemed embarrassed by her own behavior. Before he could respond, she said, "Let's take a walk and I'll show you around. Then you can answer all my questions, every one of them. I am so happy to see you!" And she threw her arms around his neck again, giving him a light kiss on each cheek.

Hand in hand, they left her makeshift office and passed by some astonished people also in khakis working the shortwave radio and stubborn mechanical typewriters under the canvas shelter.

Outside, the area was an anthill of activity, most of it incomprehensible to El Indio Jesús. It also seemed to be a colony of very young people, almost children, he thought. And yet they were playing dangerous adult games.

Nidia led him away from the noise and bustle up a hillside. The climb was steep enough to stop conversation. When they reached the top of the rise, Nidia stopped.

"Look around you. What do you see?" she asked.

El Indio Jesús' eyes followed the curve of the mountainside in the dimming light, over the several peaks to the south and down the slopes as far as possible. Then he looked more closely at the area where they were standing.

"It's a village," he exclaimed, "a village, and . . ." more slowly, "a very large village." And then, "Are those terraces? All along the slopes down there, are those *trincheras*, rows and rows of *trincheras*?" He turned to her, wonderingly.

"Yes," she smiled. "All around here. Not just this one. We have found mountainside after mountainside almost corrugated with terraces used for farming I don't know how very long ago. Maybe a thousand years ago, who knows? Maybe more.

"At first we thought the terraces were left over from the time of Pancho Villa and the revolution. You know, they could have been made for defense against the *federales*. Maybe they did use them like that. But the sites are too old, too ancient. And too large for that. There are pottery pieces all around and bits of maize and many house sites.

"No, it seems that people lived here for a long time, working the terraces for food, for ages, perhaps." She paused. "I hope you won't laugh at me, but sometimes right about this time of night, before it gets really dark, I can almost feel the villagers moving around here . . . here on this flat area above the *trincheras*, where the plaza must have been."

She stopped and turned to look at him.

"Are you laughing at me?"

He smiled. "No, Angelica *mia*, I am not laughing at you. Show me some more."

"Some say that when wildfires sweep up the mountainside burning off the shrubs and grasses, the trenches are easier to see, and you can make out their pattern, the logic of their placement. But I haven't been here all that long, yet."

"Will you stay, Angelica *mia*?"

"Oh yes. That I am sure of. It's my second chance for a home, a place where I can be helpful, absolutely full of relatives—you remember that line about 'home is where they have to let you return,' something like that—and there are other reasons, too."

"Well, I don't want to press you on that. And you may change your mind in the future. But most of all, I want you to be happy. I have some idea about what you went through in those last years in the north valley if you want to talk about it . . ."

She smiled and stopped him on the path. She put her head on his chest for a short moment, then turned back to the path. Still holding his hand, she turned and continued walking along the thin pathway amid the brush on either side.

"My mother . . ." she began haltingly, "my mother came from these *montañas*, as you know so well, since you and Tío Chewy had so much to do with it. My father thought he had found the ideal child-woman, and for many years, that's what he had: a beautiful wife and mother of daughters. All this you know.

"But you might not have known that it couldn't last forever. She was just too smart, too intelligent, to stay in the kitchen for the rest of her life. Once she learned English and began reading everything she could lay her hands on, well, that was the first crack in the strong wall of our family.

"My dad even helped her, helped her to grow and explore. She didn't neglect any of us, of course, but she became more and more distracted. That's when I found myself carrying more of the weight around the house. My sisters went off to school, to build their careers or lives away from home."

She led him to a seat on a rock outcrop where they could look across the valley to distant *sierras* beyond.

"And he changed, too, my father . . ."

Nidia looked at him questioningly.

"Look," she said, "I know you aren't my priest or judge or anything like that, but you have been a friend to all of us for so long, I feel I owe it to you to tell you these things, maybe to justify why I am here and not still back there tending my father . . ."

"No no no," El Indio Jesús quickly reacted. "No, I understand. I know some of what you must have felt back then. You don't owe me any explanations, in any case. I'm not your father confessor!"

In the waning light, her dark hair fell over her downturned face. Even her voice seemed muffled now.

"There weren't any battles, any fights between them. Oh, the struggle was there all right, but it was silent . . . and maybe that's what made it so inexorable . . . the split, I mean. Once she began taking courses at the university and meeting new people, well, the end couldn't be far behind.

"And there I was, left with my beloved dad, and he getting stranger and stranger all the time. You see, after working so hard all those years, he suffered a series of small strokes. Nothing to keep him from moving around physically, you understand, but his mind had been affected. He began to do things that put himself and me and the house in danger. Maybe you knew that?

"As for me, I won't deny that I felt some level of resentment. In my worst moments, I didn't like myself very much, feeling angry at being left to bear what was happening with my dad with little help except money from the rest while my own life was going nowhere."

They heard a noise from behind them on the path. Soon a young woman appeared, something in her arms.

"*Disculpe, Comandante Nidia, Señor. Tengo un poco para comer, tortillas, tamales, algo para beber . . .*"

"*O, gracias, Señora, muchas gracias,*" said El Indio Jesús, taking the food from her. She left then, threading her way back down the pathway still visible in the dusk.

The young woman took the food from him and placed it on the outcrop near her.

"Let's sit here for a while more then, eat and watch the moon come up, all right? Can you hear a little bit more? Be honest. I haven't given you a chance to say a word yet!"

El Indio Jesús put his arm around her. "You know I have as much time as you need and a whole lot of patience. Go on."

"Well, where was I? Oops, here's your dish.

"Oh yes. Well, I was not about to side with my mother against my father or my father against my mother. What was becoming clearer, though, was that as my dad glided into deeper and deeper depression, some resolution was needed. For as long as I could, I tried to maintain the continuity of home, of food, and of affection.

"But the day finally came when I had to face the fact that I had become superfluous, that I as Angelica, had passed the point where I was no longer useful to either my dad or myself. He no longer recognized me. He no longer even remembered by name. He called me by my mother's name . . . which was good, I suppose, in that he hadn't completely lost touch with the past, of course. But in truth, neither of us had any hope of survival if I were to continue hiding out there while he and the house deteriorated around us.

"And so," she continued, "my mother and sisters and I sat down and looked at the alternatives, of which there weren't many. In the end, we decided to place him in the home of some relatives in Las Vegas, one of whom was trained in hospice nursing and was already taking care of another elderly cousin there.

"Here's something to drink.

"Well, we were uncomfortable with the inevitability of the decision. But we had to get over that. We had to remain viable ourselves.

"Yet, I must tell you that there was hell to pay from my neighbors, especially *la vieja* who lived on the other side of the fence. She passed it all around the neighborhood among the *vecinos* that we had stuck Dad in *la casa de los locos* in Las Vegas. They turned on me then, people I had known all my life. It was hell. They clucked at me and whispered and made my life miserable, all alone in that falling-down house in the north valley. You know how community opinion can affect a person's whole life, every day . . ."

He chuckled softly. "I know exactly who you mean. *La viejita* stalked me the last time I went to your house looking for Armando. Tall? Skinny? Big nose? White hair cut really short? Loud? Voice like a parrot? Yeah, she gave me a piece of her mind, all right, and wouldn't quit."

They laughed together. She took his two hands in hers.

"Okay, there are more than two ways to look at it, I'll grant you. But for me, I had to come to grips with this new situation. My mother, as you know, remarried. In fact," she turned to gaze toward the rising moon, "her own parents—my grandparents and lots of other relatives I never knew—still live on the *estancia* over there in that direction, in the hacienda they received out of Pancho Villa's *ejido* after the revolution. And my new stepfather's people, as well." She turned back to face him. "But of course you know that. Why have you let me ramble on?"

She laughed self-consciously. The moon was rising higher.

"And every one of them, all of them here are still *revolucionarios* even to this day." She leaned toward him and kissed his cheek. "Just like you.

"It is they who rescued me from I don't know what, whatever it was that might have become of me.

"And so, at the end of this long tale," she said in a self-deprecatory way, "here I am, at last grounded in a sense of who I am. And what I must do to earn the love and respect of my remaining, my new—and old—families, and mostly, for my self-respect."

She stopped then and turned her head in the direction of sounds suddenly coming around one of the mountain peaks.

She turned back to El Indio Jesús, who could just make out a smile on her face in the glowing moonlight.

"And so, dear friend," nodding toward the sound, "here is my new world." She laughed. "Here comes Houlton with passengers probably stuffed inside his marijuana bales."

El Indio Jesús watched the single-engine Cessna skirt the slopes, landing far below where a few lights from lanterns showed the outlines of the strip.

"*Guatemaltecos esta vez, un cacique y dos curanderos*. Their knowledge should not be erased from history the way their Mayan villages were."

In the morning, El Indio Jesús would fly out with the Columbus Air Force and return to his multilayered life up the Jornada del Muerto. He would leave Comandante Nidia here with her people in the *cerros*—she had taken her new name from the Sierra del Nido, the Mountain of the Nest, where she was reborn—and where she would remain part of a crucial way station on the freedom road that went north, south, east and west. Just one of the way stations.

He wondered if the villagers who built their communities and *trincheras* here, so far from the urban centers of the region even then, performed similar services as did Nidia and the others. The high *sierras* may always have been a haven for political refugees of any nation at any time and however they might arrive there. El Indio Jesús supposed—well, felt certain—that these very mountains served as sanctuary not simply during the Mexican Revolution, when General Pershing searched for Pancho Villa and Zapata, but back into time past, past the massacre at Tomóchic, beyond the Spanish Revolution and the Aztec Revolution and the Toltec Revolution and the Teotihuacán Revolution and perhaps back into even Quimbaya times at the dawn of centralized authoritarian regimes. He believed that this area was somehow part of the soul of the Gran Chichimeca, a sanctuary that had sheltered who could guess how many refugees from all directions, the ones migrating away from intolerable pressures, always toward the dream of relief.

He thought of one of Ambrose Bierce's poems, titled "Freedom"—Ambrose Bierce, whom Carlos Fuentes called "Old Gringo," a man who witnessed Mexico's struggle from the valleys to perhaps these very mountains. It was not a good literary poem, he surmised, but its anger stayed in El Indio Jesús' mind all these years:

> Freedom, as every schoolboy knows,
>   Once shrieked as Kosciusko fell;
> On every wind, indeed, that blows
>   I hear her yell.
>
> She screams whenever monarchs meet,
>   And parliaments as well,
> To bind the chains about her feet
>   And toll her knell.
>
> And when the sovereign people cast
>   The votes they cannot spell,
> Upon the lung-imposed blast
>   Her clamors swell.
>
> For all to whom the power's given
>   To sway or to compel,
> Among themselves apportion heaven
>   And give her hell.

He interrupted his thoughts to ask, "While you are 'feeling' the ancients who lived up here, do you ever see Pancho Villa's white stallion?"

Her small laugh came now out of the dark.

"No, not me. Not yet. But everyone else around here has! Maybe I will after I've been here awhile longer, maybe after I have done a few good deeds!"

"Thinking about *trincheras*, have you ever seen the Forbes Trinchera Ranch development in Southern Colorado? at the foot of La Blanca, the Navajo's sacred northern mountain?

"It used to be a land grant for *genízaros*, I think, but I'm not sure: I'd have to look it up.

"Well, the only *trincheras* I have ever seen there were wide ugly bulldozer slashes all around the low hills where they want weekend warriors to build their cabins in the woods. But there aren't all that many woods to be seen from the highway.

"One time, I read in the papers that Malcolm Forbes might make a deal to sell the Trinchera Ranch for incredible megabucks to a Saudi investor. I was in the area, so I stopped by to see José Alfredo Maestas at San Juan Pueblo. I couldn't help but ask him whether he would prefer the Forbeses or the Saudis as owners of the Trinchera. You could predict what he'd say first, of course: that is, he'd prefer the original owners, the ones Forbes got it from . . . pennies on the dollar, probably. But with a choice between Forbes and the Saudis? José said the Saudis. He thinks they would be easier to get along with. And they have good souls, he said.

"But I'm getting off track. "You know that I only want good things for you. And maybe this is the time and place for you to find good things. For a while. Perhaps not forever. I hear positive things about you all up and down the line . . ."

"I'm not doing all that much. There are many more taking greater chances out there, accomplishing the impossible . . ."

"You are doing your part and more. Be satisfied with that. And if you need me—at any time, any time at all—contact me. You know how. Just do it. Are you listening? Will you do that?"

She was silent. Taking his hand again, she squeezed it and nodded in the half-light of the moon.

"Thank you. Thank you for listening. Thank you for being my good friend. And yes, I will contact you if I need to, you can count on that."

They lingered in the lengthening night deep in their own thoughts. Looking down the slopes ringed with *trincheras*, he felt more certain than ever that the pathways to these highlands and beyond in all directions were indelibly etched into their sides by centuries of freedom seekers. Gerónimo must have walked these hills, he reasoned. Perhaps Santa Teresita as well.

He thought also of himself, of his origins there in the moonlit village below, where he and El Chewy Jiménez and Angelica's mother shared kin ties as strong as chains.

Then he wondered if and when it would be his turn to shoulder responsibility here. It would come. Someday.

■ ■ ■

The traffic approaching the cathedral area of the city slowed his progress to nearly a walker's pace. He saw that the small plaza in front of the church had once again been sabotaged by those who feared the political education that comes about when people sit and talk to each other. The big trees were cut down. The benches were missing. Grass and dirt were replaced by ankle-breaking cobblestones. An iron fence with few gateways ringed the circumference.

From the close of the revolution until now, this little square bore the unofficial name of La Plaza de los Generales de Pancho Villa. It was where the old men, some of whom had actually fought with him and as many who had not, hashed over the battles and field maneuvers of Villa's Army of the North.

Among the real generals of Villa's forces was Sarturnino Gutierrez Durango of Sierra del Nido. It was this grizzled warlord Angelica faced when she flew into the high ranges back to her mother's homeland.

El Indio Jesús could very well imagine that first meeting, as he threaded his way through the city. It had not been so many years ago that he himself had made that same encounter when El Chewy Jiménez gripped his near bicep and firmly propelled him into the dark drawing room of the hacienda and into the presence of the old general.

■ ■ ■

El Indio Jesús eased the van into the driveway of a private home surrounded by high brick walls. A collection of silly dogs bounced around the rear entrance until a *criado* hushed them up and sent them to their corner of the yard.

"*Buenas tardes, señor, buenas tardes. La señora lo espera. Pase por aquí, por favor.*"

El Indio Jesús followed him into the interior of the large structure across glistening wood floors and deeply piled carpets. The servant indicated that he should enter a doorway flanked by a sideboard graced by a flowing menorah.

"Welcome, my good friend," said a tall red-haired matron who walked toward him, hands extended for greeting.

"Hello, Shana. It's good to see you again." He held both of her hands in his. "All is well?"

"Yes. Of course. And you?"

"Yes. Yes."

"Well, come in. Something to drink? Tea? Coffee? Perhaps some lemonade?

"Yes, lemonade would be fine."

She gave the order to the servant and then turned back to El Indio Jesús.

"Well, dear heart, I have missed your evil face these last few weeks. When will you spend some time with me that's not tied to business?"

He laughed. "You know that I have no time for playing. Not now, at least."

"Yes, I know, I know, I know," she smiled, "but one of these days, I'll catch you at exactly the right time, you'll see!"

"Good," he responded, "I'll take that as a promise."

"Do that, *mon cher*." She walked from the couch where they were sitting to a large polished desk dominating the room. She opened and closed a drawer and walked to a side door, which she then unlocked. "Knowing you as I do, let's get the business done first and then maybe I can waylay you for other things later."

She snapped on a light, which flooded a small storeroom of shelves fully stocked with items of folk art from floor to ceiling: baskets, wooden utensils, antique tools, pottery, religious items, primitive masks. "Some new stuff came in this week. It's over there," she said, indicating an unsorted pile of boxes and things wrapped in newspaper. "I've had another fight with our friends in El Paso. They insist that no one gives a damn if I pick up stuff that has been looted from the village churches and *moradas*. They want it for their customers in New York and Palm Beach. I told them to go get what they want from their Taos and Colorado contacts. My business will remain modest and legal." She reflected a moment. "I don't need headaches."

"Neither does the Fly By Night Company," El Indio Jesús added. "Let's keep things neat and legitimate. There's no need to be greedy. Especially since profit can be made by acting correctly."

He looked over the goods lining the shelves. Holding a Monte Alban figurine, he asked, "Have you cleared these with the authorities? You have the necessary *cédulas*? I'll probably not need certificates today, but when I go up-river I may." He examined some masks of recent manufacture. "Last Sunday afternoon I watched a van full of Casas Grandes and Mimbres ware being sold under a tree at Tiguex Park. One of the eager customers said she represented the university. Sure. Then why wasn't she on the phone to the police to break up this business of the *huaqueros*, these grave robbers?"

"It's hard to compete with the looters now that times are hard and getting harder on both sides of the border," she added thoughtfully. She sighed.

"Yes," she resumed. "Everything is in order. Take whatever you need."

"I will pay you in *pesos* today."

"Fine," she replied. "No problem. But try to give me U.S. dollars whenever you can. It gives me a margin to play with."

"Right."

Business done, she came around her desk and put her arms around El Indio's neck. "You come and go too quickly, *mi cielo*. You must plan to stay longer one of these times."

He kissed her forehead lightly and gently released her grip. Smiling, he walked to the door. Turning to look back over his shoulder, still smiling, he said, "We'll always have Paris."

■ ■ ■

Precisely at nine o'clock. Sister Kateri stepped down from the van and limped across the driveway to the servant's entrance of the beautiful rambling home built of hand-dressed stone, the best of Mexican craftsmanship, situated in the country club area of the city. Flowing lawns of deep, artificially irrigated verdancy were still visible in the late twilight.

She was met at the door by an Anglo man wearing a clerical collar. They embraced. Then she disappeared into the doorway but within minutes returned with a young man wearing a baseball cap and an elderly woman whose frailty required the man and El Indio Jesús to assist her into the rear of the vehicle. The cleric and El Indio Jesús then grasped each other in an *abrazo* of friendship and affection. The man then climbed into the driver's seat of the van and closed the door.

El Indio Jesús then turned to say good-bye to the nun. Silence fell between them. Slowly he lifted her hand and kissed it in farewell.

■ ■ ■

On the Interstate highway once again. El Indio Jesús spoke to the driver. "We must be at the checkpoint between eleven thirty and twelve, when our contact is on duty. If we miss that window, we will have to wait until tomorrow night."

The Reverend Frank Dutton nodded.

Foreign Service

The driver could feel through his spine and scapulae the sensation of a strip of pavement hundreds of miles long tugging him, that he was pulling along with him a highway the color of old dead blood. He drove feeling sutured to that road of memories trailing behind and he feared he would never be free of the drag and pull of those painful stitches, which bound him to a memory of himself as another person, now dead, but living then in a wounded land.

■ ■ ■

The embassy was a fortress designed by what must have been medievalists who longed to convert places of diplomatic business into unassailable castles. The act of obtaining a short-term visa to go to the United States required the foreign national applicant to commute nearly out of the city to the citadel on high ground. With a car, there was no parking area; without a car, there was no public transportation anywhere near the embassy. Nearly everyone must endure the long wait on the sidewalk outside the first concrete wall with its crown of curly concertina wire: only high officials or "important contacts" could leap the time and bureaucratic hurdles to capture prized "A" or "B" referrals, which did little more than cut the waiting test. Overhead, television cameras scanned the line, back and forth, back and forth. National soldiers stood guard around the perimeter, automatic weapons chest-high. Some were boys. Some were spies.

Throughout the year, the sun thumped down onto the pavement and back up into the faces of the hundreds who lined up every weekday from dawn until hope faded in late afternoon. This was not a ragtag collection of petitioners: it was expensive to travel to the United States for whatever reason, so those in the daily line-up were not poor people by any stretch of the imagination or prejudice but rather members of the middle class or above. Many were businessmen. And there were the wealthy who took their children to Disneyland during school holidays or visited relatives in the Miami area. The unpleasantness of the visa line was democratically shared by nearly all. It was no comfort.

As his place in line drew closer to the one-person-wide doorway to the guard's interrogation booth, the visa seeker could ponder the technology behind the twin flanks of driveway barriers, covered over by yellow and blue diagonal stripes, which in an instant could be activated to display enormous teeth capable of chomping down on the tires of most approaching vehicles. Yet for all the obvious mechanical and electronic complexity, the gate crept open and crept closed again so slowly that the Americans in their big cars and four-wheeled vehicles were in plain sight as they awaited their turn for the car-by-car search undertaken by hired security guards within. These guards just inside the gate were equipped with what looked like dentist's mirrors on a wand except that their's were large and on small wheels for the purpose of examining the undersides of each vehicle to check for car bombs. It saved them having to get down on hands and knees. The guards also opened up the hood and very thoroughly checked the trunk and back seats of each car in its turn.

The Americans in line early in the day were most often Foreign Service officers coming to work. They never looked at the people in the line. They just looked at the line itself and sighed. The Americans all seemed to be *blancos* or *rubios* and large, except for the spies and narcotics agents who must have been chosen for their ability to "pass" in the local crowds. Mixed in among the American officers were the Foreign Service nationals—the FSNs—in older-model American cars. Most of them were women, handsome women, sophisticated, international. They looked at the line while they waited, but only from the corners of their eyes. They would never "recognize" anyone, because that might lead to a plea for assistance that they rarely could give. Powerless, in the driveway with the Americans they exuded feigned power. And they reaped hatred from those standing in the sun.

Toward midmorning the wives of the Americans drove up to the gate in their turn, station wagons and carryalls bulging with out-of-control children they screamed at from time to time and then seemed to forget. This was the commissary parade. The commissary sold American food and household products such as soaps and cleansers, toilet paper, and large amounts of antacid at greatly elevated prices to its captive clients, who would die of starvation and filth before patronizing local markets. Those standing in the visa line were invisible to the commissary parade except for a few wide-eyed American children who stared out the car windows.

One Foreign Service officer did, in fact, look at the line each morning, looked at it with a small shudder of shame. As he waited his turn through the gate and the inspection, he never failed to reflect about the motives that might be compelling the visa seekers to endure the line and its humiliations. The endurance test did not end at the guard booth there at the gate: passing up the ramp lined with hired security guards and into the multifloored building, they would face the stonelike embassy guards and then the bureaucratic maze that was waiting like an electronic rat trap, ready to spring shut on your chance to escape this beautiful hell.

For beautiful this country was, he thought, beautiful to the eye. But not to any of the other senses. To the ear, it was too quiet most of the time, and when there was any noise, it was the shrill night screams of emergency vehicles. Too often, there was the scent of burning rubber, tear gas, or the aftermath smell of explosives.

Sitting in his Jeep Wagoneer, the American Foreign Service officer would surreptitiously scan the men and women in the visa line and wonder what had led this one or that one here to this place at this time. Yet he never mistook these moments of idle curiosity for genuine compassion, knowing that he would soon be upstairs at his Wang word processor, knocking out the latest reporting cable on the political climate of the nation, a cable that would be filed under ARA/GEL/pol in the State Department, where it would never see the light again.

At the end of the day, he was again uncharacteristic in his actions. He was particularly drawn to the sounds and sights in the barrios, where, unlike other Americans, he chose to wander. His coworkers and their families or the escorted wives of CODELs, congressional delegations, visited certain barrios on certain market days to buy *folclóricos*. That was their entire interaction with the native population save for the legions of household help they hired: maids, gardeners, chauffeurs, nursemaids, cooks, swimming pool maintenance men, manicurists/pedicurists, playmates for the children. He did all the wrong things, so warned the people who bothered to interact with him in the embassy: he ate local food, drank the water, learned to speak barrio Spanish, read the little newspapers, drank *caña*, hung out at cantinas, and sometimes dated the local *chicas*. About the dating, though, he was beginning to feel too old for the rigamarole involved in going through the formal steps to gain family permission. He liked women, but the female Foreign Service officers were rarely available for one reason or another: already married, or in love with someone, or too career-minded. There were complications when dating any career-woman who worked in the embassy, since the

Foreign Service nationals were notoriously quick to sniff out such a romance and turn it into public business and endless discussion.

Right now he felt challenged. His training at seminary before taking and passing the Foreign Service entrance examinations and getting his commission reinforced a certain righteousness in his character that, even as a child and a youth, made him pretty insufferable to a lot of people around him. As a Foreign Service officer these many years, he learned over and over again—since he seemed to keep forgetting the lesson—that what Ambrose Bierce said about politics was even more closely keyed to a definition of international diplomacy, that it is "a strife of interests masquerading as a contest of principles: the conduct of public [read "national"] affairs for private advantage."

At the present time he was charged with drafting this year's human rights report. He was to survey the appropriate touchstones to measure the essential freedoms of speech, press, fair and competitive elections, assembly, movement, and so on. The touchstones were visiting prisons, interviewing newspaper columnists and radio and television commentators where self-censorship was suspected, searching out dissidents of all stripes, people known or thought to be under house arrest, political party "outs" whose activities might have been inhibited from full participation in national affairs, and, trickiest of all, tracking down the *desaparecidos*—those who had simply disappeared without trace from their homes and friends.

It was in this last part of the job, looking for information about the *desaparecidos*, that he found himself working long hours not at the keyboard of his word processor but pursuing shadows through a kind of Russian doll-like series of human groups. Following up on one known student troublemaker nicknamed El Cedrito, Little Cedar Tree, who had vanished some months before at the height of his popularity in the student movement, he started his inquiries in the university. Bit by bit, as he won the confidence of the student's friends and compatriots, he was seduced into ever more clandestine, mysterious meetings until he somehow felt that he was drifting away from being a gung-ho political officer in the American Embassy to suddenly becoming a coconspirator in something of which he had zero understanding. And yet he was caught up in the intrigue and his stubborn intention to get to the bottom of it. And then, just as suddenly, he was dropped by all those who had been leading him on to where, he did not know. It deflated him.

At the embassy, both American officers and the Foreign Service nationals began making comments about his appearance and state of health.

"Hey, Frank, who's keeping you out so late at night? You look a wreck," said the section head, Bart Brown. "Want to come into my office and talk about it?"

"No." He laughed. "There's no problem, no problem at all. It's just this report I'm doing background on. It's keeping me out late. That's all."

"Well, look, Frank," said Bart, squeezing Frank's shoulder, "don't get too deep into this thing, will you? I mean, we do this exercise every year and you know what happens to it once it hits State: they'll write and rewrite till you'd never recognize you've had a hand in it. So don't kill yourself, just get the damned thing done and send it off. That's my advice."

"'Good advice. I'll take it." Frank chuckled, shoving back the shock of dark hair that habitually fell into his eyes. "It's almost done anyway."

"Good. Good man. Keep me in the loop if there's anything I should know, though, okay?"

"Sure. No problem."

It didn't end there in the office that morning. The gorgeous Consuela, married childlessly to a prominent local businessman, took up her usual teasing banter with him.

"I heard that," she stage-whispered when he left Bart Brown's doorway. "I think it's a woman. Only a woman could make your pretty brown eyes look so red." She laughed. "Come on, *chico*, you can tell *mamacita*."

Frank looked at her and then around the office, seeing the other three FSNs watching him carefully.

"How could I possibly look at other women when we have all of you beauties here in the office?"

They made sounds of agreement.

"But, *mi amor*, you don't take any of us dancing or anything like that," continued the undaunted Consuela. "If you really liked us, you'd do something about it," she cooed. "Look at Morella there. She knows that you can salsa. She's ready to dance."

Morella blushed and turned back to her Wang monitor. "Hey, leave me out of this," she demanded over her shoulder.

Consuela pressed on. "Someone so tall and nice looking like you, you should have lots of *chicas* mad for you. Come on, you can tell us: what do you do on the weekends? Do you go to the *playas* or what? Who is feeding you?"

Frank slapped his flat stomach. "Does this look like someone's feeding me? I weigh less now than I did when I came here from my last post, and that was in Africa. You women should have pity and find someone who can cook for me."

"What happened to the cook you used to have? What happened to Carmencita?"

"She went back home to her village. She said there was some kind of trouble there and she wanted to help if she could. So I need another cook. But I usually eat out anyway. There's a workman's restaurant not far from where I live that I eat in a lot. Although I'm getting a little tired of chicken and yuca all the time—"

The Embassy siren went off at that moment, and everyone listened to hear which of the three tones it was taking, signaling a fire, or that the embassy was under terrorist attack, or had received a bomb threat. The tone indicated whether they should evacuate the premises, stay in place but check around for mysterious packages, or go into the basement.

"To the basement!" Consuela shrieked, grabbing her purse and kicking the button to the surge protector for her computer monitor. Everyone did about the same and headed down the staircase as the siren drowned out shouts from person to person. Frank was last out of his office. He was floor warden, and it was his job to see that windows were closed and most of the electrical equipment was disconnected. Just as he shut the steel door to the stairway behind him, a terrific concussion rattled and shook the whole building. Frank jumped or was jolted down half the flight of stairs and sped down the remaining flights to the crowded basement.

"What was it? What was it?" several people asked all at once at the bottom of the stairwell.

"Haven't a clue," Frank answered. "Don't know."

Excited conjectures began among the people pressed together in the dimly lit underground room, but then quiet fell as they listened for further sounds from above. They strained to make sense from the noises woven into the siren's continuing wail.

A half-hour later, the embassy speaker system broadcast an all-clear tone, and the voice of the Marine Corps gunnery sergeant said: "Now hear this. Now hear this. This has not been a drill. This has not been a drill. There has been a small explosion outside the main gate. Repeat: there has been a small explosion of unknown type outside the main gate. Please report to your duty stations and resume your usual activities.

"That is all."

At the chicken restaurant later that evening, Frank added hot sauce to make the yuca more interesting and thought about the attack on the embassy that morning. How in the world some of the flying debris did not reach people standing in the second-gate visa line was a wonder. Guerilla action was nearly a daily occurrence, but it was thought to be *of* the people, not *against* the people. Why would the guerillas chance taking out so many of their own people to make such a minor point: blowing a hole in the embassy's main gate?

A young man moved over to his tiny table and sat down without invitation. Frank looked at him. The man looked straight back. They stared at each other in silence for some seconds.

"You American?" the young man, maybe a student, asked in English.

"Yes." Frank waited while the other regarded him for another several seconds.

"Why are you here? Why do you eat here?"

"I eat here a lot. What's the matter with that?"

"Americans don't eat here."

"Well, I do, and I'm an American."

The young man looked slowly around at the other diners, some single older men, a couple of families. No one seemed to be watching them.

"Well," said the young man, rising from his chair, smiling, "see you later," and extended his hand.

Puzzled beyond words, Frank automatically reached out and shook the hand. The handshake belied the challenge in the man's words.

Some days later, Frank paid a visit to the political prison outside the city. It was part of his duty in the preparation of the human rights report to visit prisons where political figures were held if, indeed, there were any. Frank had a list of about a dozen men who were thought to be incarcerated at Tombaba, a minimum-security facility, actually a showcase prison set up by a cynical regime conscious of criticism.

As the white U.S. government Ford van approached the walls of the prison, he could see many women and children sitting and standing in groups linked into a sort of line leading up to the front gate. They carried sacks and parcels and, very often, tiny babies. In the press of people, the van slowed to a crawl. The air conditioner blocked outside sound, making the crowd somehow unreal. Frank, who had been looking out one side of the vehicle, turned to check out the other side and found himself gazing directly into the face of a young nun only a few feet from him. Her eyes riveted him. What was the message? He quickly rolled down the window. The noise hit him, along with sweltering heat and putrid smells.

"Hey, hey!" he called to the retreating figure. "Hey, *disculpe: espérate un momento*. Hello? Can I help you? Hey . . ." But she was gone, melting into the crowd.

There certainly were political prisoners in Tombaba. The authorities at the prison were the soul of courtesy to the visiting political officer from the American Embassy. Nothing was denied him. He was free to see whomever and whatever he chose.

Frank interviewed each of the eleven there—they said that the twelfth had been released the day before—and though the cells were spartan, they were not inhumane. Each prisoner described his "case" and gave Frank messages and requests to deliver. There was no doubt that these were clear-cut political prisoners by any definition, a fact he would duly report in his wrap-up cable to the Department of State. But if past performance was repeated, the regime would read the next human rights report, smile, and forget the whole thing, because the United States was forever pointing its fingers at human rights violators, saying "shame, shame," and then doing nothing about it. Not only did the Americans pick and choose whom to say "shame, shame" to—calling Cuba's Castro a monster for his political prisoners while failing to mention Israel's Begin and his prisons crammed with Palestinians, for example— but they rarely took their most effective weapon to enforce their will: the U.S. never stopped selling and donating weapons and military technology. Until then, the regime need not worry: for the Americans, it was business as usual.

When Frank returned to his U.S. government–supplied furnished apartment that evening, he found a note stuffed under the door. He immediately thought about his restaurant visitor. That was a week before. The note read: "Si quiere asistir una reunión importante esta tarde, ven a las 9:00 hrs a la Quinta Lorena. Calle

La Castellana y Transversal 2ndo. Barrio Santa Rosa." It was written with an unreliable ballpoint pen on a page torn out of a lined notebook.

Frank ate at the usual chicken restaurant. He spotted his impromptu guest of the week before sitting with another young man at a table near the kitchen door. They seemed to have no interest in him.

Nearing nine o'clock, he made his way through the streets to the address on the note. It was a lower-class neighborhood but not one in poverty. There were homes and shops behind the walls that lined the street over which mango trees draped their fruit-laden branches. This neighborhood had electricity, so the way was vaguely illuminated. Though he saw no one actually watching him, he knew he was being watched: he felt it. There were people walking with plastic sacks in hand, and from time to time a car or a small bus, a *rutera*, passed by. He could hear the voices of children playing behind the walls in the deepening twilight. He was having trouble making out the names of the houses as it grew darker. "Quinta Anna," "Quinta Mariella," "Quinta Fifi"—they nearly always carried women's names, why, he didn't know. Maybe because the houses stayed with the women, no matter what happened in life's dramas. He was losing hope of finding the address and yet was reluctant to ask for assistance. As he approached the end of a dark block, a person who had been walking in front of him for some time turned and confronted him. Frank reacted by shortening his pace, not knowing whether the act was threatening or not. Slowing to a stop, Frank and the young man stood looking at each other. Frank's breathing came faster as his heart rate increased. The youth was calm and his hands stayed at his side. Then he spoke.

"*De la Embajada*? Are you the one from the American Embassy?"

"*Sí,*" Frank answered.

"*Espérate a la pared,*" he ordered. And he was gone into a nearby doorway.

Frank waited for what seemed hours as purpling darkness enveloped the street punctuated with yellow dots of low-wattage light bulbs. On the wall facing him was a grafitti message, ¿AHORA QUE VOY A HACER? Frank thought about it and agreed that yes, he too was wondering what he was going to do next.

In a few minutes, the young man returned and gestured him to follow.

The same portal the guide had used before entered into a patio lit only by the light shining through a partly opened doorway. They entered, Frank first. He faced a serape hung on nails across another doorway. The youth behind him reached forward and pulled it aside when Frank hesitated. The second room was dark and empty. So was the third room, so dark that Frank worried about banging into something. Nearly face into it, Frank found himself at a closed door from which a ringing voice could be heard. The man behind him rapped the universal "*Ta*-tata-*ta*-ta, *ta-ta*," and turned the door handle, pressing Frank into the room.

Quickly the young men in the room pulled knit masks and scarves over their faces and then assumed studied casual positions. The act of snatching up the masks was ludicrous in contrast to the poise they now displayed. One had knocked off his baseball hat in the process, displaying flaming red hair, an unfortunate genetic mutation in a world of brunettes.

But now the apparent leader was addressing Frank.

"*Mira*, Yankee, what are you asking questions about? Why are you hanging around where you have no business to be? Nobody asked you to come over here where you don't belong. What's it with you anyway, Yankee?"

Frank looked around the group of five men, no, four: one was a young woman in jeans. Unquestionably students. A single light bulb shone at the end of a cord above the table. Other than the chairs and stools they sat on, there was no other furniture. A poster of Che Guevara threatened to peel off the wall next to a calendar for the previous year featuring a big-breasted blonde offering "Julio Rivas: *Repuestas*."

"Actually, you invited me here," he responded.

"That's not what was meant, Yankee. Answer the question: why are you looking for El Cedrito? We know you are doing that."

"Look," Frank said slowly, "I'm not looking for trouble, and I don't want to get anyone else in trouble. Let's start with that, okay?"

The leader looked around the room from person to person. "*¿Entonces?*"

"I've been asking around about the student El Cedrito who seems to have disappeared. Maybe he's *un desaparecido*. I don't know. But we think—"

"'We think'? Who's the 'we' in that 'we think,' Yankee?"

"Look, I mean that I am the one who's looking for him. It's me. I think maybe because of his speeches around the university that he's gone underground or something. Maybe he's been shut up . . ."

"This does not yet make sense, Yankee. What do you care? What does the embassy of the government of the United States of America care about one small student?"

"Well, *usted tiene razón*, the embassy of the government of the United States of America doesn't really care anything about El Cedrito or any other 'small student.' It's just me: I am doing a human rights report, and I just got curious, that's all. And here I am."

The leader let out a blast of breath born of exasperation and slapped his thigh with the beret he swept off his head.

"*No puedo crearlo! Idiotas! Idiotas todas!*" He glared through his mask at the others in the room. He thrust his head forward toward one, then another, and then another. He slapped the table with his hat. "*Esto es demasiado . . .*" He broke off his rant and turned back to Frank.

"*Entonces*, you are not some kind of a spy for the embassy of the government of the United States of America." He paused and looked around the room again. "You are just a nosy person with nothing better to do than stick that big Yankee nose of yours into other people's lives. *Correcto*, Yankee?" He turned his back to the group, crossed his arms over his chest, and stood rocking heel to toe in an obvious attempt to calm himself but letting the full weight of his indignation fall on the others, who stared at his taut shoulders.

In the lengthening silence, one by one the others turned their attention back to Frank who looked back at them. He could not help thinking all the while that the smile on his face must look totally forced, insincere, stupid. He felt like a chimpanzee with a "please don't hurt me" smile that zoogoers thought meant "hi, let's be friends." He began sweating in the closeness of the small room. Why indeed, was he bothering these students? He felt no more than what the leader said he was, a meddling nosy American bored with watching "I Love Lucy" reruns in Spanish or drinking in solitude as so many of his fellow officers did in American posts around the world.

The leader swung around. He screamed in fast Spanish to the man who had brought Frank in. The man took Frank's arm and drew him back out of the room. Frank began walking through the darkened area toward where he thought the front door was located, but the man grabbed his arm again.

"*Siéntate acá*," he said, pushing him down onto something soft that Frank couldn't make out. The man stood there next to him. Waiting for something.

Voices soft and loud reached them as the minutes passed. There was little that could be deciphered from the sounds, just garbled, jumbled voices braided upon each other in argument. Then quiet took over. The minutes dragged even slower with now nothing to capture attention except that Frank now felt he need to piss. He addressed the guard.

"*Hay un baño?*"

"*Dios mío*, now what? *No puedo crearlo . . .*" He thought for a moment, and then lifted Frank's arm by the elbow and propelled him out into the courtyard. He shoved him toward the corner. "*Allá.*"

Frank's bladder was so full he felt he would urinate for an hour. Standing there, listening to the splash against brick, hoping he wasn't splashing his shoes, he began to chuckle. He began to feel laughter bubbling up inside himself. What the hell am I doing here?, he asked himself. Who the hell is El Jefe Máximo, who the hell does he think he is, dragging me here—no, luring me here on this crazy business. A bunch of kids: self-important kids who think they're Che Guevaras, one and all. I don't believe this, its just too dumb . . . I've got to get out of here. Who needs this crap? His anger turned back to humor then. Sure, he thought, a bunch of kids half my age scaring me . . . yes, they actually scared me for a while . . . and I bought the whole cloak-and-dagger thing. I really need to get out of here. I need a break. I need . . .

He finished and turned to see his guard motioning to him in the half light to return inside. Again he passed through the darkened rooms to the inner door, pressed down on the handle—not waiting for the guard to do it—and entered the meeting room. They sat as before with the leader (Frank now called him El Jefe Máximo in his mind) leaning with his back against the wall. He straightened up as Frank approached the table.

"Are you in charge of visas?" he asked Frank.

"No, I'm not."

"Do you have anything to do with visas?"

"No. Nothing."

El Jefe Máximo paused thoughtfully. He turned his head toward the masked woman, who looked back at him.

"Then, who does?" he asked Frank.

"That's the business of the Consular Section. I'm in the Political Section."

"But cannot you recommend someone to get a visa to go to the United States of America if you want someone to go there?"

"Well, yes, I guess I can," Frank agreed. "But we don't do much of that, or at least, I don't do that very often. It's not my primary responsibility."

"So it is not your primary responsibility to help people who you know are being hunted by a corrupt regime to get away to freedom when their lives are in danger?"

"Well, let's not get too dramatic here: what is it that you want with me? I told you that all I'm doing is writing a report—"

"*Basta!*" screamed El Jefe Máximo.

In the momentary silence, the woman student spoke for the first time.

"*Bueno*. We understand that you are only a little person, a nosy person, who works in an office in the embassy. We have many friends there that do your work for you. We know how you treat the Foreign Service nationals." She stood up. "We know that they do all the work and the American officers get all the credit. We know you pay them in the local money at the local rate of pay while you Americans pay yourselves in American dollars at American rates of pay. And get free housing and everything else. We know all about—"

"*Basta*," El Jefe broke in. "*Basta*."

She sat down, mollified.

"We have a friend," he began slowly, calmly, "who must leave the country now—"

"You mean El Cedrito, don't you?" interrupted Frank.

"*Sí*. He must—"

The young woman lashed out at El Jefe in a torrent of Spanish. He listened with his head hung low, patiently. When she quit, he straightened up. He addressed Frank for the last time.

"*Mira*, Yankee, this has all been a mistake. I ask your pardon. We shall not trouble you again. You may go."

At that, the guard took Frank's elbow. Frank shook off his hand and turned back to the group.

"Look, I wouldn't mind helping out if I thought it might do some good, if I knew more about what's going on . . ."

"Forget it, General Haig, you're not in control here," said the red-haired student, who now stood up face to face with Frank.

"You can't help, we don't need help, and this has been a lousy mistake. Now get lost, will you?" The young man spoke English like someone from Brooklyn.

"Okay," said Frank, walking out the door, "have it your way."

■ ■ ■

With each step toward his apartment, Frank found the whole situation funnier and funnier. Instead of playing cops and robbers or cowboys and Indians, the students were playing dictators and guerillas, caught up in the romance and excitement of play-acting. Sure, maybe El Cedrito was truly in some kind of trouble. That wouldn't be unusual for bright, loose-mouthed students: it comes with the territory. But this beret-and-mask stuff was right out of comic books and grade B movies. The level of suppression in this country hadn't gotten that bad, nor did it reach down to the level of students, he believed. At least, not yet. The students were paranoid, that was it: they just got caught up in their own adventure story and thought they could ship their friend out of the country using me, using the first silly thought that came into their heads. If this is the revolution, then the revolution is in deep trouble, Frank concluded. He laughed to himself but was jolted from his thoughts as he heard loud Salsa music coming from his apartment.

The apartment was a shambles. It had been wrecked. The first thing that Frank could think of was how upset Señor Yanis, the warehouseman, would be when he saw how the embassy furniture was all torn up and broken. His second thought was, how did they get in? The embassy policy for all American officers who lived in apartment houses was that the building must have twenty-four-hour guard service as well as alarm systems and other security measures. The perpetrators had obviously gotten past the guard, not a hard task really, and entered his apartment easily: no, he hadn't set his alarm system on the way out. He never did. The sound of crashing furniture had been drowned out with the heavy salsa beat blasting from his stereo. Thanks for small favors, he thought wryly, at least that cover-up of the noise saved me my stereo system.

Frank dialed the embassy then. He could have used his two-way radio issued to all the American officers. but the telephone system in this part of the city was presently functioning and easier to use. He reported the break-in first to the marine on guard duty, then to the regional security officer, and then a third time to the officer in charge of the security patrol that regularly cruised past all the houses and apartment buildings of the American officers each night. In turn, the local police were informed and a team from the *policía* dropped by, surveyed the mess briefly, shook their collective heads, and left after duly writing something on their pads of paper. Frank then began the job of cleaning it all up.

■ ■ ■

The draft of the human rights cable landed back on Frank's desk radically slashed with mark-outs and Xs and substituted words and phrases throughout. Whole paragraphs were deleted and strong terms were supplanted with weak terms. The whole character and intent of his draft report was lost. In its place, known and unknown hands had sculpted a completely fictitious state of affairs in that country. Gone were his descriptions—warnings, really—that there was a growing climate of repression and intimidation, that there were more and more claims of *desaparecidos*, particularly among the radical student groups, and that the newspapers cloaked themselves in a fabric of self-censorship so as to avoid conflict with the ruling—really the only—political party. He had written about how the key union leaders were no longer in the country. Gone too were opposition leaders who published broadsides from across the seas, unwilling to stick it out any longer where they felt repression would deepen.

His coworkers displayed exaggerated patience with him, being overly polite about their disagreement with the substance and implications of his report, but in the end the report would be radically rewritten to reflect their cumulative wisdom, not his. His senior officer, Bart Brown, took the report as an indication of not just political naïveté or misjudgment but also as a sign that Frank was getting caught up in the lives of "host country nationals," as the term was used to describe the people of the country. Host country nationals had surely been influencing Frank, getting him bent out of shape to the extent that he had lost his perspective, his judgment, his training, and his understanding of his own country's policy points of reference by which he should be guided. In other words, Frank was losing it: Frank was "going native," like anthropologists and missionaries who lived too long with the natives and began taking on their coloration and cultural ways. He was selling out to the natives. Didn't he realize that his country had a carefully laid out operational procedure guiding all aspects of its interaction? His report carried the recommendation that there be a moratorium on further arms sales to the regime until certain human rights questions were resolved. Didn't he understand that the aid package required that American weaponry and equipment be bought with those same donated funds? That U.S. specialists in interrogation and crowd suppression would be paid for out of those same funds? That the American military training exercises and the lessons taught were bought with "donated" foreign aid that boomeranged back into U.S. pockets one way or another? That, in sum, the dollar figure for foreign aid to this country really encompassed a whole list of items that the recipient country was required to buy from the United States as a condition of the aid?

His friends in the Economic Section argued that it was simply the price of doing business between nations, just like business at home. That goods and services such as tanks, cattle prods, and crowd control training were against what they labeled Frank's "personal values and standards" was simply a matter of his theological training getting mixed up with the real world of give-and-take of foreign relations. Someone whose past posting was in

London and had become insufferably Anglicized paraphrased Aldous Huxley to the effect that "the sociopolitical level of integration of any nation is no more developed than that of the nervous system of a fish, and one wouldn't expect morality from a fish, would one?" In short, did he really want to continue being a Foreign Service officer carrying out the policies of his country, or would he rather be a missionary to the Ungabunga in deepest Tarzalandia? In any case, the message from his fellow Foreign Service officers was clear enough: Frank had better make up his mind, one way or the other. The Foreign Service wanted janissaries, not Weak Willies with moral and ethical qualms.

Frank buckled under the criticism and typed out the human rights report cable incorporating all of the multitudinous corrections, additions, and deletions. The State Department report would not come out until the end of the year, and only then would he see what would result from further rewriting in Washington. By now, Frank was beginning not to care, or at least not to care as much as he did during the writing of his draft. He recognized that his conviction about the importance of honest reporting had been compromised more and more as time went on. He also perceived that the American officers around him would never consider him one of them again: he had shown himself not to be diplomatic corps material. Pure and simple. And the word would get around, around to other officers around the globe, to say nothing about Washington.

And he began not to care about that either.

■ ■ ■

On an American holiday not celebrated by the host country, Frank visited a different city weekday market, one he hadn't seen before. It was in a barrio that perched along a mountainside in strings of shanties reaching like fingers up to the crest. The marketplace was small, as were the goods: the sellers and buyers dealt in tiny quantities, for neither had enough capital to do otherwise. This informal economy in reality floated the whole of the economy of the nation. In Latin America, it served as one of the most stabilizing forces because it could absorb the great multitude of unskilled unemployed workers who would otherwise be a distinct threat to any government. While the marketplace and sidewalk entrepreneurs paid no taxes, had no licenses, offered no social security or medical benefits, and sometimes dealt in smuggled goods, they nevertheless created millions of jobs, fed families, and generated some of the most vibrant economic growth on the continent. Frank roamed through food stalls and clothing racks, along patches of ground with piles of Bic lighters and Jockey underwear.

He bought some empanadas from a round-faced, round-bodied Indian woman wearing a T-shirt with the legends I LIVE TO SURF, then continued strolling among the sellers, eating as he went.

For some time he had been entranced with the ingenuity of children who created toys out of wires, coat hangers, and bits of string, pieces of plastic. He had collected a few at other posts overseas: a pull-toy here, a push-toy there. Today he saw some delightful creations in the hands of a group of boys ranged around a doorway just beyond the market square. He slowly approached them, smiling. They looked up from the dry earth on which they were squatting and regarded him quizzically. He stopped near but not too near.

Pointing to a spidery automobile with windows of clear plastic, he asked the boy, "*¿Hiciste esto?*"

"*Sí, señor,*" he responded shyly. He was proud of his work but not sure his friends approved of his talking with a gringo.

"*A mí me gusta mucho, bien hecho.*"

"*Gracias, señor.*"

To another, Frank asked if he could see his *jugete.* The boy thought about it for a moment and then pushed his airplane closer on the ground. None of the boys stood. Soon Frank had been shown each of their creations, marveling at the clever use of discarded materials to produce their models. One boy had worked out a system whereby he used batteries to run the propeller of his airplane. Another used flashlight bulbs and batteries to rig up headlights that flickered on and off without much predictability.

He was sitting in the dirt with them in the afternoon sun when he noticed that a shadow had fallen over his shoulder and onto the ground before him. The boys looked up at someone behind him with smiles and questions on their faces. Frank swung around but couldn't make out the person behind him because of the sun's glare. He turned back toward the boys to return the model he was holding in time to see them struggling to their feet: each one of them was crippled in the legs, some in their arms and spine. The sticks lying around the play area were props by which to stand and stay standing. Frank was shocked in a flash of understanding.

He jumped up then and, turning once again, discovered that the shadow had been that of a small dark woman, a nun by the cowl she wore, the same nun he had seen at the prison months ago. She spoke quickly and quietly to the boys, who hobbled off up the street.

"*Adiós*," one after another called back to him, one waving his model car in good-bye.

"*¿Perdón, Hermana, disculpa la molesta, pero estos chicos son . . .?*"

"Yes," she answered his question in English, "they are all crippled from poliomyelitis. We have a small clinic and orphanage here. In your country, you think polio is dead, but here it is a strong monster eating up the futures of the children."

"Your English sounds too good to be secondary: are you an American?"

"Yes, I am an American, but no, I am not a citizen of the United States. I'm Canadian. But I have lived in the U.S. a fair amount of my life. You seem to forget that there are Americans and Americans . . ."

"Yes, I'm sorry. North Americans, Central Americans, South Americans, Latin Americans, et cetera, et cetera, et cetera. What a bore I am."

"I know who you are, Mr. Frank Dutton. You are a political officer in the U.S. Embassy."

"How do you know that?"

"I have seen you a few times, that's all."

"Really? Where? When?"

"It doesn't matter. We can meet formally now." She held out her hand to be shaken.

He grasped her hand, finding it tiny.

"How do you do?" he smiled at the studied politeness of the moment. "I have seen you before, too."

"Oh? Really?" she looked suddenly worried.

"Yes, at Tombaba Prison. I saw you when I went to visit the political prisoners."

"Ah, yes."

They stood silently for a few long moments.

"Well," he started up again, "tell me more about your clinic and orphanage."

Her dark eyes shot directly into his face, and he felt their strength probe into his.

"Perhaps, if you have a few minutes free . . . they're not far from here, just up the way . . ."

"Yes, of course. Lead the way."

She did not move but stood in place as though weighing her decision. Then she moved forward, lurching on a wasted leg that Frank had not noticed until then. Yet she moved quickly, and Frank took large paces to catch up with her. Soon she turned a corner and passed into a doorway. There she paused.

"This is the courtyard to our clinic and orphanage both. You'll see that we are very poor. Don't pity us."

Frank smiled. "I promise."

The boys had placed their models in a row along the inner courtyard wall before entering the building to the left. The chatter of young voices filtered out through the doorway as Frank and the young nun went in.

"Say," Frank said, drawing to a fast stop, "I don't know your name yet!" The noise neatly drowned out his question, but she heard it anyway.

"Kateri."

"What?"

She shouted above the boys' din. "I'm Sister Kateri."

He shouted back. "Pleased to know you, Sister Kateri."

"And I you, Mr. Dutton," she responded, and they shook hands again.

The orphanage and clinic run by the Medical Sisters of the Poor was indeed poor and small and graceless. But over the next months, Frank became a frequent visitor to the point where he was no longer considered a guest but a comfortable friend to the boys and to the nuns, of whom there were three in addition to Sister Kateri. Their focus was on crippled children, on those who had contracted polio, for the most part, since rehabilitation of shrunken limbs ranked high in their skills. Usually there was not much that could be done with bodies already tightened with the disease, but some therapy was possible, and the prostheses where needed could be sought from benefactors in Canada and the United States. Much of their time was spent setting up day-long clinics in various parts of the city and into the countryside to administer polio vaccine to long lines of children. Fortunately, there was always a supply of vaccine available to them, even when food seemed short to Frank. He soon came to know that their single white Volkswagen van could be seen throughout the nearby mountain ranges at any time and in any season, come rains or not. He went out with them from time to time, or with either Sister Kateri or Sister Lupe alone, and discovered that his primary responsibility was to push the van up, down, or in any case out of trouble at fairly regular intervals. His chino pants all seemed to be red from the knees down where the red clay mud had permanently painted them. Sister Lupe, a Navajo from Arizona, threatened to marry him because she was "born for the red earth clan people," of which he was clearly a member.

■ ■ ■

Frank went on home leave in June. It was a break that he very much needed in order to do some deep thinking about his life. Home leave meant one day's vacation in the United States for each month he had spent overseas. He had used up earlier accrued home leave just before coming to this post, so now he had only twenty working days to sort things out, twenty working days plus the weekends. He hoped it would be enough to decide what he wanted to do with himself and, what might be more telling, what he did not want to do with himself for the foreseeable future. He disliked leaving the boys at the orphanage and saying good-bye to Sister Kateri and the rest. They had become important to him in ways he could not yet describe.

He was drawn back to the seminary, where once he thought he would find a vocation. Somehow that didn't happen. He never quite understood why he left, or fled. But now, after more than two decades in the Foreign Service, living in Africa, Asia, and Latin America on his various tours, the lessons he had learned overseas seemed to be sending him back to where he started.

He sought counseling with his former teachers at the seminary. They were irritatingly balanced in their discussions with him about the two worlds he was comparing and contrasting. A lot of things going on in the United States at that time flung most precepts up against the wall for spotlight examination. Overseas it was easy to avoid internal politics, the things that were every-day newspaper topics inside the United States. He had left the country before the advent of hippies, before the years when the counterculture was flourishing, when free love and free grass were the standards of the day. He missed out on the marches protesting the Vietnam War; he missed the gay parades and the feminist demonstrations. He was in many ways very virginal where U.S. politics and social movements were concerned.

So it was a shock to him to visit his former roommate, the Reverend Raul Sena. His friend sat in nearly absolute silence for long, thick minutes, and then would spew out question after question: What had happened? Why did his people desert him? Why was the church deserting him? Who was tapping his telephone? Why? Who are the men in that car across the street? (Frank saw no car, saw no men.) Exhausted, Raul would sink back into his chair and finger the frayed upholstered armrest. He failed to understand how much a demand for a civilian review board threatened police hegemony.

Frank did not have much of his leave left, but of one thing he became certain: it was time for him to come back to his first love, the ministry. Here with Raul he could be of help, could make some positive difference in his life and maybe in the lives of others at the same time. The Foreign Service, with all its travel and perks, seemed unimportant in contrast to working with real people with real-life problems and joys.

Before he left the little mission, he assured his friend Raul that he would return soon. Raul must not become too downhearted in the meantime: it would all work out. "Have faith," Frank said, half in jest and half in utter seriousness.

■ ■ ■

When Frank returned to post, he gave notice of his "retirement." Although he had served the necessary twenty years, he was still too young to collect annuities on his retirement, so he would definitely have to find gainful employment. But his first plan was to join Raul to help him over the tough spot, and he would look for some permanent parish position later.

With all the paperwork to catch up on, plus all the tasks necessary to be completed in the process of checking out of the Foreign Service, Frank did not visit the orphanage and clinic for some weeks after he returned. When he did, he found the boys inside behind the closed front doors instead of enjoying the afternoon warmth of the plaza. There was no laughter. There was a sense that something had converted this place of joy into something else, something not right. The quiet was thick and looming.

Sister Kateri appeared gaunt, her dark eyes ringed with mauve creases. She was glad to see him but talked to him more like a stranger than a friend. He was puzzled.

A young man wearing a baseball cap rushed into the room but stopped when he saw Frank.

"*Disculpe la molesta, pero tengo que hablar con usted, Hermana Kateri.*"

"Please excuse me, Frank, this will take just a few minutes." She left with the young man, who, Frank could now see, was violently red-haired.

"He came to help us shortly after you left, Frank. He's from the student organization," Sister Lupe explained. "I confess I sort of captured him myself. We need all the help possible, as you know. Well, it just so happened that one evening I surprised him painting a graffiti slogan on our street wall, and as they say, the rest was history. I threatened him. I sweet-talked him. And I begged him to apply his revolutionary instincts into something worthwhile, like helping us with our work in the mountains. We came to appreciate your help, Frank, and began to see that we really needed a driver—"

"You mean a van-pusher."

"Well, yes, probably. Anyway, he's been taking Sister Kateri up into the high mountains, where she's doing immunizations, and it has worked out very nicely. Except lately."

Sister Lupe looked at her hands, which were characteristically stained with paint from one project or another.

"Lately," she continued, "there has been trouble. We have run into problems on the road that were never there before. The government has set up roadblocks, cut off roads entirely, and set up checkpoints with soldiers who have been given instructions not to let anyone through without passes. And you can't get passes, most of the time. They say it's because of guerilla actions. But although that's been growing, there's no reason to stop us from giving our shots to the children. There's no reason to stop us . . ." She ended uncertainly.

"But our new recruit has been a real benefit," she brightened. "He seems to be able to get us where we need to go much, if not most, of the time. We are glad to have him on board. Sometimes he brings along others of his group, too. We hear that he is the son of a famous man, but we don't know who that is. And we don't really care, come to think of it."

Sister Kateri returned alone. Sister Lupe excused herself and left the two of them sitting across the kitchen table with nothing being spoken between them.

Finally Frank broke the silence. "Okay, what is it? Why is this place like a graveyard? What's going on?"

Sister Kateri looked at him for a long moment and then dropped her eyes. Then she looked back at him again, drew a breath, and responded.

"The government has given us—me—thirty days to leave the country."

"What? Why?"

"They say I'm helping subversive elements here, and that the orphanage is a training ground for tomorrow's guerillas."

"But what nonsense!"

"Of course. Of course. We've all been through the absurdity of it. But that doesn't change the picture. Oh, Lupe and one or two others can stay for a while—who knows for how long?—but they seem to have targeted me as the threat to the established order. They sent some bullies here while you were gone, and they pushed us around a bit and accused me personally of being involved with 'the wrong people' in the mountains. I don't even know what village or villages they are talking about. They just kept warning me to stay out of the mountains and get packed up to leave. Period. And then they left. But they are outside: they've set up an observation post beyond the gate to spy on us.

"So you might be in trouble for coming here, Frank. That's one more problem I didn't have an hour ago," she ended, trying to put a touch of humor to what was clearly dismay.

Frank looked around the modest kitchen with its *fogón* hearth, which could cook full meals for chronically hungry boys using just a few sticks of wood or pieces of charcoal, the pile of cheap battered metal pots and pans, the packed-earth floor. He thought of the happy mealtimes. He considered how the boys had time and space to be creative, to learn, to grow, in the atmosphere provided by the good sisters. He hated the thought that it would come to an end because of taking a wrong road in the mountains. It made no sense. It was cruel.

"I came to say good-bye," said Frank.

Sister Kateri was startled. "What did you say?"

"I said, I came here to say good-bye to you. I'm leaving next week." He did not meet her eyes.

"But is your tour really up? I thought . . ."

"No, it's not that. I'm leaving the Foreign Service."

"Leaving?" She looked around the room as if for an answer he wouldn't, couldn't give.

"Look," Frank began slowly, "I have watched you work. I have seen what you and the others are doing. I love what you do, your dedication more than anything. You are really doing something. In my work, I do nothing. I write cable number 001542 and so what? Nobody reads it. Nobody cares. It makes no difference whatsoever.

"And then I push a Volkswagen van up a mountainside for you and I feel as though I've accomplished something worthwhile.

"Can't you see what I'm getting at? I need more out of life, and that means I have to put more into living. I'm returning to the States. I'm going to work with a friend of mine who has a small parish that's in trouble. Maybe I can make a better decision after that, but that's my first step."

■ ■ ■

A letter informed him that the Reverend Raul Sena had committed suicide a week after his visit. He made one more unsatisfying visit to the orphanage before he left. He could hardly bear the looks in the eyes of the boys, and the faces of the sisters imprinted themselves on his mind forever.

Only the redheaded driver seemed unconcerned, even pleased, with his departure. Frank knew he had met him before.

1 2 3
4 5 6
7 SUNDAY

Checkpoint Carlito

There will be too much moonlight once this line of squalls passes through, thought the large man sitting at a desk near the door of the light green trailer. There should be only a little traffic, though. By now the campers are probably bunked down in the parks for the night and won't be on the move until midday tomorrow. This much moon will carry too much light into the creosote and tumbleweed desert between El Paso and here, he mused, pacing along the windows at the checkpoint stop of the Immigration and Customs Services on the Interstate highway.

Bill Haywood Williams had a great deal of time for thinking while at work as an agent assigned to the Truth or Consequences gateway to the north. Winter especially left long gaps of time for reading and for reflecting on the matters and problems that came to his mind. Things moved more swiftly in the warm months, when the Texans began their migrations, but often enough this stretch of highway could be empty for long periods of time nevertheless, whether in summer or winter.

Tonight Big Bill was thinking about the grandfather he had never met in life but who hung like a ghost around his family all his years. While the feelings of his parents always remained permanently closed off from him, his father kept trunks full of newspaper clippings and photographs telling about social foment in days gone by. When he asked his mother about the contents of the storage, she only shook her head and clenched tight her jaw. But the trunks and boxes were never off limits.

By the time he entered high school he had figured out that his parents were the offspring of union workers who had somehow ended up in Texas in the 1930s following years of intense and sometimes dangerous activity throughout the country. Like many other children of activist parents, neither his mother nor his father wanted any part of that life. Leaving Texas for New Mexico, they constructed a world for themselves almost immune to outside events. Every day they went out to teach in the local schools—his father a biology teacher and his mother in the English department—and every evening they returned home together, where after dinner and dishes were done they attended to their own affairs. In short, political issues were never a topic of discussion at the dinner table.

As a child, Little Bill, as he was then called, would sometimes ask who the people were whose faces were fading to yellow on posters downstairs in the basement or who posed in cracking photographs hung on the walls there. Men in these photos often held their arms high in victory salutes, happy and exuberant. None of the pictures carried more than a name or a set of names, and none of the names meant anything to Little Bill.

They had no relatives near Carlsbad, where they lived. There were only a few special occasions when someone from the family passed through and stopped by. It was then that Little Bill put his ear to the door or stood quietly by in order to glean what he could about who he was and where his parents really came from. It was important for him to learn these things, but he did not quite understand exactly why it became so important to him. Further, it seemed that the more he was determined to find answers, the more remote his parents became.

One could not really say that Little Bill grew obsessed with the question of his origins. In truth, his interest came and went, and years might go by without flashes of interest developing into insistent questioning of his parents. If anything, he was absorbed throughout his childhood with another family, the Trujillo family, which lived across the street.

Little Bill could not remember a time when he was not involved with the activities of the Trujillo family. When he was a baby and before entering kindergarten he spent every day all day long with the numerous children and adults who made up the always noisy and boisterous family. In time he himself felt to be one of the many children of the brood. He could not recall when he was not in the Trujillo swirl of things, even when he was at home with his parents, since he would be either arriving from or returning soon to the Trujillo household. The home of his parents, his own house, was merely a quiet haven where he would remain until he could leave again for the whirlwind life of the Trujillos.

Looking back at those days it seemed to him that his very existence depended on the Trujillos. His own home was neat, white, ordinary, and benevolent but stolidly remote and emotionally distant. In his memory of his childhood years, his own home by contrast was only a place to sleep and to have Sunday dinner. That was all.

He had no dog.

In the Trujillo household, everything was utterly chaotic. The fields in back of the house were an enchanted garden of rusting cars and trucks, an alfalfa patch, rabbits, sheep, dogs with continuous litters of puppies, cats and kittens, fighting cocks and hens and chicks, a tank of goldfish guarded over by a plaster *Virgen* in half a bathtub upended, and piles of boards, firewood, and pipe. In other words, the Trujillos had everything any boy could want, including seven boys and three girls. Nothing was lacking. And what was more, in the Trujillo household anyone could touch, move, inspect, and use anything, anything at all. Nothing was inherently sacred and untouchable. Nor was orderliness considered something essential in the conduct code of the Trujillos.

But passing through his high school years, he found himself spending more time at home, mostly because it was a quiet place in which to read, something nearly impossible to do in the busy Trujillo home, where too many distractions took time away from homework. Sometimes in his own house he would spend time with his father in the basement workshop fashioning a table leg or a footstool. It was then that he tried again to learn more about his family, his predecessors. Yet it was difficult to break the silence of his father, who was always evasive though never angry.

By the time he reached his first year of high school, the name Little Bill no longer made sense. Almost overnight he grew larger than his parents, who, for whatever reason, seemed dismayed by it. He knew so little about what went through their minds, yet he somehow sensed they were not surprised that he grew so tall and massive. It was not they who first called him Big Bill, but once it started, it stuck with him forever.

The football coaches pleaded with him to join the team from the time he was a seventh grader. The coaches did not know what kind of life he led either in class or outside school hours. They didn't understand that Big Bill had been rejected permanently and irrevocably by the Anglo kids because of his close association with the Trujillos and their Chicano friends. It was clear to Big Bill that he would never be welcome in the locker room under those circumstances. The only way he could conceive of joining a team would be if his family moved to another town or city where he could start anew and not be pegged as a "greaser lover." But there was no possibility of that.

Furthermore, Big Bill was no hypocrite. He was grateful for the fullness of life that the Trujillos had openheartedly given him. He came to recognize, too, that although his large exterior was Anglo, his interior was to a large extent Chicano.

Having decided where his loyalties lay, Big Bill passed through secondary school pretty much an alien to most of his classmates, especially when his Chicano companions began to quit school or were pushed out onto the job market in their junior or senior years. He was a member of the marching band, though, towering over the rest of the musicians, mostly Chicanos, by at least a foot. There were no uniform trousers with long enough legs to fit him, so usually he was allowed to wear blue jeans with the pseudo-military jacket, to the enjoyment and occasional laughter of the spectators at the games. This did not bother him. He played the tuba, and they laughed at it. This did not bother him. His roll call name was William Williams, which evoked mirth, too. This did not bother him either.

His addiction to reading intensified as the Trujillo children went off into the military, got married, or looked for work in other towns. The house was almost always empty, and it was during this time that he followed his curiosity into the attic and the dusty trunks under the eaves. There he finally met his family's history or, at least, the principle members of his antecedents. His parents neither urged him to explore the trove nor discouraged him from investigating.

It took weeks, even months, to pore over the books, pamphlets, journals, and newspapers that had been thrown hurriedly and helter-skelter into the boxes. He found a multitude of pamphlets and literature produced by unions, radical groups, and political parties. In addition to flyers of all sorts, there were crepe paper streamers tucked into the corners and flags designed with hammer and sickle. A cap carried the legend WORKERS OF THE WORLD. There were several copies of a little red book titled *Songs of the IWW: To Fan the Flames of Discontent*. In one copy Big Bill found an inserted leaf laying out the philosophic stand of another group, which included the mandate "Abolition of the System of Salaries."

Whatever emotion Big Bill may have felt, he found himself smiling darkly at the notion that his cautious and reserved parents ever had such radical spirits as those in the attic. Nothing that he saw or read had any continuity with what he knew of his parents. These trunks contained mementos of an explosive epoch in the country's past when unionism and revolutionary movements flourished throughout the world. Sometimes while leafing through the yellowed papers, he almost sensed the roar of the crowds and the clang of metal against metal.

But the most intriguing material he came across was the large quantity of newspaper clippings that spoke of a Big Bill Haywood, a name almost like his own—Bill Haywood Williams. And he, too, was a "Big Bill," naturally so. How could he not ask who this person was whose name he carried? This could be no coincidence.

In addition to this startling find, he pulled out many clippings about a Joe Hill. Who could this be? Who exactly are all these people, what were they up to really, and why store away this thrilling archive of documents and souveniers? About Joe Hill, there was a story describing his trial and execution in Utah. A story from Chicago said that when his body was taken there for the funeral the crowd numbered thirty thousand. Clipped to it was a copy of his will sent to Bill Haywood, which he found quaintly old-fashioned but so very human and without pretensions.

> My will is easy to decide,
> For there is nothing to divide.
> My kin don't need to fuss and moan,—
> "Moss does not cling to a rolling stone."
> My body? Ah, if I could choose,
> I would to ashes it reduce,
> And let the merry breezes blow
> My dust to where some flowers grow.
> Perhaps some fading flower then
> Would come to life and bloom again.

This is my last and final will,
Good luck to all of you,

Joe Hill

Once he had gone through all the papers stored in the boxes, the moment came when Big Bill felt it necessary at last to confront his parents and demand explanations. This was the hard part: they had spent so much time shielded by evasions that it would be difficult to interrogate them. But finally the day arrived, and even though he did in fact receive some actual responses, more questions were raised than were answered. Unless he wanted to dedicate himself right away to the study of unionism in the United States, Big Bill would have to settle for the minimal responses that his parents deigned to give him.

For now he had to stitch it all together as best he could, knowing at last that he was grandson of the most powerful and influential man in the history of the North American union movement, the legendary Big Bill Haywood. The woman who was his grandmother was an organizer, a friend of Emma Goldman, and a fighter for women's rights. She refused to marry Big Bill Haywood and held on to her own name even though she gave birth to his son, whom she named Joseph Hillstrom Williams after Joe Hill, whose real name was Joseph Hillstrom. This man, this Joseph Hillstrom Williams, his own father, met his mother at Blair Mountain, Justice County, West Virginia, where President Harding's troops massacred the striking miners, extinguishing the bloodiest workers' rebellion in the history of the United States. His parents were too young to be recognized and marked for death among the leaders of District 17 of the Miners Union. They fled and survived by going into hiding, keeping invisible at first out of fear, and later, when there was no longer any danger, by habit. Their spirits crushed by having witnessed the suppression of the labor movement, they drew together and distanced themselves from the world in which they had once lived.

His father shared a few other things with him, a copy of the letter that Joe Hill had sent from prison to young Bill's grandfather and a red kerchief. The letter read:

GOODBYE, BILL:

I die like a true rebel. Don't waste any time mourning—organize! It is a hundred miles from here to Wyoming. Could you arrange to have my body hauled to the state-line to be buried? I don't want to be found dead in Utah.

Joe Hill

His father explained that the red bandanna was the insignia the strikers wore around their necks at Blair Mountain and that it was from this that the term "red neck" came about.

"And so," he smiled warmly at Bill with a twinkle of light dancing in his eyes, "when someone calls you a redneck, son . . . be proud of it!"

■ ■ ■

With time, Big Bill earned a scholarship to the university and commenced his search for the political origins and philosophies of unionism. He was active during the 1970s when still a student in anti-Vietnam demonstrations and various civil rights efforts. He would tramp through the mesas and valleys of Rio Arriba looking for the hidden soul of this beautiful land. It was during one of these forays that he met Pablo Martínez, who was then deeply engrossed in the struggle for the preservation of the Hispanic land grants. He also met Pilar Valles y Martínez.

The meeting was by pure happenstance. Big Bill was walking along the river on a dusty path through the falling golden leaves of the cottonwoods one autumn day. He approached a set of menacing signs meant to keep people away. He smiled at the first ones and began laughing out loud as he progressed from one to the next. His laugh was strong and deep. By then he had reached a small ranch house in front of which stood a woman who seemed planted in the soil, hands on hips in a belligerent manner.

He hailed her in Spanish and wished her good day. *"Buen día."*

She looked at him with hostility in her eyes.

He asked her if last night's frost had hurt her tomato crop.

She remained quietly hostile.

Angry barking dogs stormed up threateningly near.

He bent toward them to scratch their ears and stroke their shoulders.

She watched in indignation.

Then she addressed him. In English.

"Can't you read your own language?"

He let off stroking the dogs and straightened up. "Of course," he replied.

"The signs say 'Keep Away Gringos!'"

"Yes, that's what I read."

"So, what are you doing here? Why don't you go away and leave us alone?"

He replied, *"Porque no soy gringo."*

The woman dropped her arms to her sides and looked at him guardedly. Her eyes told her one thing and her ears another.

"Wait here," she told him, shrugging her shoulders and walking away toward the barn. There she called out her husband, Pablo Martínez. They approached Big Bill.

"Tell that to him," she instructed Big Bill.

■ ■ ■

The friendship between the Martínezes and Big Bill began with that storm and continued thereafter through the years as calmly and strongly as a deep river. They often worked long into the night on pamphlets and newsletters about land grant issues which they distributed through contacts up and down the valley to both borders.

It was Big Bill who found his friend Pablo's body pinned under a car on the west mesa.

After that Big Bill moved to Washington, D.C., to study at Georgetown University and to use the library at the Department of Labor. He returned to Rio Abajo knowing at last who he truly was, where he came from, and what he wanted to do in his life as a result of his studies.

With time he married a Chicana who appeared to be Anglo but was in fact one of the Belén Castillos, known along the river for their special beauty.

Big Bill was considered an incredible find by the U.S. Immigration and Naturalization Service—La Migra—which was always on the lookout for Anglos who could speak the local Spanish, those few whose native language was Spanish and not simply veterans of four years of language classes in high school. He was expected to rise rapidly through the ranks.

His first posting was situated south of Truth or Consequences. He and his wife were now neighbors of the Valles family in Mesilla. Slowly and thoughtfully they constructed a traditional ranchito of eighteenth-century style with the help of skilled Mexican nationals.

Their friendship took off immediately when Carlos mentioned that he was the grandson of Big Bill Haywood, a man that El Indio Jesús considered one of the great heroes of universal history. Not much time passed before they were hashing out the tragic story of Big Bill's death in Moscow, where he had sought asylum from political persecution in America. Because he had run out of money, the radical journalist John Reed returned to Russia to deliver the ransom required by the bondsmen when Big Bill was detained there. El Indio Jesús, Carlos, Pilar, and Big Bill argued endlessly over the concepts of asylum and sanctuary, on which so many immigrants to America had counted for their survival. Somehow, they thought, the ideal of sanctuary had become redefined beyond recognition through the years. It needed fixing, they believed. They discussed the gross inconsistencies in the perception of politicians who demanded the U.S. borders be closed except to a chosen few, forgetting that most of their forefathers—Irish, German, Jews, Hungarians, English, whatever nationality—had fled political and economic oppression in the same way as those now seeking the same from Latin America and Southeast Asia. What caused them sadness was the apparent amnesia of second and later generations of immigrants, amnesia that allowed them to dictate without humility the conditions with which later would-be immigrants must cope in order to enter the country.

It was long conversations such as these with people holding ideas so much like his own that finally brought Big Bill to enlist in the informal sanctuary movement.

And now, this night, he would supervise the transfer to a place of relative security some of the most desperate and worthy refugees of the twentieth century.

■ ■ ■

The moon sailed high while the van crawled along the highway toward the government trailer. Big Bill got up off the chair from behind the desk, walked to the doorway, and signaled the van to go on. The van with its human cargo continued to climb the Jornada del Muerto.

It had passed safely through Checkpoint Charlie.

La Majada

"Paginas diez y once, diez, diez . . . y once! diez y once, diez, diez y once . . ."

The young man leapt out of a terror-filled space that could not have been sleep. He swung his head about, wondering where he was. He began to rise. His red hair looked black in the dim light.

El Indio Jesús slid from the passenger seat in the front of the van and grasped his struggling shoulders. He made comforting sounds, gentle sounds, to calm, to soothe.

The refugee's eyes were like a horse's in a fire, beyond sense and reason.

He and El Indio Jesús wrestled behind the pastor's seat, the driver's seat.

Then the frantic movements stopped. There was no noise save the drone of the van motor. The old woman in the far corner of the van did not move.

El Indio Jesús spoke in a language that mixed Spanish with the universal sounds of caressing the wounded.

The young man breathed deeply.

In Spanish he shed pieces of his terror.

■ ■ ■

You must understand, he said, that the elections which your country forced upon our people gave those whom you keep in power a most effective tool to find out who and where the people are who oppose the regime. What was created was a census of death. The elections allowed us to choose among those who had brought such evils to our land. We were to choose one of the men who had brought us to this terrible time.

When the election time came, we were torn between two fears: that the census being taken would identify those of us who would be considered threatening, and that if we did not vote, we would certainly die soon because our *cédulas* failed to have the voting stamps on pages ten and eleven. Without the stamps, the death squads, the hired killers, the police, or the army could stop us and do with us what they wished.

You must understand that I am the last male of my family. My father was a government minister deposed by political forces controlled by your country. He refused to flee to Mexico or Cuba, but chose to stay. He said that he would stand like a tree in a city park whose fall, if it came, would be seen by everyone, and those who used the ax against him would be recognized by the people. He said this many times. It appeared in the newspapers so often during the period of the overthrow that the people began to call him "El Cedro," the cedar tree.

In the years that followed, my family was hounded out of the cities where we had spread, our modest family of shopkeepers, a dentist, a university professor. It seemed as though everyone who carried our family name was considered to be the enemy, and once the faceless ones who made such decisions had done so, there could be no hope for our future. Not that we understood at the start what was happening: we did not. But when one or two of my uncles lost his business, my cousins in city government were fired, the neighbors closing their doors when we came near, we came to recognize that something far beyond our abilities to change was taking place.

Then they began killing us. First, we lost our little stores or little jobs. That was one thing. And we began moving back to the mountains and the village where our family began. It was time to gather. But many did not arrive home. Some we heard about, some we did not. Others came in slowly, perhaps not whole families anymore but just a mother with my little cousins or an old father-in-law. About eight of our families came.

My father remained in the city. El Cedro would not be moved.

As the day came nearer for the elections, he spent much time deciding the course he must take. Without telling me his decision, he took me into his study and told me what I must do.

He said that although he had served his country to the best of his ability, for reasons he did not understand, the political powers had turned away from him and, because of who we are, from all of our family members. There was no further hope for trying to change things, because he had tried all the ways he could think of and they had failed. It was like some blind thing, something that kills without seeing, hearing, or feeling. But he was certain it would not stop until we were all dead.

And so he had made arrangements for as many family members as possible to look for asylum in other countries. While some of the family members who did not appear in our village where we gathered were presumed dead, others had already fled over the borders.

With the help of many nameless people from my country and yours and elsewhere, his plan had been put into action. On a *ranchito* called La Majada small airplanes were making regular stops to leave off supplies for the villagers and to take out our people, a few at a time.

He did not know how many had been evacuated by then, but this he insisted I do: that I must be responsible for his mother, my grandmother, who carries in her heart and mind the history of our family. He said the history must not be lost.

And he said that our blood must not be lost for all time. There-fore, I must save myself as the carrier of the blood.

He placed this responsibility upon me when I am not yet a man and would rather fight with the mountain people against those who have killed my family members for reasons we have never known.

■ ■ ■

He wept then. He wept with searing rasps threatening to tear out his lungs. El Indio Jesús held him in his arms.

In time, he continued.

■ ■ ■

I did not go into the mountains yet but stayed in the city with my father.

The day of the elections came. The law said that every person in the country must vote except the children. But in the city, the government set up only thirteen voting places for more than a million and a half people.

As I said before, it was difficult to decide whether to vote or not. Our papers are examined many times each day by anyone who thinks they are in authority, whether it is the army or the police or even the fire department. There is no help for it, and there is no point in resisting when asked, no matter how ques-tionable the person's authority may be. I have been stopped for my papers by the army, the national guard, by the treasury police, by everyone, it seems.

Pages ten and eleven must be stamped on our *cédulas* or we can be detained forever. Perhaps until executed. So the lines at the voting places began to form long before the sun reached the edge of the farthest hills above the city. When the sun got clear of the hills, it was suddenly hot, and it became hotter. The people in line were wiping their foreheads but were generally patient to creep forward toward the voting boxes.

I argued with my father about the importance of getting the stamp on his *cédula* no matter how he felt about the elections. He argued with me point for point. At last, he simply ordered me to go to the voting place and cast a ballot. It did not matter for whom the ballot was cast so long as the stamp was affixed to the pages.

It was late afternoon when I joined the line. The government reported that the people were so eager to vote that they began pushing and shoving each other in a demonstration of patriotic cooperation. But that was not the truth: they knew full well that it would be considered an act of treason if they did not vote, and that the stamp meant the difference between life and death.

I carried my father's *cédula*, not my own. He did not know that I had taken it. Our names are the same and in the press of people trying to vote, I hoped that I could pass it through without challenge. It was more important to me that he have the correct identification papers: I would work out something for myself later. It was he, not me, who stood in the greatest danger without credentials.

But it was no use.

Before I reached the boxes, night had fallen and the people in charge let the soldiers take the ballots to their headquarters to be counted. They would not let the rest of us vote. Nor would they stamp our *cédulas*.

They turned us away, laughing at us. They thought our despair was funny.

Perhaps my clumsy attempt to protect my father would not have worked. I will never know. But what happened then burns in my mind like acid.

A few days later, late in the day, some of the militia who were from our neighborhood came down our avenue shouting and firing off their rifles at anything that caught their attention. They were no more than corrupted *campesinos* who still carried their *machetes* slung from their belts. They now lived in a style quite different from before and they were as drunk on their good fortune as if they were on *pulque*.

My father turned the corner just then, returning from the library where he sought answers in the writings of the past. The militiamen stopped shooting and fastened their attention upon him. They swaggered down the cobblestones to where he had slowed to a stop.

The leader recognized him, not from his past life as a government minister but as a neighborhood man of distinction. His calm disdain infuriated him. He shouted at him that he knew who he was and that it amounted to nothing now that the correct people were in charge of things. He became reddened and his voice climbed higher and higher until his harangue became screams of rage.

From my window I could do nothing but watch as they marched my father into our courtyard. I ran to another window—and will regret that I did for the rest of my life.

The leader was screaming that if my father was indeed El Cedro, it was time that he be cut down to make way for the younger trees of the country. Pleased with his cleverness, he carried his joke farther. He had the others tie my father's hands above his head and then raise him off the ground where he hung in the gateway. He then ordered them to use their *machetes*, to start at his feet and chop the old cedar down "for the good of the country." My father lived as pieces of himself lay about on the ground until their chopping reached his heart.

■ ■ ■

Again the young man was stopped by a flush of despair that threatened to smother him. El Indio Jesús cradled him in his arms.

Yet he insisted on finishing.

■ ■ ■

I ran. I ran as far and as fast as I could. I gave no thought to anyone else. My own safety was all. It was everything.

I am not certain how long it took me to reach our village. I found my grandmother in an ocean of blood.

She told me that army troops came again and again to the village and each time killed more of our family members and neighbors. They killed not only in that village but in other nearby villages, too, and on the more isolated farms in the region. Even as she talked to me I could see wisps of black smoke spiraling up from a number of places on the side of La Majada. The troops burned the bodies as they went along.

■ ■ ■

The grandmother had been listening to the young man's recitation in the darkness. She pulled herself into a sitting position now and cleared her throat before speaking.

■ ■ ■

My grandson has told you much, but I would add what happened in our villages.

Our family came together as best we could. There were nearly fifty of us there. I know because I directed the cooking and other preparations. It was a strange time. We were happy to see each other all together for the first time in many years, but at the same time, death hung around us. Many were missing.

The army came with no warning. The soldiers never talked with us. They just began shooting. They kept shooting until no one moved anymore. Then they left.

I crept out from my kitchen wood box and found some of my neighbors leaving their hiding places to see what was left of our people. There were bodies everywhere: old, young, it did not matter. A big pile of bodies was at the edge of the plaza.

But then we heard the soldiers returning and we hid again. When we came out this time, the bodies in the pile were on fire, with kerosene smoke filling the village.

Over the next two days, the soldiers came back several times. We were too afraid to find out what other villages and farms they went to. We made guesses from where the smoke made black chimneys.

On the third day, the guerillas came into the village to tell us that they were sorry they did not protect us from this ugly thing. They said that they were farther away in the mountains and could not get back in time to be of help.

Our people just looked at them. There was nothing to be said.

We learned from the guerillas that one of their most important leaders had been killed in the massacre, as well. She and some others who were involved with bringing weapons in and taking people out to safety had been slaughtered at the small farm high up on the side of La Majada. They said that there was a Catholic nun among the dead, too, and someone who was an American, perhaps Spanish or Indian, they did not know. And the farmer was hacked to death—Señor Augustín.

■ ■ ■

La Señora dropped into her thoughts and remained silent for many minutes. Then, as if rousing herself from a bad dream, she plucked her grandson's sleeve.

"*Pregúntales.*"

"*Después. Después.*"

La Jornada del Muerto

La Jornada de Muerto was as empty as bones for as far as the eye could see in the lustrous moonlight. No lights of villages or truck stops pricked out of the distance. Off both shoulders, endless drifts of sterile sand begrudgingly put up creosote bushes so smart that they sealed themselves off from others of their kind by poisoning a ring around their root system so that nothing could grow nearby, even their offspring.

The driver sat hunched and tense over the wheel, his eyes aching from vigilance, covering the highway behind through mirrors and the highway ahead with a mixture of vision and imagination. He could not say which landscape was eerier. Each set of headlights that stung the mirror from behind could be a possible interception, and every vehicle pulled off to the side of the road when they approached could be danger in waiting.

Danger came from more than just the Immigration people. In fact, La Migra was in some ways a lesser consideration. Even the state and county police could be handled occasionally if one kept one's head. Compounding and confusing the danger was the possibility of vigilantes stoked up on beer and bravado in saloons bent on "cleaning out them damn wetbacks once and for all." Different from them but more ruthless were bounty hunters, who had preyed upon travelers on this stretch of terrain for time out of mind. These jackals carried a heritage as long as there have been refugees seeking sanctuary on the Jornada del Muerto. Each of these acted with impunity.

Their vulnerability meant only one thing: they must not under any circumstance be stopped by anyone. The point was simple: being stopped could mean death, death now or death later. It was all the same.

This was not the pastor's first run. Each time became more difficult for him, more laden with tension, because now he could imagine more ambush sites, more places where they could be waylaid. The seeming flatness of the land was deceptive. There were countless arroyos cut by rainstorms but dry now where vehicles could be waiting to intercept them.

Headlights shown in the rearview mirror suddenly. Truck? Car? If a truck, what kind? Pickups and vans must be closely monitored. A car? Headlight conformation: model? make? recent? Was that a luggage rack on top or a bank of bubble lights?

There must be no variation from the fifty-five-mile-an-hour speed limit, neither faster nor slower. Either held the possibility of being stopped by the police for a routine check. Did a taillight go out? Did a nail in the customs driveway pierce a tire? What about the clutch and pressure plate? Did the van really have another thirty thousand miles? or one mile? The sound of the engine, was there something different, a new sound added to the others? The headlight on the left seems dimmer than the other, than before: an electrical problem?

The fuzz buster glowed from the visor above his forehead. Its hum was alternately comforting and maddening. Was it really working? Was the hum masking other noises that should be heard—the motor or an approaching car or truck? Could it detect *every* police radar unit?

It was a hot night, but a thankful coolness flowed in the open windows. Behind him whispers rustled through the sticky blackness—the tenor voice of the young man. When the whispers stopped, the humming silence was oppressive, and the pastor wished with all his might that the young man would continue his story, even though the pastor could not hear him. He was certain from experience that whatever the story, the whole of it must be told, and that there was no one better to disclose it to than El Indio Jesús, the man of measureless compassion. Sometimes he could hear the older man's soothing voice almost crooning along with the climbing terror of the young man's rasping phonemes, gliding him back to safer ranges.

Each time, each flight to sanctuary, there was the compunction for a refugee to tell the story that their conveyors in truth did not wish to hear. They did not need convincing that their effort was needful, was correct. The narrations only inflicted additional pangs of care and fear for their ward's safety.

The pastor knew that guilt drove these confessions in the back of the van, guilt that safety may be near while lives of horror still continued for those left behind. The burden they placed upon the listeners, so often El Indio Jesús, had become mountainous. It could crush.

The old woman whimpered out of her sleep that was nearly coma, punctuating the young man's thread of sounds. The pastor could hear them move toward her to soothe the pain.

Lights behind, again. Two sets. Three. A convoy? A staged raid about to descend on them? Now a helicopter whisked over the crest of a dune. It paused, then headed toward the vehicles gaining on the van.

He lost sight of it. The vehicles also vanished behind a slow curve and dip. He began to sweat profusely. Imagination flirted with the instinct to be prescient. Either one could help or hurt.

Up a rise, the lights were seen again, a bit closer. Were they at equal distances from each other, traveling together? Why would three vehicles be bunched together on this empty Interstate? It could only mean they were a convoy. It must mean that. Yes.

No. The second one seems to be pulling into the left lane. No. Wrong. It was the curve that made it seem so. They are still pretty much together. Equidistant, perhaps.

The helicopter. Where is it now? It's not in sight. Yes, it is. Over to the southwest, skirting the low hills. It has a spotlight on, raking the hilltops there. What are they looking for? Who are they looking for?

Ahead, his headlights picked out red rear reflectors. A slow-moving vehicle or someone stopped along the side of the highway? Too far to tell yet, dropping into a small arroyo that blocked his front and back views.

El Indio Jesús climbed into the passenger seat next to the pastor.

"I am beginning to smell you, my friend. It is the smell of worry."

"Yes, perhaps. Back and front. Tell me how you read it."

They peered intently through the windows and into the several mirrors. El Indio Jesús slipped out of his seat and made his way through to the back of the van to look out the rear. He crouched there a long time, using the peephole drilled through the back door to survey the oncoming vehicles.

So intent were the two men that they failed to see that they had driven into a desert downpour of enormous virulence. It was upon them with crashing power and blinding cracks of lightning. Wind and water became one, flinging pounding waves against the side of the van with such force that it seemed surely to be in danger of being turned over. The pastor swiveled left and right over the steering wheel, attempting to keep the van on the highway. But nothing, absolutely nothing could be seen through the windshield, the darkness now shimmering as sheets of hail mixed with rain slid faster than the wipers could clear. Enough water came in the side windows before they were rolled up to leave the smell of wet earth and ozone to mingle together. The staccato of rain and hail on the van's roof and sides, added to the roar of thunder and smash of lightning, came to be nearly deafening. The van could not proceed another yard.

The pastor edged the van over onto the sloping shoulder in blindness, hoping that he had not chosen a place where a flash flood would come through and sweep them away. In such blindness there was no way to tell. They could not see one inch beyond their windows save for dim glowing coming up from the headlights.

He turned off the motor. He glanced at El Indio Jesús, whom he could barely make out in the gloom. Turning toward the rear of the van, he could barely perceive the whites of the young man's eyes, and he wondered if he actually saw them or was merely sensing his presence and giving shape to it with perceptions beyond sight.

The red reflectors they had seen before could be picked out from time to time now that the rain blasts were coming more in waves than as a solid sheet. The car appeared abandoned and perhaps stripped.

Now the lights of the three vehicles that were behind them inched past, going no faster than five miles an hour. The caravan turned out to be snowbirds, retirees presumably, traveling from Arizona to Michigan, as their license plates gave reason to assume. They often traveled in such convoys up this Interstate.

The pastor and El Indio Jesús looked at each other and took deep breaths, smiling wryly at the expenditure of needless tension. There was no profit in discussing it even if there had been enough lessening of the storm's roar to allow for it.

In twenty minutes the worst of the barrage was over. Lightning strikes on transformers illuminated the terrain, showing that a roiling flood was passing not more than ten yards in front and five yards below. When the van's headlights were flipped back on, they could make out debris of all kinds churning down the arroyo.

The storm slackened off nearly as fast as it had come upon them. They continued northward. Through thinning rain they made out lights up ahead and knew they were approaching the rest stop south of Socorro, named for the merciful pueblo it once was.

As soon as they cleared the crest of the last dune before the rest stop, however, they saw that a roadblock had been set up funneling all northbound traffic into the parking area. State police cars lined the barricades. Officers with flashlights motioned the incoming vehicles to pull over and stop where they indicated.

The pastor and El Indio Jesús glanced at each other. A split-second decision must be made.

El Indio Jesús slid into the rear of the van saying, "Let's try to face them down."

The van rolled to a stop and all was silence save the thrum of the motor. Reverend Dutton switched off the ignition and rolled down the window. The rain had stopped.

To the far right was a knot of squad cars with several officers standing by. The one who had signaled them to pull over now approached the van.

"Good evening, sir," he said.

"Good evening, officer."

"We won't detain you long. May I please see your license, vehicle registration, and proof of insurance?"

"Yes," responded the pastor, "of course."

The state policeman played his flashlight over the documents he was given. He walked to the rear of the van to see if the registration and license plate matched, then returned.

"Thank you, Reverend Dutton."

He handed the documents back through the open window, into which streamed the sultry creosote-scented air now conflicting with the artificial air inside the van. The sudden cessation of highway sound and motion left a kind of tingling feeling in the ears, in the feet, at the ends of fingers. The exchange of documents seemed unnaturally slowed, as though underwater. The van occupants were pitched to excruciatingly high tension in the viscous dark.

The officer stepped away from the window. Very slowly, very deliberately he circled around the entire vehicle, taking time to illuminate the sides, the undercarriage, and the rear of the van. When he completed the round he returned to the driver's window.

"Will you step out please, Reverend Dutton?"

The pastor suppressed an urge to look over his shoulder toward El Indio Jesús in the rear.

"Of course, officer," he replied.

He unbuckled his seat belt, opened the door, and stepped out onto the parking area's tarmack, shutting the door behind him.

"Please open the door again, Reverend Dutton," he asked.

The pastor hesitated just long enough to telegraph alarm.

"Of course, officer."

He took his time, deliberately fumbling with the door handle. The door opened but the cab light did not illuminate. Carlos had disconnected it intentionally.

The officer approached the vehicle once the pastor had moved away from the door as he had indicated. At the open door he ran the light beam along the front of the cab area and then into the rear of the van as far as the angle would permit.

His flashlight caught one thing and held: El Indio Jesús' face.

There was no movement. There was no breathing. Time stopped. The thousands of muscles holding the bodies of all four people tightened to the breaking point, the officer, El Indio Jesús, and the two refugees. Hot wet pungent air continued to roll into the van.

The flashlight snapped off. The officer withdrew from the driver's doorway.

"Please ask everyone in the van to step down, Reverend Dutton."

There was a pause.

"My grandmother needs to use the restroom, officer." Reverend Dutton's voice was suddenly authoritative.

The officer nodded. He pointed toward the toilets.

Reverend Dutton strode to the rear and threw open one of the doors. Long minutes passed before the tiny fragile woman appeared. He gently helped her down to the wet pavement. There she clung to the slender man. Slowly they paced to the restrooms.

Next El Indio Jesús stepped down.

"*Buenos tardes, Don Jesús.*"

"*Buenos tardes,*" El Indio Jesús replied.

At that moment the young man descended.

"May I introduce you to the next Diego Rivera? This is a muralist in the making," gesturing to the youth.

"*Con mucho gusto. Sería un placer.* Yes indeed," replied the officer.

"Would you like to see a small sample of his work? There are a few pieces here in the van. He will be exhibiting in Pojoaque next week."

The officer gestured with his flashlight that El Indio Jesús and the young man should step back away from the van. He then opened the other door. He stroked his light around the interior. Briefly it touched the boxes and suitcases inside.

"May I see some identification, *por favor, Don Jesús?*"

"*Por supuesto.*" He handed over some cards, a license.

The officer scanned the documents under the ray of the flashlight and returned them. He looked thoughtfully at the youth for several seconds but did not ask for his identification.

Reverend Dutton and his "grandmother" returned from the restrooms. He and the officer helped her up into the van and settled her in a seat. With a nod from the officer the young man joined her.

"You may board now, Reverend Dutton. Thank you for your cooperation.

"*Don Jesús,* will you come with me please? Only one more thing . . ."

As the two moved to the front of the van a car with flashing lights and siren blaring splashed past them and drew up so close to the other officers gathered together that some of them jumped away. It idled there, sound and lights still activated. The men in the group moved restlessly, randomly, but stayed close. No door opened.

Then the lights and siren ended abruptly. So did the motor. Nothing else happened for long minutes. Everyone's attention was fixed on the car sitting dead in the roadblock's pulsing signal lights.

The door on the driver's side opened slowly. A long lean figure emerged. In one smooth motion the man placed a white Stetson on his head. Leaving the car door open he walked over to the group of men. The officer with El Indio Jesús motioned for him to stay where he was and then left, approaching the tall man.

El Indio Jesús stayed put, watching.

The tall man appeared to be listening to the officer. His height and the white hat made his movements easy to make out as he looked at the van and back to the officer and once again to the van.

Then he disengaged himself from the officer. He walked toward El Indio Jesús slowly, almost languidly.

El Indio Jesús smiled and addressed him. *"Buenos tardes, Capitán Beserra. ¿Que tal?"*

Jack Spencer laughed quietly.

"I don't think I will ever get used to your polite insolence, *mi amigo.*"

They stood looking at each other in the gloom, taking each other's measure once again as they had so many times before.

Spencer spoke. "It appears that you are on another of your useless missions of mercy, saving drowning rats from the swill of their own countries."

"Perhaps not rats but birds," El Indio Jesús rejoined, "birds who will fly and sing again someday."

"*¡Aii! Que dolor!* I am impressed not only by the high tone of your mission but also by the beauty of your imagery." But there was mockery in his voice. After a pause, he continued in a more serious vein.

"And what is so special about these particular birds that you would risk ten to twenty years of your life for them?"

El Indio Jesús reflected for a moment, then responded, "Nothing. Nothing at all. Or everything. I trust others. Unlike you, I can trust others. I don't make their judgments. My decisions are based on the goal, not so much on the means to the goal so long as I stay within my own standards."

"But if the means to your elevated goal are against the laws of this state and country, what then?" He paused. "I also have life-and-death responsibilities."

"Yes, I know," El Indio Jesús shot back quickly. "I know all about them. I know everything about your life-and-death responsibilities."

Spencer rolled back on his heels as he looked more intently at El Indio Jesús. Then, as if to lighten the tone, he chuckled. "Well, now, let's get back to your rats or birds. *¿Ahora que vamos a hacer?* What shall we do with them? I need to say but one word to these men here and—"

El Indio Jesús held up his hand in caution. "Back in Barelas you were taught many lessons as a child. Please forgive me if I sound like one of your teachers. But one of the lessons you missed or forgot was that this Interstate highway is less than fifty years old, and that it was the Camino Real—the Royal Road of the Spanish crown—for four hundred years, and before that it was the road to Chaco Canyon and freedom for centuries beyond memory.

"So what makes you and your ilk think you own, control, the conduit north and south used by people as their 'inalienable right' since the dawn of time? You and your laws—"

Spencer interrupted. "Look. You know what the law says. And I intend to see that it is enforced . . . with these men here."

El Indio Jesús took a breath and fixed his eyes on Spencer. "What if this law you speak of had been enforced at the time that your father was brought north from Chihuahua as a railroad scab? What then? Where would you be today?"

"That's enough. That's just enough." He looked over toward the group of officers to see if they had heard El Indio Jesús. "This garbage about the old days means nothing anymore. Barelas was leveled with urban renewal projects years ago. It doesn't exist . . . and neither does—"

El Indio Jesús raised his hand again in caution. He spoke quietly. "What you fail to understand is that Barelas is not a place. It is an idea. A spirit. What was once a place that we loved and that was destroyed has now been reborn from seeds sown throughout the valley and farther.

"And what is more, with each new so-called illegal alien the spirit of Barelas is strengthened. Each one who seeks freedom along this ancient road makes us all the stronger.

"But," he pauses, "none of this has any bearing on you any longer."

Spencer tensed. "What do you mean by all that? What are you suggesting? What's the point of all this?"

El Indio Jesús turned to the group of officers. "I will let them say it for me. Look." He pointed his chin toward the men. All of them were staring at El Indio Jesús and Spencer, focused on the two even though they were too far away to hear what was said.

Despite the half-light, all the men were unmistakably mestizos, descendants of Indian and Hispanic unions, male with female, female with male, across five centuries of intermingled blood and culture.

The men were waiting. They were patient.

Spencer turned back to El Indio Jesús. El Indio Jesús could not see his face now, the Stetson's rim casting too dark a shadow.

Spencer's voice was smaller now, but measured. "*¿Entonces? Que quiere decir?* What exactly are you implying?"

"The message should be clear even to you by this time, *Capitán.* You are among the people here, *la gente, la raza,* as you were in the barrio. You never learned to listen then. Nor did you learn to see with your eyes."

"See what? What are you raving on about?"

"Graffiti, Waldo. You are Waldo. Have you forgotten that?"

"That? That was just a kid's game . . ."

"The barrio has never forgotten. It never forgets."

"Forget what? What are you talking about? I am becoming very pissed with all your—"

"On the playground, you molested Miguel Olson's sister. That was Waldo I. Then, the second time—Waldo II—you betrayed Miguel Olson again so your gringo football team would win the tournament. You failed to understand that football was not the issue. What made it important on the one hand was the community's need, desire, to beat the gringos at their own silly game. For the first time.

"But no, your betrayal had everything to do with your own ego and very little to do with your football team. That is why you turned Miguel in to the police.

"You earned Waldo II then. The graffiti warned you. It was everywhere. And even all these years later, it can still be seen on some walls.

"Finally, when Waldo III went up on the walls—you must have seen it, you are not that unaware of the system—it meant that the community knew exactly who was responsible for the flood of drugs poisoning the minds and bodies of the youth in the barrio, your airmail deliveries, all that.

"Every time, you were warned about your behavior. Three warnings. Three Waldo warnings. Like Yankee baseball, three strikes and you're out.

"In this way, you have struck out, Jacobo Beserra. The barrios warned you with the public newspaper, the graffiti. The barrios have judged you. You will do the community no more harm. *Quien no oye consejos no llega a viejo.*"

Again El Indio Jesús turned toward the group of officers. He made a slight movement of his head. An officer, the one who had intercepted the van, detached himself and joined him.

Taking something out of pocket, El Indio Jesús said, "Here are two invitations to the Pojoaque exhibit opening. I hope you and your lovely *señora* will enjoy it."

With that he turned and walked back toward the van, leaving Spencer alone in the wet darkness.

Still walking, El Indio Jesús looked over his shoulder at the men once again. So did Spencer, rooted to the spot where he stood.

The men straightened up. They were ready. They knew what they would do next. Their dark eyes glistened in the pulsing light.

El Indio Jesús climbed into the van. The engine caught and the van slid out of the rest stop, swinging north into the night.

Silence bathed the van for a very long time.

Then the pastor drew an audible breath, which seemed to have tracked its way up the length of his body before expulsion.

"All right. What happened back there?" He turned to look quickly at El Indio Jesús and then back to the road.

After a considerable contemplative silence, El Indio Jesús answered.

"There," he said, "there we have witnessed the tragedy of the *grafiteros*. The best of them. Officer Trujillo, one of our very best. A tragedy. But today, perhaps, a blessing."

Again silence except for the road sounds filled the van as they continued to climb the concrete ribbon northward, ever maintaining the correct speed limit.

From the back of the van came the voice of the old woman directed to her grandson.

"Mijo, ¿estamos en los Estados Unidos?"

"Sí, Abuela."

"Pregúntales."

"Después, Después."

And Again

El Indio Jesús fought to come awake. He lay in Pilar's bed, tracing with his eyes the knots in the *vigas* above him for some minutes. Then he pulled himself up and went to take a second shower in as many hours as he had been there.

He found Pilar in the kitchen. Her face was gray and stony.

"You know, then."

"Yes."

"How?"

"Shortwave. I was monitoring it."

"Yes."

"All of them?"

He shrugged.

"Who? Tell me what you know."

He rubbed his face with a gnarled hand.

"Uncle Augustín. Angelica. Tony the World Traveler. Sister Lupe. Others."

"Who?"

"I don't know. Villagers. Dozens of them." He poured himself another cup of coffee. "No planes, though. They didn't intercept the flight."

"Your passengers told you? They saw it? They were there?"

"They are the last of their family. They were the last two to be taken out. The others were at the farm ready to go, by twos and threes. All dead. All." His hands roughly scrubbed his face. "And another La Majada stinks of death."

He leaned back in his chair at the table.

"Each thinks they are bringing the other out. La Señora thinks she is delivering her grandson to safety, and the grandson thinks he is saving his grandmother's life." He made a short chuckling sound. "All along the way, for miles and miles—and maybe for years, I don't know—she has wanted to ask us two questions."

"Us?"

"Not just you or me. The American people. The inhabitants of the United States of America."

"What are the questions?"

He sighed. "I couldn't see her very well in the darkness, but it felt as though her eyes were stabbing into me. She asked me, 'Don't your people know what your government is doing to my people?' And then she asked, 'If your people know what their government is doing, do they agree with it, support it?'"

Sipping his coffee, his mind flashed back to the concrete's whine under the tires along the endless Jornada del Muerto and the thick stillness of the inhabitants inside the van. Sometimes he could make out the old woman's face, ghastly green from the dashboard glow. She awaited his answer, but as the pause grew longer and longer, her eyes closed, then opened, and then closed at last into an exhausted doze.

His mind probed the questions tentatively, not bravely, because the answers to the questions went to the heart of what motivated him, caused him to live this strange life, a life so full in its experiences of, its witnessing of, the love of good people for one another while, at the same, driven by surging, roiling waters of anger—yes, hatred—for the thick band of brutality in the genetic makeup of the American culture and its people. His own bloodlines mocked his pretentions of being inherently, devotedly altruistic, because he recognized the glassy-eyed faces of the crazed Spanish looters who sired him over the shame of the ancient owners of this New/Old World who birthed him in anguished dread for the monsters or angels they were forced to create. Sometimes he forgave his heritage when he could see that by using the mental pathways of the dominating Europeans, he could transform the outcomes into helpfulness instead of selfishness. In this he understood the poignancy with which so many Americans and Europeans sought to rescue an old tarnished silver soul line nearly worn through.

■ ■ ■

El Indio Jesús drove his *caro troquita* south on Rio Grande Boulevard past Wells Market in Duranes. A whirring siren sailed out to him from behind. In the rearview mirror he could see the squad car gaining on him. He pulled over to the curb and stopped. So did the police car.

"Good morning, sir."

"Good morning, officer."

"May I see your license and vehicle registration, please?"

"Of course, officer."

Examining the papers El Indio Jesús gave him, the officer pushed his hat back from his forehead and said, "This is no registration. What is this?"

"It is a bill of sale, officer."

"This thing? He waved a dingy creased piece of paper.

"Yes, sir, it's a bill of sale."

"Well, it doesn't look like any bill of sale I've ever seen. And it sure as hell ain't no registration. Where's your registration?"

"That's all I have, officer. I just bought this car and the Motor Vehicle Department hasn't mailed back the title yet."

"And where's your proof of insurance? This state requires you to show that you have it, or else you have to have a surety bond or show me a cash deposit in the amount of twenty thousand dollars. Failure to have evidence of . . ."

He droned on and finally came to the end of his recitation.

"In other words, I'm going to have to take you down to the station. You have a right to . . ."

While waiting for the tow truck, they sat in the patrol car. The officer had one hand on the steering wheel and with the other he grasped the barrel of the shotgun that was pointed toward the ceiling.

Looking over his shoulder at El Indio Jesús seated in the back of the car, he said, "I just don't know about you people. Do you realize that you have been endangering the lives of good Christian people on their way to church this morning with that thing you call a car? It looks to me like you've been on a two-day drunk."

El Indio Jesús lowered his head and sighed.

■ ■ ■

On Monday morning, El Indio Jesús was released by the judge and placed on his own recognizance while serving out time in community service not with the Plaza Vieja priests but at the pleasure of the director of the mayor's graffiti removal campaign.

Glossary: Terms and Phrases

Abogado(s) — Lawyer(s)
Abrazo(s) — Embrace(s), hug(s)
Abuela — Grandmother
Acequia(s) — Irrigation canal, main canal
Adelante — Come In!; go in!; let's go!
Adiós — Good bye, (go with) God
Adobe(s) — Mud, mud bricks
Adobero — One who works with adobe
Ahora que vamos a hacer? — Now what are we going to do?
Ahora que voy a hacer? — Now what am I going to do?
Álamo(s) — Poplar tree(s)
Allá, allí — There
Amigo(s), amiga(s) — Friend(s)
Amiguito — Little friend
A mí me gusto mucho — I like it a lot
Amor, mi — Love, my love
Anglo — Non-Hispanic, Euroamerican
Aquí viene tu daddy — Here comes your daddy
Arroyo — Streambed, usually dry
Asociación de Señoras de la Sangre de Cristo — Women's Blood of Christ Association
Atufado — Maddeningly stoic

Auto intelectual	Originator of idea or plan
Bajada, la	Place where the land drops down
Barrio	Neighborhood, community
Basta	Enough, that is enough
Bien	Good, it is good
Bien hecho	Well done
Blanco(s)	Whites, Euroamericans
Blondi, la	The blond woman
La Blondi desbarató la compañia; a mí tambien	Blondie destroyed the company, and me, too
Bosque	Woods
Buena suerte	Good luck
Cabrito	Young male goat
Cabron(es)	He-goat, cuckold, fool
Caliche	White clay soil
Calientita	Hot tortilla
Camino Real	Royal Road
Campesino(s)	Country person, farmer, worker
Caña	Beer made from sugarcane
Cantar bien o cantar mal puede ser indiferente; pero estando entre la gente cantar bien o no cantar	To sing well or to sing poorly doesn't really matter; but among the people sing well or not at all
Capitán	Captain
Carga	Cargo, load
Carito	Little car
Carnal(es)	Blood brother(s)
Carne al carbón	Barbequed beef
Caro troquita	Handmade combination of car-truck; El Indio Jesus employs the local vernacular dropping the double r of carro
Carreta	Ox cart
Casa de los locos	Crazy house, home for the insane
Casita	Little house
Cedrito, el	Little cedar tree
Cedro, el	The cedar tree
Cédula	Identification certificate
Chico(s), chica(s)	Young man, men; young woman, women
Chicano(s), chicana(s)	Hispanics
Chili, rojo, verde	Chili, red, green
Chipita	Little jeep, pun on "jeep"

Chisme	Rumor, gossip, deliberate (?) lie
Chismero	Gossip monger
Chota, la	Slang for police
Cielo, mi	My heaven
Compadre(s)	Close friend(s)
Comandante	Major, commander
Como un trampe	Like a tramp
Con mucho gusto	With pleasure
Con su permiso	With your permission
Consentida	Pet, preferred one
Copita, la	Little cup, (brand of wine)
Correcto	Correct
Creo que sí	I believe so; I think so
Criado(s), criada(s)	Servant(s)
Cuate	Twin, brother, buddy
Cuidadito	Be a little careful
Culebras mestizas	Mixed species of snakes
Desaparecido(s)	Person(s) who have disappeared
Después	Later
Dichos son dichos	Sayings are only sayings
Dios, Dios mío	God, my god!
Disculpe la molesta pero	Sorry for bothering you but . . .
Don	Gentleman
Duende	Fearless, spiritually protected
EE.UU. fuera de America Central; de America del Norte	U.S. get out of Central America; of North America
Ejido	Landholding
Embajada	Embassy
Entonces	Then, well then, then what?
Entre una pasión y una locura estas tu	To me you are somewhere between passion and insanity
Escúchame	Listen to me
Espérate aqui	Wait here
Espérate un momento; . . . a la pared	Wait a moment; wait here at the wall
Esposo(s), esposa(s)	Husband(s), wife, wives
Esta bien, esta bien	It is okay; you are okay
Estamos en los Estados Unidos?	Are we in the U.S. now?
Esto es demasiado . . .	This is just too much . . .
Famila que vendieron dos veces, la	The family that was sold twice
Fati, me electrizas	Fatty, you electrify me
Federales	Federal troops
Fogón	Kitchen range, wood hearth

Folclórico	Folk art, crafts
Gabacho	White, Anglo, mainstream culture
Genízaro(s)	Hispanicized Indians; janissaries
Gente, la	The people, the community
Grafitero(s)	Wall artists, messengers
Grafitismo	Art of wall writing or drawing
Granaria	Granary, storehouse for grain
Guatemaltecos esta vez, un cacique y dos curanderos	Guatemalans this time, one headman and two medicine people
Intelectual	Intellectual
Ha sido una estancia muy bueno, muy feliz, pero tengo que irme	It has been a nice visit, very pleasant, but I must go
Hasta el última cartucho	Until the last cartridge
Hasta muy pronto	Until the very next time
Hasta pronto	Until the next time (soon)
Hay un baño?	Is there a bathroom?
Hermano(s), hermana(s)	Brother(s), sister(s); also nun
Hiciste esto?	Did you make this?
Historia	Story
Huaquero(s)	Grave raider(s); archeologists
Huevos rancheros	Eggs with chili
Idiota(s)	Idiot(s)
Indigena(s)	Native person(s), American Indian(s)
Jefe, máximo	Chief, big chief
Jolla del Rio Grande	Jewel of the Rio Grande
Jornada del Muerto	Journey of Death
Juanabago	Pun on Winnebago travel vans
Jugete	Toy
Kati, un viejo? Que triste!	Kathy, an old man? How sad!
Lastima que seas pura bulla	It's a shame that you are nothing but noise
Lo siento mucho, compadres, pero tengo que irme	I am sorry, my friends, but I must go
Magonista	Follower of Mexican Magón brothers
Majada, la	Sheep corral
Malinchismo	Acting like Doña Malinche; traitorous behavior
Manito	Mexican slang for U.S. Hispanic
Mierda	Garbage, manure, shit
Migra, la	Immigration, border guards
Mijo	Contraction for "my son," "grandson"

Mira	Look, look here
Montaña(s)	Mountain(s)
Morada(s)	Small chapel(s)
Movida(s)	Move(s), maneuver(s)
Muchas cosas son arenas en el reloj de la vida	Many things are merely sand in the clock of life
Mujer(es)	Woman, women
Mujeres Muralistas	Women muralists
Nationals, Foreign Service	Host country staff in American embassies
No puedo crearlo	I can't believe it
No vale una chingada	Not worth a damn
Norte, El	The North, the United States
Nuestra(s) Señora(s)	Virgin or Virgins
Oficina	Office
Otra calientita, por favor	Another hot tortilla, please
Pagina diez, once	Page ten, eleven
Pase por aquí	Come this way
Pendejo	Jerk, fool
Para el esposo	For the husband
Pinche gringo	Annoyingly insistent gringo
Playa(s)	Beach, beaches
Pochteca	Guild of pre-Columbian traders
Por supuesto	Of course
Plaza de los Generales de Pancho Villa, la	Plaza of Pancho Villa's generals
Plaza Vieja, la	The old plaza, Old Town
Porque no soy gringo	Because I am no gringo
Pregúntales	Ask them
Primo	Cousin, buddy
Puede usted acompañarme?	Can you come with me?
Pues, a mí también	Yes, and me too
Pues sí	Of course
Pulque	Drink with low alcohol content
Que no	Isn't that right?
Que caballero!	How gracious! how chivalrous!
Que dolor	How sad
Que estas haciendo?	What are you doing?
Que hay de nuevo?	What's new?
Que quiere decir?	What are you trying to say?
Quien ganó?	Who wins? Who gains?
Quién no oye consejos no llega a viejo	He who fails to listen to counsel will never reach old age
Quinta	House, home, dwelling, cottage

Raza, la	The people, the Hispanic race
Regalo	Gift, present
Repuesto(s)	Spare part(s)
Rico	Rich person
Rio, Arriba, Abajo	River, Upper River, Lower River
Rubio(s)	Light, blond
Rutera(s)	Vans used as taxis
Santo(s)	Catholic saint(s)
Señora le espera, la	The lady is waiting for you
Sería un placer	It would be a pleasure
Siéntate, aquí, acá	Sit down, sit here
Sierra del Nido	Mountain range called the Nest
Si quiere asistir una reunión ven . . .	If you would like to attend a meeting, come to . . .
Somozista(s)	Somoza follower(s)
Suave, muy suave	Smooth, very cool
Tanto tiempo!	(It has been) such a long time!
Taquería	Mexican fast food enterprise
Tengo gusto en conocerle	I am pleased to meet you
Tengo que hablar con usted	I have to talk to you
Tengo que irme a las damas	I need to go to the ladies' toilet
Tengo un poco para comer; algo para beber	I have a little for you to eat; something to drink
Te quiero mucho	I love you very much
Tío	Uncle
Tipo(s)	Type, kind, kind of person
Trinchera(s)	Trench, also terrace
Turista(s)	Tourist(s)
Unica, La	The one, the only one
Vaca	Cow
Usted tiene razón	You are right, correct
Vato(s), vata(s)	Youth(s); male(s), female(s)
Vecino(s)	Neighbor(s)
Vendido(s)	Sell-outs; traitors
Vieja(s)	Old lady, old ladies
Viejita(s)	Little old lady, ladies
Viga(s)	Log(s) used in house construction
Virgen, La; Las Virgenes	Referring to the Virgin Mary and other Catholic virginal saints
Voy a comprar los fierros de los que tiraron la toalla	I am going to buy the tools of those who have thrown in the towel

Ya no las puedes	He can no longer do what he should; one can't do it anymore
Ya verán	They will see
Yonke	Mexican version of "junk"